THE BECKONING HILLS

Ruth Elwin Harris began storytelling when, during the last war, she and her brother went to stay with their grandfather in his isolated Somerset house: "We led a very solitary existence," she says. "Not that we minded. We read a lot and made up stories to entertain each other. We both loved the house and were very happy."

It is that house, christened Hillcrest, which plays an important part in *The Beckoning Hills*, the second book in the *Quantocks Quartet*. "My grandfather bought it in the 1930s from three elderly sisters – all of whom had been painters. Their murals still remained on the stable walls. I used to think about those sisters and wonder about life in the village when they were young." *The Beckoning Hills* tells the story of the eldest Purcell sister, Frances, and her struggle to become an artist.

Ruth Elwin Harris lived abroad for several years before and after her marriage – at one time accompanying her husband to India where she helped out at an orphanage run by Mother Teresa's nuns. She now lives with her family in North Yorkshire. She has written stories for magazines and radio and two other novels in the *Quantocks Quartet: The Silent Shore* (shortlisted for The Observer Teenage Fiction Award) and *The Dividing Sea* (Julia MacRae Books 1989).

Also by Ruth Elwin Harris

The Silent Shore
The Dividing Sea

RUTH · ELWIN · HARRIS

The Beckoning Hills

WALKER BOOKS
LONDON

First published 1987 by Julia MacRae Books
This edition published 1989 by Walker Books Ltd
87 Vauxhall Walk, London SE11 5HJ

© 1987 Ruth Elwin Harris
Cover illustration by Emma Chichester-Clark

Printed in Great Britain by Cox and Wyman Ltd, Reading

British Library Cataloguing in Publication Data
Harris, Ruth Elwin
The beckoning hills.
I. Title
823'.914[F]
ISBN 0-7445-1356-1

FOR JENNY

CONTENTS

1910

Chapter One

Rain fell against the study windows, hiding the Rectory garden outside, drop chasing drop in a constantly changing, soundless pattern across the pane.

Behind the desk tiers of photographs looked down from the wall onto Frances. Teams and groups, of schoolboys, of young men, of clergymen, watching her. Crossed legs, folded arms, stiff-necked, their eyes focused on her.

Everyone, watching her.

Julia and Gwen yesterday, sitting in the train coming home from school for the last time, their eyes helpless and frightened: "What's going to happen to us, Frances? What will we do, without Mother?"

The headmistress, two days ago: "Your mother ... a chill ... pneumonia." Her eyes cold and unsympathetic. She had never liked Frances; would be glad to get rid of her. "The Rector of Huish Priory is to be your guardian. A Mr. Mackenzie." Watching Frances, waiting for her to break down. "'In the midst of life we are in death,' Frances. Remember that."

Mr. Mackenzie's eyes as he looked at Frances now, sitting in his study, were grave. Grave but kind. If only she could think properly, Frances told herself, if only she could take in what he was saying, if only she understood the will ... More than any of these, if only it were still Christmas and everything as it had been then. How could it have happened that Mr. Mackenzie, almost a stranger . . .?

"I don't understand, Mr. Mackenzie," she said. "Why should Mother ask you to be our guardian? We hardly know you."

The Rector clasped his hands together, his fingers long, thin, bony-knuckled. "Try to put yourself in your mother's position, my dear. She was dying. She knew it. Dying, and leaving four children, four daughters, the youngest only seven . . . What else could she do? Who else could she turn to? She had become something of a recluse, had she not? No friends. No-one to call on."

"It was different when Father was alive," Frances said. "I remember when he was stationed at Greenwich . . ."

"It's true," Mr. Mackenzie said, "that there are two aunts, living in Bristol – your great-aunts – but they're too old, too infirm. They could not possibly take you in. And I was there, you see, at your mother's bedside. We've known each other for a long time. Not well, perhaps, but we respected each other." He was silent for a moment. Someone, somewhere in the house, was practising scales on the piano. Up and down. Another key. Up and down. "It was a privilege to be asked," Mr. Mackenzie said.

"So you," Frances said, "and Mr. Baynham, you're both our guardians?"

"Joint guardians, executors and trustees. Mr. Baynham, of course, has been a guardian with your mother for some time, since your father died. Have you met Mr. Baynham?

Frances shook her head. "Mother didn't like him."

"I may be wrong," Mr. Mackenzie said, slowly as if reluctant to criticise, "but I fear that Mr. Baynham has little knowledge of the young. Another reason, no doubt, why your mother asked me to be guardian. Mrs. Mackenzie and I have a daughter, as well as three sons. We are well used to children." He smiled at Frances. "How old are you, my dear?"

"Seventeen."

Last summer she had put up her hair and let down her skirts. She was a child no longer. Her three sisters were children still — her responsibility now. It was she who would have to take their mother's place.

"There's nothing we can do at the moment," Mr. Mackenzie said, "until probate has been granted. Mr. Baynham expects little difficulty — your mother's will is quite straightforward. The estate is divided between the four of you, in trust, with specific bequests, such as pieces of jewellery, left to each. Her painting things come to you."

"Yes," Frances said, "I saw that," and read again that astonishing paragraph, the only paragraph that had made sense to her on first reading:

To my eldest daughter, Frances Mary Purcell, my brushes and paints, canvases and all such painting equipment ...

"Mr. Baynham will be coming to Huish Priory for the funeral tomorrow," Mr. Mackenzie said. "Mrs. Mackenzie and I have invited him to stay on afterwards. It would seem sensible to have a meeting here to give you and your sisters the opportunity of meeting him. He'll be able to explain then, in more detail than I, the position you find yourselves in." He smiled at Frances. "Is there anything else you want to know?"

She shook her head. Later, she knew, she would remember the questions she should have asked.

Mr. Mackenzie stood up. "Let us go and fetch your sisters."

She stared. "Fetch ...?"

"Mrs. Mackenzie has rearranged the bedrooms and had beds made up for the four of you. I believe she's even found one or two toys in the attic to please Sarah."

Shock made Frances abrupt. "We're not coming to the Rectory, Mr. Mackenzie. We're staying at Hillcrest."

"My dear child!" Mr. Mackenzie said. "You can't stay there on your own."

"We're not on our own. We've got Annie. And the maids."

"Of course, but ..."

She had not meant to sound rude. She tried to be conciliatory. "It is our home, Mr. Mackenzie. Please."

He hesitated. "For one night then."

She stood in the Rectory hall, waiting for the maid to bring her coat. There were Indian rugs on the floor, thick and richly coloured, and Indian pictures on the wall. Oak panelling gleamed in the light of lamps already lit. Comfortable, well cared for, but not home.

Through a half-open door she glimpsed a young man in the room beyond. He stood without moving, watching her. His face was shadowed but it seemed to Frances that his expression was severe, even hostile. She gave him a tentative smile. It was not returned.

Guardian and ward walked up the hill from the Rectory in silence. The rain had stopped, but water still gurgled in the ditches beside the road. Frances turned her head quickly away from the churchyard as they reached the top of the hill. Too late. She had already caught sight of the heaped line of red earth that marked the newly dug grave.

She stood outside the gate to Hillcrest and looked up at the house; at the apricot-coloured walls covered with winter skeletons of creeper and shrub roses, at the grey-green slate roof and elm trees beyond. She shivered with apprehension. She could never leave Hillcrest to live at the Rectory.

As the Rector let the heavy knocker drop onto the door she tried to summon the courage to speak. "Mr. Mackenzie," she said at last, "don't you think it would be better to have that meeting here tomorrow instead of at the Rectory? The one with Mr. Baynham."

"I think not, my dear. Mrs. Mackenzie is quite prepared, indeed happy, that we should hold it at the Rectory."

"But I'd rather have it in our own home. It's our future we'll be discussing. We should be here. It'd be easier for the others, too, particularly Sarah."

He looked at her in surprise. Perhaps he sensed her determination. "If you feel strongly . . ."

"I do." She heard Annie fumbling with the bolts of the front door. "It's not that I'm not grateful," she said quickly. "Don't think that. I think it's more sensible, that's all."

The door opened. The hall behind Annie was smaller than that of the Rectory and darker, but light from the living-room fell across the unpatterned carpet in a cheerful bar of colour. The steady *tock*, *tock* of the grandfather clock on the half-landing greeted and consoled. Hillcrest was home as the Rectory could never be.

"Very well. As you wish." He took Frances's hands in his. "I'm sorry, my dear, that there is so little comfort I can give at such a time, but we shall be happy together, I know it. Take each day as it comes, child, and believe that life will get better, however unlikely it may seem to you now. Remember your prayers. You'll all be remembered in ours at the Rectory."

It was hard, coming back to Hillcrest. Life at the Rectory had been as it must always have been – maids coming in to stoke the fire, the piano player, teacups tinkling in another room. Had Mrs. Mackenzie been expecting the Purcells to tea, Frances wondered?

At Hillcrest life would never be the same again. There was the empty chair by the fire, that everyone avoided but no-one mentioned or had the courage to move. The white faces of the younger Purcells, watching and waiting. "What did Mr. Mackenzie say, Frances? What's going to happen?" Maids snivelling in the kitchen, and Annie, red-eyed. "Do you know what's to do, Miss Frances? It's you who's giving the orders now." All of them looking to her, for comfort and guidance, for direction. Only Willis in the garden was condescending, faintly insolent: "Leave it to me, Miss Frances. No need to worry your little head . . ." He would never have dared speak to her mother so.

Worst of all was Sarah, sitting on Frances's lap before going to bed, white-faced, lips quivering, looking up at Frances with sad grey eyes, full of trust. Frances looked down at her youngest sister and realised for the first time that she knew nothing about seven-year-olds, did not know what to say to them, nor how to comfort. She had never paid Sarah much attention, yet Sarah's future happiness now rested in Frances's hands.

She could pretend to be brave in Mr. Mackenzie's presence; could hide her fears from the maids and from Annie the housekeeper, only a few years older than Frances herself; with an effort she could even pretend cheerfulness in the presence of her sisters, but in the privacy of her room that night, misery, uncertainty and fear overwhelmed her. And rebellion, that she should have been burdened with such responsibility.

It's not fair, she cried at the open window of her bedroom. The cold, damp air floated in under the sash, unheeding, uncaring. I can't do it. Why did you have to die? The doctor told Annie you'd get better. Why didn't you get better? Why didn't you tell me what I must do? It's not fair. Why now? Why me? Why? Why? Why?

The quarter moon slithered out from behind the clouds, shining down on its reflection in the glass roof of the verandah below Frances's window. For a moment Frances glimpsed her mother down by the trees beyond the lawn. Hair dripped onto her shoulders, clothes clung to her body. She looked as she had that last morning of the holidays, coming in from the rain after planting the catalpa to commemorate the beginning of a new decade.

Frances leant forward to call out.

It was an illusion. There was no-one there. Frances was on her own.

Chapter Two

Mrs. Purcell had refused to let her daughters meet Mr. Baynham. "I don't see the need," she told Frances. "He and I don't get on. He thinks women should be weak, biddable creatures with no mind of their own. You can imagine what he thinks of me."

A vulture in mourning. That was how she described him and had drawn a cartoon of him as such to entertain her daughters.

Frances remembered that drawing now as she faced the lawyer in the Hillcrest living-room. The stooped, black-clad figure, those hooded lids, the pouched skin under the eyes – yes, Mrs. Purcell's few black lines had caught him precisely on paper.

"Mr. Baynham," said Mrs. Mackenzie, "may I introduce Mrs. Purcell's eldest daughter? Frances."

The lawyer studied Frances. "Indeed. You're very like your mother." It did not sound like a compliment.

"And this is Julia," Mrs. Mackenzie continued, "who is fifteen."

Julia, face still swollen with tears shed at the graveside, made a brave attempt to smile.

"Gwen is thirteen."

Gwen choked back a sob.

"And last of all, Sarah. Come along, Sarah. Mr. Baynham won't eat you."

Mrs. Mackenzie, majestic, formidable, had taken charge.

A managing woman, Mrs. Purcell had thought Mrs. Mackenzie. Mrs. Purcell liked managing women as little as she liked lawyers.

Frances was calmer this afternoon than she had been yesterday. She had lain awake for most of the night, trying to think, to plan. Now she watched the Rector's wife. A managing woman like Mrs. Mackenzie would take charge – was taking charge. Mrs. Mackenzie would manage the Purcells. I won't let her, Frances promised herself. I'll fight her. We can look after ourselves. As long as we stick together we'll be able to look after ourselves.

Another visitor had come with Mr. Baynham and the Mackenzies. Frances recognised him at once – yesterday's silent watcher from the Rectory.

"My eldest son," Mr. Mackenzie said. Pride and affection sounded in his voice. "Gabriel."

[15]

The hostile expression had gone. Today Gabriel smiled as he held his hand out to Frances. "I know it's impertinent," he said, "to come uninvited. I thought I might be able to help. I thought I should know what's going on for my father's sake. If you'd rather I went you have only to say . . . "

What did he mean, Frances wondered? Did he think Mr. Mackenzie would need help? What sort of help? "Of course not," she said. "It's kind of you." She looked defiantly at Mrs. Mackenzie. "Won't you sit down?"

They arranged themselves. The lawyer sat at the head of the table, under the portrait of Commander Purcell in tropical uniform on the deck of his ship. The three elder Purcells kept together. Sarah, to Frances's astonishment, turned down Mr. Mackenzie's invitation to join Annie in the kitchen and climbed up onto Gabriel's lap.

Mr. Baynham laid his papers on the table in front of him. He adjusted his spectacles. He cleared his throat. He began to talk.

He told them how Commander Purcell had appointed Mr. Baynham as executor of his will, and joint guardian of the Purcell children. He deplored the fact that Mrs. Purcell when widowed had failed to make her own will until she was dying, despite his exhortations to her to do so; explained that since it was necessary to have a second executor and guardian, Mr. Mackenzie had kindly agreed to take on these positions, there being no-one else to do so. The Purcells, Mr. Baynham pointed out, were fortunate in being provided with guardians able to supervise both their material and moral well-being. He mentioned the only relatives Mr. Mackenzie and he had been able to locate – the two great-aunts in Bristol. The Misses Ellison.

"Of course if it is true – as we undertand – that your mother ran away before her marriage and was disowned as a result, the lack of relatives is hardly surprising . . . "

The expressions on Gwen's and Julia's faces had become glazed. Sarah slept with Gabriel's arms around her. Frances listened in bewilderment. Why had her mother never told her about her family, she wondered? The Ellisons had written at Christmas as far back as Frances could remember, but never once had Mrs. Purcell even hinted that they were related. And running away from home – could that really be true?

The lawyer was talking about income now, and trusts and trustees, naval pensions and children's allowances, the difficulties of calculating how financially sound the Purcells might be.

"Of course," he said, "once the house has been sold and the proceeds invested we shall have a more accurate idea of your likely income ..."

The implication passed Frances by at first. It was Gwen's tears that alerted her ...

"I don't want to leave my garden," Gwen sobbed.

Frances stared at the lawyer. She could not believe it. "Where do you expect us to live?"

He hesitated. "We assumed ... in Taunton. The trustees would rent a house and put a housekeeper in charge."

It had never occurred to Frances that they might lose Hillcrest. Watching Mrs. Mackenzie at the graveside that morning, her fears had been centred on the possibility of the sisters being gathered into the Rectory household. She had assumed, if she had assumed anything, that Hillcrest would remain over the brow of the hill, waiting until they were old enough to return. The enormity of what was being so casually proposed – selling the house that had been the family's base during her parents' wandering marriage, selling the only real home that the Purcells had ever known – was so great that she was momentarily made speechless. Then she thought of Hillcrest, the comfortable, rambling house, and all that it meant, the history laid out in the trees of the garden that marked birthdays and anniversaries, promotions and successes, the memories of father and mother contained in house and grounds, and speech returned. She was scarcely aware of what she was saying. She knew only that she must fight for herself and her sisters, that she must do everything in her power to prevent such a loss.

She stopped at last. Mr. Baynham cleared his throat and tugged at his cuffs. She realised that she had embarrassed him by a display of such emotion. In the silence that followed despair enveloped her. There was nothing she could do. She was powerless.

"There's the financial aspect to consider, Miss Purcell," the lawyer said. His voice, cold and distant, reproved her. "Hillcrest is a large house and the garden must be – what? Two, three acres? There's the running of it, the upkeep, the *expense*, Miss Purcell."

She must keep calm. Shortage of money she could understand, but their wants were few: to be together, to have a comfortable home in which to live and paint, to have enough to eat. That was all.

"There'd be expenses if we lived in Taunton," she said. "Rent. Food. A housekeeper, you said – her wages. If we stayed here we could keep Annie on. There'd be no rent. We grow most of the food we need. If the garden's too big we could let some of it grow wild, or have more orchard." Ideas tumbled into her head. "We could rent some out to Mr. Escott for his pigs. Or have pigs ourselves. Why should size be a problem? It doesn't cost any more. You don't know us. We aren't extravagant, we don't want expensive things. We want to stay here."

"It would need careful consideration. Mr. Mackenzie and I . . ."

And there, she suddenly realised, was the strongest reason possible for remaining. "Ah yes. Mr. Mackenzie. Of course I know you're our guardian too, but Mr. Mackenzie's the one Mother wanted, isn't he, the one she chose. We should be here, near Mr. Mackenzie, not seven miles away in Taunton."

She was so thankful that for the first time she smiled at the lawyer.

Relief came too soon. There was the question of education. She need no longer attend school, nor Julia, but Gwen and Sarah remained.

"There's the village school," Mr. Baynham suggested.

Frances's heart sank. Mrs. Purcell had always said Sarah was clever. Mrs. Purcell would never have agreed to Sarah attending the village school.

"I suppose I could . . . " Mr. Mackenzie began. He sounded diffident. "I taught my own daughter at home. I still teach my youngest son. The girls could come to me."

Even then victory was not assured. The lawyer had his doubts still. The size of the house, upkeep of the garden, the youth of its would-be occupants, the need for somebody, a housekeeper . . .

Quibbles, quibbles, Frances thought in despair. Couldn't he see they'd need housekeeper and food wherever they were, in Huish Priory or Taunton?

Annie was summoned from the kitchen. It had never occurred to Frances that Annie might be interviewed. Had it done so she would have warned her, and told her what to say. Annie avoided Frances's eyes, bobbed at the lawyer, smiled at the Rector and answered Mrs. Mackenzie's questions, quietly and with respect. Her face softened as she went out at the sight of Sarah asleep in Gabriel's arms.

"I know that Mrs. Purcell thought highly of Annie," Mrs. Mackenzie said. "And Frances is seventeen, old enough to run a home – under supervision, of course. The Rectory is only across the road." She smiled graciously at Frances. "I would consider it my duty to do what I could to help."

Frances did not smile back.

"The evening's drawing in," Mr. Baynham said, and put a hand over his papers. "I must get back to Taunton before dark. I believe we have discussed all that it is possible to discuss at present. Decisions will come later. Meanwhile . . . "

"There is something else," Frances said. She gripped her hands together under the table and took a deep breath. "Would there . . . is there enough money for me to go to art school?"

The reaction was worse than she had expected. She might have asked for permission to murder. Even Mr. Mackenzie appeared shocked. Frances looked hopelessly round the table.

Only Gabriel, and he seemed . . . amused? Surely not. She had to take the risk.

"You haven't said a word this afternoon," she said to him. "What do *you* think about my going to art school?"

"It's a matter of talent, isn't it? I don't know. Are you any good?"

She was annoyed that he should doubt her. "I'm not as good as I'd like," she said, "but, yes, I have got talent."

"Then I think you should go," he said, "but only if you can win a place at a decent school."

Silence. She tried to control her trembling, tried to think . . .

"I believe," Mr. Mackenzie said, in a voice that lacked conviction, "that the art school in Taunton is quite respectable."

She could not hide her scorn. "I wouldn't be seen dead in an art school in Taunton. I was thinking of London."

"How do you intend to run a house this size," Gabriel said, "*and* look after your sisters, if you're more than a hundred miles away in London?"

Her first instinct had been right, but even so, he seemed to be her only supporter; she appealed to him again. "I don't have to go at once. If I worked at home for a couple of years Julia would be seventeen. She could take charge during term-time then, couldn't she?"

"That'd be much more sensible," he said. "It's a mistake to do anything in a hurry. Give yourself – and everyone else – time to consider." To Frances's astonishment, he added, "I could see what I can find out about the various schools, if you like."

Mr. Baynham gathered up his papers, tapping the edges together with nervous fingers as he said, quickly as though fearing that Frances might introduce another unwelcome subject, "I think we've covered all the points we need this afternoon. I shall continue, of course, with the necessary formalities . . ."

Frances wondered whether she should be offering tea and was annoyed with herself for not discussing it earlier with Annie. There was so much she didn't know, she thought wearily, so much to learn.

Mrs. Mackenzie smiled down at Sarah, lying asleep in her son's arms. "Let the poor child wake in her own time," she said to Gabriel. "You can follow us later."

Frances went into the hall to help Annie with the coats. Now that the meeting was over she scarcely had energy left to force the necessary smile. Mr. Mackenzie stayed behind for a moment, his hand resting lightly on Frances's shoulder. "I wish you'd come back with us, my dear. I don't like to think of the four of you here on your own at a time like this."

Tears pricked behind her eyelids. "We're all right," she said. "We can manage."

"I'm beginning to think that you can." His smile, shy, kindly, lit up his face. "Good-night, my dear."

She thought, I wish we'd given him tea.

She went reluctantly back into the living-room. Annie was pulling the curtains across the French windows. Sometime, Frances thought, I shall have to talk to Annie. Perhaps now is as good a time as any.

"I should have asked you last night, Annie," she said. "Do you want to stay, now that my mother's no longer here?"

Annie gave the heavy velvet curtains a final tug before turning round. "I wouldn't want to leave Miss Sarah," she said. "Not at a time like this. Do *you* want me to go, Miss Frances?"

I don't know, Frances thought. You've never approved of me, have you? You always sided with Mother when she and I quarrelled. I don't see how we can do without you, all the same. Not for the moment, anyway. "No," she said, "I don't want you to go."

"I expect we'll manage all right then," Annie said. She sounded doubtful.

"We must manage," Frances said. "Make no mistake about that. If things don't work out here that man'll sell Hillcrest and settle the four of us in Taunton. You know what that means, don't you? You'll be out of work. Without a reference from Mother, too."

Annie pursed her lips. "I'll fetch the tea," she said at last and went out.

"That wasn't very kind," Julia protested. "Annie wouldn't want to be out of work any more than we'd want to live in Taunton. Less – she's got that sick mother and her brothers and sisters to look after."

"Oh well. You know Annie and me," Frances said wearily. "At least she knows what's what now. I don't suppose they'll let us stay here, anyway."

Gabriel shifted in his chair. "It sounded to me as if they intend to consider it," he said. "Tell me, how do I wake your sister?"

"Can't you let her sleep on for a bit?" Frances said. "She's been having bad nights, Annie says. She's tired out. You'd better stay to tea."

The invitation sounded grudging, even to her own ears. Gabriel must have thought so too, for he raised his eyebrows. "Are you angry with me?"

"Why should I be angry?"

"I don't know. For saying what I did about London, perhaps."

She felt a spurt of irritation. "It was a bit tactless, wasn't it? You didn't have to say it. You could have kept quiet."

"So could you. What made you bring up that art school idea? You were doing so well, you'd almost persuaded them to let you stay on in this house and then you go and spoil everything. You're obviously not stupid. You must have realised the sort of reaction you would get from a fellow like that lawyer."

She was annoyed by his criticism. "It was important."

"Not that important, surely?"

"Yes, it was."

She knew that she could not expect him to understand. She put a log on the fire and knelt on the hearthrug watching the flames wrap themselves round the rough bark. Perhaps he was right. If she had talked to Mr. Mackenzie first ... But Gabriel would not understand the pressure of time, the way in which she felt the years were passing her by ... Mr. Baynham's approval would have to be given eventually, on financial grounds if nothing else. The sooner he was told the sooner he might be persuaded.

"May I give you some advice?" Gabriel said.

She looked up. "If you want. I don't promise to take it."

"Take things slowly. You all want to stay here apparently; I think you should concentrate on that. If you get them to agree to that and things work out satisfactorily, and they can see that they do, then you can start mentioning art school. Not ... how shall I put it? ... belligerently."

She was taken aback. Was that what he thought her – belligerent?

Sarah stirred, yawned, stretched out her arms. Gabriel lifted her down on to the floor, releasing strands of hair that had twisted themselves round his jacket buttons with a gentleness that surprised Frances. He refused her second invitation to stay for tea.

"If my parents are discussing matters with that man I think I should be present to put forward your views." He said hopefully, "Perhaps you could invite me another day?"

She went with him into the hall, reluctant to return to the subject but knowing that she had no choice. "Did you mean what you said about art schools? I do need to know. The Slade sounds the best place for me – but I don't know how you get in."

"I'll see what I can do." He sounded amused, as if recognising her persistence. "There shouldn't be any difficulty once I'm back at Cambridge. I often go down to London. I'll write and let you know. Think over what I said, though. I wouldn't talk about it too much if I were you. There's plenty of time."

She stood on the doorstep and watched him disappear into the January mist. Suddenly, irrationally, she felt better. She had endured the first day, coped with the funeral and in this afternoon's meeting had stood up for her sisters and herself. The more she saw of Mr. Mackenzie the more she liked him, and in his son she sensed that she might have found an ally.

Mr. Mackenzie had been right. Life would get better.

Chapter Three

Frances was taken aback by Mr. Mackenzie's suggestion when he came over to Hillcrest next morning.

"Don't you think it's a bit soon?" she said. "I mean ... why not let them get over things first?"

"Study will occupy their thoughts and stop them brooding," Mr. Mackenzie said. "It'll help them recover more quickly. They'll be able to make friends with Antony, too. No, my dear, I'm sure it would be best. Send them over tomorrow morning. Half past nine. I shall be back from prayers and bible study at the school by then."

Frances gave Gwen's and Sarah's hair an extra thorough brushing after breakfast and checked hands and fingernails while Annie put indoor shoes in one bag, pencils and handkerchieves in another.

The hours until their return seemed endless.

"Well?" Frances said.

"It was nice," Sarah said.

Gwen glared. "Antony's cleverer than me *and* he's a year younger," was the only comment she would make before disappearing into the garden.

"Mr. Mackenzie has a *lovely* room," Sarah said. "It's got lots of books – the walls are *covered* with books. And photographs. Mr. Mackenzie told me about the photographs. They're Mr. Mackenzie and his friends a long time ago. Mr. Mackenzie used to row in a boat, did you know? He keeps the oar over the fireplace. He showed me a picture of a tiger, too, a dead tiger. Mrs. Mackenzie's father is standing on him. When Mrs. Mackenzie was seven she used to live in India – that's what Mr. Mackenzie said."

Frances was amused, and grateful to the Rector. The morning seemed to have been a success; she heard Sarah telling Annie about it in the kitchen that afternoon. "I had to sit on a big pile of cushions, Annie, that *prickled*. And I've got my own inkwell and my own pen and my own table . . ." She had not talked so much since her mother's death.

The relief was enormous. Gwen's feelings about lessons were unimportant – Gwen would have to bear with them as Frances had borne with boarding-school. It was Sarah, with all those years of schooling ahead, whose feelings mattered.

There was another reason for relief, as Frances realised watching Sarah leave with Gwen the following day without a backward glance at her sister and Annie standing on the front doorstep. If Sarah were happy studying at the Rectory and Mr. Mackenzie happy to teach her, it would be impossible for the Purcells to live in Taunton. The seven miles that divided town from village would see to that.

Frances's fears of being managed by Mrs. Mackenzie could not keep the Purcells out of the Rectory for ever.

"I don't see why you object to her so much," Julia said. "I thought she was nice. She did offer to help – you know, supervise and all that."

"That's it," Frances said. "She wants to take charge."

Their first visit, for lunch, was easier than Frances had expected. Mr. Mackenzie was welcoming, Mrs. Mackenzie gracious. The difficulties of conversation were eased by Gabriel, who sat next to Sarah and entertained her, and by Antony, the youngest Mackenzie, a thin, fair-haired boy who talked throughout the meal without hindrance from his parents. Precocious, Frances decided, and wondered why he should be kept at home for his education when Geoffrey, the middle son, was away at school. Lucy, the remaining Mackenzie, tall and fair like her eldest brother and probably only a little younger, was very much quieter, smiling at the Purcells but saying little.

"You promised to invite me to tea," Gabriel said when he escorted the Purcells back to Hillcrest.

[25]

"I don't think I promised," Frances said.

"Oh yes, you did. How about tomorrow?"

She was reluctant. "I suppose ... oh, all right, if you insist. Tomorrow then."

He came, and within minutes it seemed as if he had known them all their lives. He teased Sarah, even succeeding in making her smile, and taught her Old Maid; marvelled at the advanced growth of Gwen's bulbs; admired Julia's embroidery, and asked about Commander Purcell's portrait on the wall. Before Frances could stop them Gwen and Julia were giving him their family history, as far back as their father's death somewhere off the coast of China when the family had settled permanently at Hillcrest.

"Before that we only lived here when Father was at sea," Gwen said. "We've lived in Plymouth ... and Greenwich ... and ... Portsmouth, was it, Frances? I can't exactly remember where else at the moment."

"What well-travelled young ladies you are," Gabriel said. He lay back in the big armchair, now and then glancing across at Frances as she sat beside the fire. She had an uncomfortable feeling that he could read her thoughts. She wondered whether he would report back to the Rectory all that he had been told. Mr. Mackenzie must have sent him ...

She had considered Gabriel's advice about art school and decided that he might well be right in recommending silence for the time being. It was Gabriel himself who brought up the subject when he came to tea the day before returning to Cambridge. He was building a house of cards for Sarah at the time, slowly and painstakingly placing card against card, layer on layer, and didn't look up as he said, "A friend of mine went to the Slade."

Frances stared. "Why didn't you say before?"

He shrugged. "I wanted to get to know you better first. Let's have another card, mouse. Don't breathe, now, or you'll blow it down."

Frances watched in silence. If Gabriel already knew

someone – a friend, he'd said, not an acquaintance – surely he wouldn't think her own wish to attend so preposterous. "Could you ask his advice?" she said.

"Hers, not his. It's a woman. Yes, of course. I shall be seeing her when I get back to Cambridge."

He placed yet another card with a steady hand. One card too many – the building slithered down onto the table, turning itself into nothing more impressive than a heap of coloured cardboard on the baize.

"Oh no!" Sarah cried. Her lip quivered.

"Don't cry," Gabriel said. "Here. You try. See if you can do better than me." He tipped back his chair and regarded Frances with a smile of . . . what? Amusement? Mockery? She wished that she felt more at ease in his presence.

She was sorry when he left, all the same, and not only because Sarah missed him. He provided a touch of lightness in a world grown suddenly grim. When she had protested so vehemently at the proposal to rent she had not understood the economics involved. She was dismayed when they were explained to her by Mr. Mackenzie, but determined still. Remaining at Hillcrest was what the Purcells wanted: if doing so meant making economies, economies they would make. She began by dismissing young Ted, Willis's boy in the garden, and two of the maids.

"We can't do without help altogether, Miss Frances," Annie complained, "not in a house this size. Don't think Mrs. Mackenzie won't come in and run her finger along the picture rails, because she will. She won't be letting our standards slip, help or no help."

"We don't have any choice, Annie. You've still got Harriet for the rough. We'll get someone up from the village to help with the housework and the three of us will have to do more. If we make our own beds . . . and I wouldn't mind doing some cooking. Julia always has in the holidays. You'll have to teach me to make bread. Don't you understand, Annie? We must learn to live on as little as we can until Mr. Baynham has sorted things out and we know how much money there is. You do want to stay, don't you?"

Mr. Mackenzie took Frances down to the Manor to talk to Sir James Donne. Sir James owned most of the village and the land round it; nothing in the neighbourhood was outside his interest. He was sympathetic in a firm, practical manner that was easy to deal with, unlike the condolences of Miss Tuck, the postmistress, who had wept on Hillcrest's front doorstep and reduced the younger Purcells to tears in a matter of minutes. Sir James asked sensible questions, wanted to know what was happening about education, and discussed the upkeep of Hillcrest with Mr. Mackenzie, offering the occasional services of his agent to look the house over and ensure that it remained in good order.

Frances was encouraged by her visit. She thought it unlikely that Mr. Mackenzie would have troubled Sir James had the Purcells been about to move away, and Sir James himself appeared to take their permanence at Hillcrest for granted.

No-one suggested nowadays that the Purcells move into the Rectory, although they went there frequently for meals. Mrs. Mackenzie came to Hillcrest as Annie had predicted, to run her fingers along the picture rail, see that all was as it should be in the running of the household, and to go over the weekly accounts with Annie and the eldest Purcells; while Mr. Mackenzie called in most evenings on his way back to the Rectory from evensong.

Life had slipped into a pattern, comforting and comfortable in its routine. Only Frances was tormented by thoughts of her undecided future.

She could not remember a time when she had not drawn or painted. The only presents she had ever looked for – whether for birthdays, or Christmas or on those never-to-be-forgotten occasions when Commander Purcell came home from sea – were paper, pencils and paint; the only lessons to hold her attention at school the art lessons. It was the art mistress who took her up to London to see an exhibition of work by Holman Hunt. The memory of that day remained with Frances still, the sight of those astonishing paintings on the walls, the suffocating crush of people and the excitement seething through the gallery, but more than anything else she remembered the blinding experience of sudden knowledge. She knew then. There were no doubts. She was going to be a painter.

Gabriel was home only briefly at Easter but he came over to tea on the day of his arrival, pleased, he said, that Annie had had an extra baking session, 'just in case'.

"You do realise, don't you, that it's not the thought of you girls that brings me over to Hillcrest but Annie's fruitcake? How are you, Annie? Keeping them in order, I hope."

Annie blushed. "Really, Mr. Gabriel. What a thing to say."

He took the chair that had been Commander Purcell's and smiled across to Frances sitting behind the teapot. "Well?"

There was no need for her to reply. Gwen and Sarah vied with each other in their eagerness to tell him all that had happened since his last visit. Frances, watching, was touched by the attention he gave them and Julia too, treating all three as equals rather than children, listening to what they had to say as if it had real importance for him. She noticed, as she had on his previous visits, how Sarah blossomed in his presence, and was reassured by it.

He looked at Frances when tea was over and said, "I haven't seen the garden yet. Why don't you show me round?"

She opened the French windows and took him out onto the verandah. Easter was early this year; there was not much warmth in the sun but daffodils were out at the edge of the flagstones and the narcissi beginning to drop their heads.

"It was really an excuse to get you on your own," he said, as they walked across the lawn towards the rose garden, "though I'd like to see the garden anyway. How are things going?"

"All right. At least, I think they are. What's your father told you?"

"Nothing yet. I'll see what he says tonight. Sarah's looking better anyway."

For the first time she was aware of his sympathy and forgot that anything she said might be repeated at the Rectory.

"Do you think so? I do worry about her."

"Do you?" He sounded surprised. "Why?"

"I don't know ... I'm not used to small children. I don't know what to say to her half the time. I don't know what she's thinking. I wish ... if only I knew what Mother would've wanted me to do."

"You'll have to forget your mother," he said, "and do what you think's best. You know my parents want to help – more, I think, than you're prepared to let them."

He stood looking down on the face of the sundial, tracing the letters carved round its border with one finger.

> *"Stand with your face to the sun*
> *And the shadows will fall behind you"*.

He smiled at her. "A sound piece of advice. Isn't it?"

She smiled back. "Yes."

Walking under the shadows of the pink sandstone wall she tried to see the familiar, well-loved garden as a stranger might. Pale green shoots peered beneath the black and white stalks of last year's delphiniums in the bed by the path. Ferny leaves of poppies stretched up to the light. So different from the Rectory garden, ordered and organised, a garden of spring and summer bedding. This was a garden of shrubs and trees, of plants allowed to grow as they were meant.

"There's a fair bit of land, isn't there?" Gabriel said. "Do you have much help?"

"Willis, full-time, and a boy who comes in after school. Gwen's the gardener in our family. She's been interested in plants for as long as I can remember. She tells Willis what to do. He hates it, mind you. I'm sure he thought he'd be able to take things easily when Mother died but Gwen won't let him. It's difficult for her, though, being so young. Still, Sir James's agent did give him a talking-to the other day."

Gabriel laughed. "You are a surprising family," he said. "I remember seeing you on those rare occasions you were at church and thinking you were nothing out of the ordinary at all. How wrong I was!"

"We have to go to church every Sunday now," Frances said ruefully.

They went through the gate in the wall and came out into the vegetable garden. The earth, rich, red and unplanted, stretched away to the rhubarb plants that grew under the elms separating Hillcrest from Tinker's Field.

"Gwen gets very cross with Willis," Frances said. "The broad beans are through the ground already at the Manor, she says, and Willis only sowed ours last week."

"You'd better tell her to be careful," Gabriel said, "or you'll have him giving notice out of pique and then you'll be in a pickle."

She saw that the seedtrays in the greenhouse were beginning to sprout. Gwen was going to prove to Willis that plants did better under glass. "She's very determined, Gwen," Frances said. "You can't get her to change her mind if she's set on something. She wants to give up lessons with your father. She says her time'd be better spent here."

"How old is she?"

"Nearly fourteen."

"It'd be ridiculous, at her age."

"I did tell her she should carry on."

"Shall I talk to her? I don't mean, to lecture, but if the subject came up in the course of a general chat I could probably say something ..."

She was surprised by his suggestion and grateful. "Would you mind? I'm sure she'd pay more attention to you."

They climbed the crest of the hill that gave the house its

name, now gold with daffodils in bloom. Rooks screeched in the trees of the copse over the wall, seagulls in the field beyond. Soon the buds on the magnolia in front of the stables would burst out into waxy white flowers. Hens scratched the bare earth at the far end of the stables and scrabbled through the long grass under the walnut and copper beech.

She stood looking round her, at the distant view of the Blackdown Hills and the rolling Somerset countryside between, at the grey-green pattern of low roofs made by the outbuildings and the warm apricot and red of house and garden walls, and wished that she could make Gabriel understand how she felt about Hillcrest. She watched him as he stood silent beside her. Perhaps he glimpsed it.

The living-room was empty when they returned. Gabriel settled himself back in the armchair. She felt at ease with him for the first time. She did not even mind the teasing way in which he looked at her.

"All this time with me," he said, smiling, "and you haven't yet mentioned art school. Lost interest?"

She tilted her chin. "I was waiting for you to bring it up."

He laughed. "All right. What do you want to know?"

She discovered that he had found out a great deal on her behalf and in doing so had come to agree with her: that the Slade was the place to which she should apply. The Royal Academy schools had deteriorated, he said; they had become illustrative with little to say, while the Slade during the past decade had produced artists astonishing both in number and quality.

Frances's fears, that she was not clever enough for an art school that was part of London University, he dismissed. Her youth worried him more. "You're only seventeen; it's the same situation as Gwen."

She was indignant. "It's not. Gwen wants to stop learning. I want to go on."

He laughed. "I suppose you're right. So, the Slade it is. Have you discussed it with Father yet?"

She shook her head. "You told me not to."

"You'd better come over while I'm home and we'll see what he says. Not at once; give me time to prepare the ground. He might agree to your trying for an interview this summer. It would give us some idea of your chances."

Her heart began to flutter with excitement. "Do you mean it?"

"I can't promise anything."

"Oh, Gabriel."

She could have hugged him.

Chapter Four

Once it had been agreed that Frances should apply for a place at the Slade there was the problem of the journey to be overcome.

"Anyone would think I was a package from the Army and Navy," Frances grumbled to Julia and Gwen. "Why such a fuss when we've been travelling to school for years without any trouble?"

At last, after much discussion, Mrs. Mackenzie's disapproval of girls travelling unescorted was overcome. She was persuaded that convention would be observed if Frances were put on the train at Taunton by Mr. Mackenzie and met in London by Gabriel, who would come down from Cambridge for the purpose.

There was no question of where to stay in London: Mrs. Mackenzie's sister had returned from India to present her eldest daughter at court, and would be delighted to put Frances up.

"It will give her some distraction," Mrs. Mackenzie said. "It's so unfortunate that she should have chosen this year of all years. Court mourning is bound to spoil the season."

The unexpected death of the King had upset the Purcells too. The long winter was over, spring had come. With the onset of fine weather they had begun to recover from the shock of Mrs. Purcell's death. Now the muffled bells, the black draped church and mourning clothes around them brought back memories of their own loss. Surprisingly Frances was the worst affected. It was almost as if the tears she had held back earlier in the year could be contained no longer. "It's ridiculous," she said to Julia. "Why can't I stop crying? I didn't care about the stupid old King. Why should I go on like this?"

But tears were forgotten, the King's death long past: it was June when Frances went up to London. Gabriel was waiting on the platform when the train steamed in.

"I'll take you to my aunt," he said in the cab, "and leave you. I'm supposed to be at a meeting, so I can't stop. I believe Aunt Mildred has arranged some sortie after dinner this evening, so I shan't be able to be around with you then either, I'm afraid. I'm going back with you tomorrow, I expect you know that. I thought we might catch the early train." He glanced at the portfolio she was clutching in her lap. "What have you got there? May I see it? I haven't seen any of your work yet."

She shook her head. "Later." Any criticism now and what little confidence she had would disappear for ever.

He took her refusal without protest and looked out of the cab window. "Here we are. It's pleasant enough, the house. They've rented it for the season. Very useful, really."

'Pleasant' seemed an understatement. The entrance hall alone was larger than the Rectory drawing-room and dining-room combined.

"Ah, Squires," Gabriel said to the butler who opened the door. "This is Miss Purcell. My aunt's in, I take it?"

"In the morning-room, sir."

"Here we are, Aunt Mildred. Frances Purcell. All right, Frances? Good luck with this afternoon. See you this evening, Aunt."

Frances watched him go with dismay. She was daunted, by the size of the house, by Mrs. Strong's likeness to her sister, by fears of the afternoon. She found it difficult to sit down and make the polite conversation that Gabriel's aunt evidently expected.

"It's time I took you upstairs," Mrs. Strong said at last. "Nursery lunch is served earlier than ours; you don't want to miss it." She saw Frances's expression. "My dear child! You're not yet out; you can't stay downstairs. Nanny will see to everything. She knows all about you; and I've arranged for my own maid to take you to University College this afternoon."

Nanny was kind and welcoming, her charge less so. Alexandria was almost rude. "We're a bit of a madam, I'm afraid," Nanny whispered to Frances. "It's these nannies they have out in India, you know; armers I think they're called. Spare the rod and spoil the children, I always say."

Frances played with her food at lunch. Her hands trembled as she picked up her portfolio afterwards. Walking to the Slade with Mrs. Strong's maid she contemplated changing her mind, waiting until next year, working on her own. She looked at the sweep of grass in front of her as she went through the gates of University College and at the magnificent buildings. Would she be looking at this sight every day for the next three years or would she never see it again? Waiting outside the Professor's office she wondered, for the first time, whether the talent she possessed was enough, or whether she had stood out at school only because of the mediocrity of her fellow pupils.

The office was surprisingly drab, badly in need of decoration. The walls were bare, the carpet dull. There was nothing exciting, nothing artistic about the three men who interviewed her, though the Professor's shabby frock coat, Frances noticed, was engagingly smudged with paint. Behind him, the two remaining men leant against the mantelpiece as they watched her, resembling a drawing in *Punch*: one as large and bulky as a shaggy bear, the other astonishingly tall and thin. Frances knew, from what Gabriel had told her, that the latter must be Professor Tonks, a teacher whose sarcasm, according to Gabriel's Slade friend, was legendary. It was not, thankfully, evident today. While all three men treated her kindly they were more discouraging than she had expected, not so much about her own ability but about the help she could expect. They could teach her nothing new, they told her; they could only show her the methods of the Old Masters. If she wanted to learn it was up to her to do so.

"We *say* we have classes at the Slade," Professor Tonks said, looking down at her with mournful eyes from his great height. "In point of fact all we do is draw all day long."

When she finally emerged with the offer of a place at the school in the autumn she could not believe it to be true.

By the time she reached the Strongs she had recovered her senses. She thought of the Mackenzies and knew that it was important she talk to Gabriel before returning to Somerset the following day.

"We'll send a note down to Mr. Squires," Nanny said, when Frances asked her advice, and however ridiculous having to write a letter to someone in the same house in order to get in touch seemed, there was nothing else Frances could do.

She helped Nanny bath Alexandria and put her to bed. After an hour of what Nanny termed 'miss's high spirits', Frances decided that Sarah must be an extraordinarily quiet child, and was thankful for it. Supper over, she sat with Nanny in the day nursery and waited for Gabriel.

"Like a cat on hot bricks you are," Nanny complained, looking up from her smocking. "You should have learnt to sit still at your age. Why don't you do some drawing if that's what you're going to spend the rest of your life doing?"

The best thing that could be said about drawing at such a time was that it calmed the nerves and occupied the thoughts. Frances had almost forgotten Gabriel by the time the maid knocked on the door and said, "Mr. Squires says I'm to take you to the library, miss."

The swish of rich material and the hubbub of talk came up

from the hall to the library on the first floor. Frances glimpsed the sparkle of jewels and a gleam of satin through the stairwell.

Gabriel was alone. "What is it?" he said. "You'll have to be quick; we're about to leave."

She hesitated. She had not seen him in evening dress before. It made him seem remote, someone unknown, someone grand. "It's about the Slade ..."

"Oh, yes. How did you get on?"

"They'll take me. In the autumn."

He sat down. "Lord," he said, "that's put the cat among the pigeons. What do we do now?"

She stared at him, at first with surprise, then disbelief and as the meaning of his words dawned, with fury.

"What do you mean? You don't mean ... ? You *do* mean ... You didn't think I'd get in, did you? You thought they'd turn me down. All these months I thought you were helping me and all the time you were just ... just *humouring* me, like a child. 'Let her try for the Slade.' – that's what you said. 'She won't get in, of course, but let her try if it keeps her quiet.' – that's what you told your parents, isn't it?"

"Frances – listen."

"I thought you believed in me." She mustn't, mustn't let herself cry. "I know your parents never did but I thought you ... How *could* you ... ?"

"Frances, for heavens' sake! All this drama! How could I believe in you – I've never seen anything you've done. All I know is that you're determined."

"You said if I could get a place at a good art school I must go."

He was silent.

Perhaps he hadn't meant that either. Perhaps he'd said it to pacify her, to placate her. Oh, but she would fight him, fight them, make them see ... if only she could hold back the tears.

"Gabriel, I *must* go. It's the most important thing that's happened in my life. If I lose this chance because of you and your parents ... You've got to help me."

[37]

"What is it you want me to do?"

She waited a moment until she had stopped trembling and then tried to talk calmly. "I thought ... if you went to the Slade tomorrow and found out the details — I mean, they have lists of places to stay in, hostels, things like that, as well as fees and timetables — and if you could talk to Professor Brown or someone else as well, it might be easier for you to tackle your parents. Mightn't it?"

"I'll think about it," he said and stood up. "I can't stay, Frances, I'm holding everyone up. We'll have to catch the afternoon train tomorrow, not the morning one, if I'm going to go to that place. All right?"

When she went out onto the landing he was already downstairs in the hall, being greeted with a kiss by one female, taken by the hand by another. He went out of the front door without an upward glance.

In the day nursery Nanny was looking through the sketches Frances had made. "No-one's ever drawn me before. Eh, is this how you think I am?"

"Don't you like it?" Frances asked. It never mattered to her what lay people thought of her work, but tonight she was anxious not to offend.

Nanny held it out at arm's length. "I do, indeed I do."

"You can keep it, if you like."

"Sign it for me then, there's a good girl, then when you're famous I can show it to people."

At least someone believes in me, Frances consoled herself, even if it has to be someone who probably hasn't the faintest notion about drawing. But as she lay in bed that night, listening to Nanny's stertorous breathing from the other bed, such belief could not compensate for Gabriel's betrayal: Gabriel, in whom she had placed her trust and all her hopes.

They sat opposite each other on the train back to Taunton. Gabriel's mouth curved upwards in a lopsided smile as he watched her, one corner lifting higher than the other, giving the impression of inner amusement, even of mockery. She was still not sure of his friendship. There were times – today was one of them – when she was sure that he was laughing at her. She knew that he was waiting for her to ask whether he had been to the Slade. Childishly, she refused to put the question. In the end, though not until long after Reading, she gave in.

"Did you go this morning?"

"Of course."

"Well?"

"I was given a pile of information from the office. Oh, and I saw your Professor Tonks. Odd sort of chap, isn't he? Bit like a cadaver, I thought."

She was shocked by such irreverence. "What did he say?"

"He didn't seem to think Michelangelo the second had arrived on his doorstep, if that's what you're hoping."

"Don't be silly. What I meant was ... Oh Gabriel, you will speak to your parents, won't you? Please."

"I'll do my best but it's not going to be easy. You're so young. We may well persuade my parents to agree in the end, but I wouldn't be surprised if they insisted on your waiting a year."

She was alarmed. "I couldn't do that. It would be a whole year wasted – worse, a year going backwards. I'd get into all sorts of bad habits without realising and then when I did get to the Slade I'd have to spend all my time trying to get rid of them."

He shrugged. "If it's a case of that or not going at all ..."

"It's your mother that matters, isn't it? If she doesn't approve ..."

He considered. "I don't think so. Mother won't approve, ever, but if Father says yes, she'll have to agree."

Frances was surprised: she had thought it was Mrs. Mackenzie who held sway in the Rectory.

"You're forgetting," Gabriel said, "that it's Father who's your guardian."

"That's true." She wasn't sure whether the fact comforted

or depressed her. A clergyman, and old-fashioned, however kindly: what hope had she of gaining his approval?

Gabriel left her on Hillcrest's front doorstep. "I'll let my parents know what happened. You'd better come over later and tell Mother about Aunt Mildred and Alexandria. I shan't be able to give her the details she wants to know – fashions, the sort of thing I never notice. See what you can do. Don't mention the Slade unless they bring it up. If they do, be sensible. Don't behave as if it's a matter of life or death."

"It is, to me."

He looked exasperated. "I'll do my best. Don't make my task more difficult, that's all I ask."

She never knew what he said to his parents or how he set about persuading them. He was coming and going for most of the summer, involved, according to Lucy, with something called the Minority Report. When the Purcells, curious, tried to find out more Lucy said that it was to do with the Poor Law, at which Mrs. Mackenzie, thin-lipped, hastened to change the subject. The Purcells, rapidly learning discretion in their contacts with the Mackenzies and conscious of the particular need of it for Frances's sake at the present time, reluctantly refrained from further questions.

At night Frances lay awake and fretted. What was Gabriel doing? Were the Mackenzies any nearer a decision? Were they even considering one? Did they not realise that time was rushing past, irretrievable time, gone for ever?

One afternoon Mr. Mackenzie came out to the Rectory tennis court where Frances was watching a long drawn-out duel between Geoffrey, back from boarding-school, and Julia.

"Frances, my dear, I think we should talk. Won't you come into my study?"

He settled into the depths of his armchair, elbows digging into the leather, fingers pressed together to form a triangle above his knees. Expecting him to bring up financial matters, or the children's schooling, Frances was taken by surprise when he sighed and said, "It means a great deal to you, doesn't it, going to the Slade?" She began to shake with apprehension.

"Yes. Yes, it does."

"I wish I could help you understand how difficult a decision it is for us to make. If you were our child Mrs. Mackenzie and I would have no hesitation in saying no. Especially as you're a girl."

"I don't see what difference that makes," Frances said, and wondered for the first time whether Gabriel would have found the idea easier to accept had she been male.

"Had it been university . . . " Mr. Mackenzie began.

"The Slade is part of London University," Frances pointed out.

There was a trace of a smile. At such times the relationship between the Rector and his eldest son was unmistakable. "I'm sure you'll agree that it's not the same."

"I suppose not."

The regular thump of racquet on ball stopped. Antony shouted from the bushes.

"Gabriel has friends who've been to the Slade," Frances said. "They didn't come to any harm."

"Friends more worldly, I think. And London, Frances . . . when you're so young."

"I'm sure I'm old for my age, Mr. Mackenzie, with Mother dying and my having to be responsible . . . "

When she had first suggested art school, on the day of her mother's funeral, her fears of refusal had been on financial or practical grounds. It had never occurred to her then, even after the Mackenzies' shocked reaction, that she might be prevented on moral grounds.

"Mr. Mackenzie, all I want to do is learn. I'll be working, not . . . not doing whatever you're afraid I'll be doing in London. There won't be any money, anyway, for anything except work. I'd go to that place in Taunton, I'd be happy there, truly I would, if I thought it was suitable. I must have the best training, that's all."

"I suppose I might be considered old-fashioned. Certainly Gabriel is very insistent . . . if only you could understand the position I am in, Frances, the difficulty of being responsible for someone else's children, of not knowing what their own parents would have wished."

Frances thought of her own position towards Sarah. "I do understand, Mr. Mackenzie, really I do."

"I admired your mother, you know," Mr. Mackenzie said. "She was an exceptional woman, widely read, interesting, intelligent. I greatly regret now that we never discussed education, nor her aspirations for the four of you. As a result there are times when I feel very much at a loss. Tell me, Frances, would she have allowed you to go?"

Frances stared at the Rector, remembering bitter quarrels with her mother on that very subject. She wondered now, as she'd wondered then, why Mrs. Purcell had been so against the idea of art school. It was not possible to tell Mr. Mackenzie the truth, but neither could she lie. She searched desperately in her mind for a reply.

"She did leave me her painting things," she said at last.

Mr. Mackenzie's face lightened. "So she did. I had forgotten. That puts quite a different complexion on the affair. My dear, I can't tell you how relieved I am. I had no wish to hold you back, yet as your guardian . . ."

Frances had the grace to feel ashamed.

Chapter Five

Mrs. Mackenzie had been astonished to discover, not long after Mrs. Purcell's death, that Annie had one day off a week. Rectory staff were allowed only three half-days a fortnight. Even worse, Annie took her free time as one full day rather than two afternoons.

Mrs. Mackenzie complained to the Purcells, to Frances in particular, mildly at first, more firmly later, about Annie's free time. The Purcells were taken aback. Annie's Friday off had been part of the Hillcrest routine for as long as they could remember; they knew, and told Mrs. Mackenzie so, that Annie went back to her old home each week to wash and clean for her bedridden stepmother and the half-brothers who still lived with her.

"I'm sure it's very commendable," Mrs. Mackenzie said, "but a servant's first duty is to her employer. Then, too, it sets such a bad example to other households in the neighbourhood."

Frances was never quite sure whether she supported Annie because Mrs. Purcell had allowed it, because she thought Annie was right to do it or only because she knew it irritated Mrs. Mackenzie. Her own relationship with Annie might not always be harmonious but Frances was not going to have Annie ordered about by someone outside the Hillcrest household and least of all by Mrs. Mackenzie.

As the autumn term approached Frances gave more thought to Annie and her day off. It seemed to her that Mrs. Mackenzie might well try to take charge during her absence, browbeat Julia and Gwen and forbid Annie to leave the village. She decided that she should investigate for herself before leaving for London so that if it came to a battle with Mrs. Mackenzie she would know the situation exactly.

"It's a tidy step," Annie said doubtfully, when Frances announced one Thursday that she intended to accompany Annie the following morning.

"That's all right," Frances said. "You took Mother once, didn't you?"

"Your mother had her paints with her. Better bring yours too."

She became visibly apprehensive as they approached the Blackdown Hills next day. "You mustn't mind my step-mother, Miss Frances," she said. "She warn't an easy woman before her accident and now ... well, she's in pain most every day. She gets a bit crotchety like."

Mrs. Sampford lay in bed in the downstairs room. The air smelt indefinably of patent medicines. She complained that Annie was late, the stew Annie had left the previous week too salt, and when introduced to Frances said querulously, "We don't get any vegetables now. We used to get vegetables in the old days. Your mother always sent Annie back with vegetables. Fruit, too, in the summer."

"That's enough, Mother," Annie said quickly. "The Purcells have to watch the pennies themselves these days. You be quiet now. Better leave me be, Miss Frances. No, it's kind of you to offer, but I know what's to be done. You take yourself outside and get on with your painting."

Frances was thankful to escape from the sickroom. Illness frightened and repelled her. Poor Annie, she thought, having to cope with Mrs. Sampford every week.

The long narrow garden was overgrown. Apples on the unpruned trees were small and hard. An attempt had been made at vegetable growing but thistles flourished between the potato rows and carrots and beetroot had been suffocated by weeds. The runner bean supports lay in a tangled mass on the ground, the beans themselves growing curled and dirty from too close contact with the soil. Gwen would have been horrified. So was Frances, but she thought it picturesque too and was glad of the opportunity to paint it.

The shadows were long across the garden by the time Annie had finished, the dusty road dark between the high Somerset hedges as she and Frances walked slowly home. All that work, Frances was thinking, and not a word of thanks. Nothing but grumbles, audible even from the garden, and not one protest from Annie, not one word of complaint.

"Get yourself into the living-room, Miss Frances," Annie said when they reached Hillcrest, "and I'll bring you a cup of tea."

"Don't be silly, Annie," Frances said. "I'll have it in the kitchen with you."

They sat in silence, Annie slumped in a chair, eyes closed. Frances had never seen her look so weary. She wondered why she had never thought of painting Annie before — not as she was now, exhausted, but sitting at the kitchen table one morning, with her broad arms spread over the scrubbed wood, a mug of tea in her hands and the result of her baking laid out in front of her – bread, baps, scones and cakes – and the range glowing in the background, or sitting in the yard outside the kitchen window, peeling potatoes or slicing beans, with the sun slanting across the cobbles.

"Your stepmother said Mother used to give you vegetables," Frances said. "You should have told me. I didn't know."

Annie opened her eyes. "It made me cross, that, her mentioning the veg. There was no call for it. 'Tis true your mother let me take what I could carry, but that was in the old days when there was only her and Miss Sarah in the house and no worries about money. And our lads were younger then. They could do more if they tried – Miss Gwen gets more out of her vegetable plot than the three of them put together and she's but a child. Great lumps they are. I blame her, mind. If she spent more time hustling them, and less time moaning..."

"They take advantage of you," Frances said. She added quickly, "I don't mind your having the time off, don't think that, but it does seem hard. She's no relation of yours and they're only your half-brothers."

"She was good to my father," Annie said.

"It's not right, you know," Frances said. "You ought to have some proper time off. You must have a half-day..."

"Now then, Miss Frances," Annie said firmly. "We both know what Mrs. Mackenzie would say to that. I'll not be the cause of trouble there."

"I don't care what Mrs. Mackenzie says."

"Well, you should. She's a good woman. Not easy, maybe, but she means well. We shouldn't be here without her, that's certain."

"I still think..."

"That's enough, Miss Frances. I don't deny there's been times when Bertha and I've fancied an outing together... but there'll be time for that later."

"Bertha? From the Rectory?"

Annie nodded.

How little I know about her, Frances thought. I'd no idea she was friendly with Bertha. And I suppose I should have found out about her home months ago. It never occurred to me.

She watched Annie pour out more tea. "You've never said what you thought about my going to London."

"'Tweren't for me to venture an opinion, Miss Frances."

"But you knew Mother wouldn't let me go to art school. If you'd told Mr. Mackenzie that, or even Gabriel . . ."

"Ah, well. I never understood your mother, not about that. *She'd* run away to art school. You'd think she wouldn't mind."

Frances stared. "*Mother?* Was *that* why she left home?"

"That's what she said."

"But she never went to art school, I'm sure she didn't."

"Seems there weren't the money. Father cut her off – that's what she told me. She finished up with artists all the same, leastways that's what I understood, so it seemed funny to me, her being against you doing the same. Not that I agreed with the way you went about things, mind. Downright rude to her most times you were. I don't hold with that."

"Oh, Annie," Frances said.

"We'll manage. When you've gone, I mean. It won't be easy, I daresay, but we'll manage." She took the mugs over to the sink. Her back was to Frances as she said, "There's just one thing, Miss Frances. I know it's not my place to say it, but I'll say it just the same. Mr. and Mrs. Mackenzie aren't happy about London, even now. They're letting you go because they lay store on what Mr. Gabriel says. It's him they'll turn on, if it goes wrong, not you. Don't let him down, that's all I ask. I wouldn't want this house to cause bad blood between the Mackenzies."

"Of course I won't," Frances said. "I'm not a fool, Annie."

She paused in the doorway before going out to find Sarah. "You are, though. You should know by now that you're entitled to say whatever you want in this house."

Annie's mention of Gabriel brought to the surface a problem that had worried Frances for some time: how to thank Gabriel. She knew that without him as an ally she would never have achieved her ambition to go to the Slade, knew too that words of thanks alone were inadequate.

To decide on a present was one thing, to choose the form it should take quite another. Julia suggested asking Mr. Mackenzie's advice but Frances refused.

"He'd want to know why. I couldn't very well tell him, could I?"

It was Gwen who suggested a drawing, and Julia the subject – a portrait of Mr. Mackenzie himself. "They're very close, don't you think, Gabriel and he? When you see them together ..."

Frances started work with enthusiasm, seeing what she wanted in her mind and knowing what she hoped to achieve. She refused to ask Mr. Mackenzie to sit for her. She had never shown the Mackenzies her work, whether from shyness or humility, or because she did not trust their judgement, she did not know. Mr. Mackenzie would have to be drawn without his knowledge.

The only opportunity she had to observe him without being observed herself was during church services. She made sketches during morning service, with Gwen and Julia on guard to nudge her should Mrs. Mackenzie show signs of turning round to check the behaviour of those in the Hillcrest pew, and rushed home the moment the service ended to continue working there. It was not the most satisfactory way of drawing a portrait.

Julia was the one who showed talent at portraiture, rather than Frances. The walls of the school artroom had been covered by Julia's sketches of her schoolfellows, all instantly recognisable. Frances preferred the larger scene. She soon realised that what she really wanted to do now was to paint the church interior itself, with Mr. Mackenzie as only a small part of the whole, but because that was not what she had intended for Gabriel she persisted with the study of Mr. Mackenzie himself. The result depressed her deeply.

"How can I give this to Gabriel?" she asked Julia. "It's awful."

Julia propped the drawing against the back of a chair and stood back.

"It's not as bad as all that," she said after a while. "It's a good likeness. It's from the wrong angle though. You should have done it from the opposite choirstall."

"Oh yes? During the service?"

"If you're not prepared to ask Mr. Mackenzie to sit for you what else can you expect? You'll have to promise Gabriel to do another when you don't mind Mr. Mackenzie posing, that's all. You must give it to him, Frances. It'll mean a lot, being of his father, and you thinking of it, too. It's not that bad. I expect we're more critical than most people. And Gabriel . . . I know he always seems sort of, well, amused all the time but I think he cares a lot underneath. He'll like it, I know he will."

"I hope you're right," Frances said, unconvinced. "It's too late to do anything else now."

She gave it to him in London. He came down from Cambridge to take her up at the beginning of the term. With Gabriel at her side she was forced to be cheerful, to smile and pretend that she had no doubts or second thoughts, but leaving Hillcrest and everyone in it, Annie as well as the other Purcells, was very much worse than she had anticipated. She was relieved when Gabriel appeared happy to read in the train rather than talk – Greek, as far as she could tell from a curious glance over the edge of the book.

"Do you read that sort of thing for pleasure?" she said, when he glanced up and out of the window.

"Yes, of course." He sounded amused.

"You really enjoy it?"

"I write it too, sometimes."

"You're clever, aren't you?" she said.

"Well . . . I didn't get as good a degree as I should have done. Too busy with other things, I'm afraid."

"What sort of things?"

"Theatricals. And the Fabians."

"Fabians? What are they?"

"You haven't heard of them?"

She shook her head.

"They're ... political, I suppose."

"Oh, politics." She lost interest at once.

Mrs. Mackenzie and her sister had chosen Frances's digs during the summer, visiting each one on the list supplied by the Slade and selecting the most suitable.

"So embarrassing," Gwen and Julia said, when they heard. "Think of all the questions they'd ask. Just as well you weren't there, Frances, you'd have died. Or said something dreadful."

Frances looked round now at the bare room that was hers, saw the thin line of soot beneath the window, the dismal view of house backs and plane trees sagging in the rain and wondered how she was going to endure the next three years.

"It's very nice," she said, coming downstairs to where Gabriel waited in the hall.

Something of what she felt must have shown in her face. "Cheer up," he said. "Why don't I take you out for a meal before I catch the train back to Cambridge?"

He insisted on ordering for her despite her protests that she wasn't hungry. "Food will buck you up. I know how you feel: I've always hated going away the first time. Prep school, public school, even Cambridge. It gets worse, if anything. I've always envied Geoffrey being the second one, having someone ahead of him knowing the ropes."

She tried to smile.

"If you didn't come up here," he said, "if you took the easy way out and sat at home painting pretty little watercolours you'd regret it for the rest of your life, wouldn't you?"

"I suppose so."

"You told me it was a matter of life and death, your coming to the Slade."

She said, "Do you think I'm being selfish, leaving the others on their own? You don't think I should have stayed and looked after them?"

"Of course not. They'll be all right – they've got Annie ... and Mother across the road." He leant across the table. "I'm going to give you some advice. I know you don't like being given advice but it worked last time, didn't it?"

"Yes."

"Try to see my parents' point of view. As far as Mother's concerned, going to art school is the first step on the slippery slope to moral disintegration. If not the third or fourth. Even Father can be a bit conservative sometimes. And I know he's your guardian but what Mother says does carry a lot of weight. If either of them have second thoughts or doubts about your being up here they can whip you back home and there'll be nothing you can do about it, nothing at all. So, please, Frances, be careful. Don't do anything to make them change their minds."

"You must think me very stupid."

"Impulsive, let's say."

"Annie gave me a lecture before I left. The same sort of thing."

"Did she? Good old Annie."

Surprisingly, his concern made her feel better. "Is that all? Lecture over?"

"One more thing. Write to them every week."

She was dismayed. "What would I say? I'll be writing to Hillcrest – Julia can tell them what's happening."

"That's not enough. There's no need for lengthy epistles, just regular notes telling them you're all right. Promise?"

"I suppose so." She looked at him. "Will you write to me?"

"Well ... do you want me to?"

She nodded. "Please."

"All right then. And if we're writing, it might be a good idea ... Father will have talked to you about finance. If you have any problems about money or your allowance then you must get in touch with him but if you're worried about anything else why not tell me first? We might be able to sort it out between us without having to bother my parents."

Surprise at the extent of his concern, and gratitude, reminded her of the drawing still in her trunk. "I'd forgotten. I've got a present for you back at the digs."

"For me? Hurry up then and let's go back."

The hall seemed a very public place for present-giving but the landlady had said nothing about entering downstairs rooms.

"I'm not very good at saying what I feel," Frances said awkwardly. "It's ... well, a thank you for all you've done, I suppose. I did want you to know ... going against your parents ... all that. I am grateful."

He looked down at the drawing and up at her. "Did you do this?"

She wished desperately that it was something of which she could be proud. "I'm sorry it's so bad. I know one shouldn't make excuses but it was difficult, being in church and trying not to let people see what I was doing during the service."

His lips twitched. "I should think so."

"It didn't come out as I meant. I'll do something better when I'm more experienced, I promise."

"Don't. I like this as it is. I'm ... touched. Not ... not just by the portrait, but by the thought. I ... well, thank you."

For a moment he sounded as inarticulate as Frances. She realised with surprise that Julia had been right, that the fact of the present, and perhaps the subject, meant more to him than the quality of the drawing and that it would have been foolish of her to have kept it back out of pride. In bed that night she had the remembrance of his pleasure to overlay her fear of the next day.

Chapter Six

Frances never forgot her first encounter as a student with Professor Tonks. He came up to her as she worked before a cast in the Antique Room and studied her drawing in silence for several minutes before saying, "Is that the best you can do?"

Frances's heart thumped with apprehension. "I . . . I think so."

He looked at her with sad eyes. "Then why do it?"

The class tittered.

Frances felt colour flood into her face. Tears filled her eyes. She picked up the drawing and tore it into pieces.

"You shouldn't do that," said the girl next to her after Tonks had moved on to another pupil. "Don't mind him, he's always saying that sort of thing. He wanted to see if he could make you cry. Look him in the face next time. He likes courage."

It was the shame of that moment that stayed with Frances, the humiliation of knowing that the man who mattered most at the Slade considered her work not worth the effort. Only gradually did she come to understand that Tonks was a perfectionist, and as such did not care what means he used to instil the passion that he felt into the minds of his pupils. Sarcasm was a favourite method, and yet – as Frances slowly came to discover – beneath the forbidding exterior, the severe countenance and cold hooded eyes there was a delightful, kindly and sympathetic man.

He was obsessed with the need to draw – bad drawing was like living a lie, he said, and frowned at Frances as he said it. The Slade was a school for drawing. Colour was unimportant, painting secondary. Once a student had been promoted from the Antique Room he could spend the rest of his Slade days in the Life Room without ever touching a paintbrush. Frances was dismayed. She had never paid much attention to the preliminaries, had always been anxious to start with colour or crayon. It had never occurred to her that draughtsmanship mattered.

Everything about the Slade she found strange, from the moment of arrival on the first morning when the top-hatted beadle standing in the hall expected her to know that she must sign in and out, morning and evening, in the register by the door. Her signature, she was ashamed to see, wavered over the page . . .

The high-ceilinged echoing corridors and large rooms lit by huge, draughty windows were the outward signs of a place that seemed to her to be chilly and remote. When a fellow student remarked that it brought back memories of his old public school days she could believe him. Christian names were never used. To be known always as Purcell only increased her bewilderment and loneliness.

It was the brilliance of those around her that dismayed her the most. She was under no illusions about her own talent but it seemed to her that she was surrounded by students, women as well as men, who were able to produce with ease drawings that she knew she could not hope to emulate however hard she struggled. She wondered why she had ever come, why the Slade should have accepted her when she was so obviously out of her depth. She had expected, through being one of the minority, that she would find companionship, but discovered that men and women were more or less equal in number and many of the women were more gifted than most of the men. Frances was lost as well as homesick, but the homesickness was the worst. At school she had had Julia. Here she had no-one.

She returned to her digs, when the Slade closed at lunchtime at the end of her first week, wondering how she was going to survive the long, empty hours of the weekend – and found Gabriel waiting in the hall.

"Oh, Gabriel . . . how . . . it's *wonderful* to see you!"

He removed her arms gently from round his neck. "Well,

well. What a welcome! Are you all right or does this greeting signify something amiss?"

"Of course I'm all right." Heavens, she thought, another moment and I'll burst into tears. "It's just ... I don't know ... oh Gabriel, everything's so strange."

He put an arm round her shoulder and gave her a little shake. "I never expected to find Miss Purcell homesick. I'd better take you out and feed you. It seems to be my mission in life these days."

It was surprising how cheerful she felt after a couple of hours spent in Gabriel's company. The events of the first week, the doubts and humiliations, could be made light of when recounted to Gabriel's sympathetic ears, could indeed be made to sound almost funny. To see that quirky smile she would exaggerate, and by exaggerating diminish her unhappiness ...

She had suffered from homesickness at school but she had hated school. She had thought, because she was at the Slade by her own choice, that the homesickness in London would pass. It remained with her for the whole of the first term. One of her fellow students travelled daily to the Slade from his home in Berkshire and was known as 'Cookham' as a result and teased, though not by Frances. She envied him. Every evening she watched him disappear through the gates, and walking back to her digs she pictured him arriving at Paddington, saw him travelling westwards on the train, imagined him reaching home ...

It was Gabriel's weekend visits that helped her most. He was usually amused, sometimes teasing, and always kind. He showed her London, took her to the South Kensington museums, on fine days took her further afield to Hampstead Heath, Box Hill, Newlands Corner, the Pilgrims' Way. He promised to take her walking on the Quantocks when summer came and they were back in Somerset. He let her talk endlessly about Julia and Gwen and Sarah, listened to her worries about Hillcrest and when she was at her most miserable said, "You don't have to stay, you know. You can always go home; there's nothing to stop you. Except the thought of Mother's face if you do. Imagine that look of triumph."

It was not only the vision of a triumphant Mrs. Mackenzie that kept Frances in London. Gabriel had supported her and encouraged her; she could not bear to disappoint him.

Strangely enough, many of her doubts and fears were put to rest by an exhibition she visited towards the end of that term, an exhibition that had almost as much influence on her as the Holman Hunt one had had four years before. It was of Post-Impressionist work, much of it French, held at the Grafton Gallery. Frances had seen nothing like the paintings that hung on the walls and was overwhelmed – by the images, the shapes, the intensity of colour, the effect of light. She went round in a daze, and when she had reached the end began again. Her reaction was largely instinctive – she could not have expressed her feelings in words – but for the first time she knew with absolute certainty that this was her world and her future.

She insisted on taking Gabriel to see it on his next visit. "You *must* come. It's *wonderful*. I can't tell you how wonderful."

He couldn't believe that she was serious. He thought that she was teasing him; that no-one could admire such work. She was amazed by his reaction and deeply shocked. They argued bitterly for the rest of the day. It was their first quarrel. She could not understand why he could appreciate none of it, not one canvas.

"You're a *Philistine*! You are. You're as bad as your mother. You'd rather have a Landseer – a *Landseer* – over your mantelpiece ... " She saw that she had made him angry and was triumphant. "You should stick to the Royal Academy if that's your level of appreciation." She could think of no worse insult.

He was stiff and very adult. "You're being childish. I may

not appreciate art's finer points – it's not a subject that I've ever pretended to know much about although I'm always ready to learn – but this isn't art. Black outlines filled with splodges of colour, most of it. A child could do better," and when she denied it and said that he was not merely ignorant but patronising as well, he was irate. "I'm not alone, I'll have you know. I haven't read a decent review yet."

It was true. The exhibition had many critics, not least among the staff of the Slade itself, Tonks, indeed, having gone so far as to forbid his pupils to visit it. It was an edict that was obeyed by few. Until now Frances had been well on the way to hero-worshipping Tonks. The discovery that her god had feet of clay did not upset her; she still prayed for favourable comments on her work, dreaded his disdain or, worse, his indifference, but after the Post-Impressionist exhibition she never revered him with the same intensity as that of many of her fellow female students.

She was astonished when Gabriel suggested on his next visit that they should return to the Grafton for another look.

"Well," he said, sheepishly, "I suppose ... if it means so much to you ... "

On their way into the main room they met a couple of men Gabriel knew from Cambridge, who not only – so they told him – regarded the paintings favourably, but had themselves helped set up the exhibition. Thinking back to the meeting later, Frances was sure that their opinion had helped open Gabriel's mind. She tried to explain to him, as calmly and rationally as she could, the effect such paintings had on her but she was trying to put into words emotions that she barely understood herself: she knew that she would never be able to make him understand.

"I daresay they grow on you," he said when they came out into the street again. "I do think there's a lot more to that fellow Cézanne than I did at the beginning. I don't know that I'd care to have one of Gauguin's efforts hanging on my wall, but you do want to go on looking, I admit that. You'll have to educate me, I can see, only don't bring anything like that home to Mother. She really would think you'd gone to the devil."

"What else could you expect of someone who considers Landseer the greatest painter the world's ever seen?" Frances said, but she was laughing. She was happy: it mattered to her that Gabriel should approve, however half-heartedly, of something that affected her so intensely.

Chapter Seven

Frances had hoped that her sisters might meet the train at Dunkery St. Michael on her return for the Christmas holidays. It had never occurred to her to wonder whether they might come all the way in to Taunton. She could scarcely believe her eyes when they rushed up to greet her as she descended from the London train.

"It was Mrs. Mackenzie's idea," Gwen said as they hurried over to the Minehead platform. "She said it'd be nice for us . . . though she did want Lucy to come too to look after us."

"But Lucy hasn't . . .?"

"She said she'd got to get ready for Sunday School."

"She hadn't really," Sarah said.

"She knew we wanted to be on our own," Julia said, and smiled. "Well? How was it?"

"Splendid. Really." She meant it. Now that she was back in Somerset she could forget the dirt of London and the fog, her loneliness and longing for home, and remember only the good times. "Oh, but it is nice to be back. Goodness, Sarah, you've grown!"

"Annie says I'm going to *burst* out of all my clothes any minute now," Sarah said. "She wants you to sort out Gwen's old clothes for me." She jumped up and down. "Guess what, Frances! You're going to a fancy dress dance at the Manor on New Year's Eve."

"Oh no, I'm not," Frances said. "What could I wear?"

"I rather think you have to," Julia said. "A royal summons, more or less. You're going with the Mackenzies – not Geoffrey or Antony, but the others. Mrs. Mackenzie's hired costumes."

"Has she indeed?" Frances said. "And what am I to be, may I ask?"

"Boadicea," Sarah said. "It was *my* idea, Frances. I wanted you to be Boadicea."

Hillcrest was as she remembered. Ridiculous to think it might have changed. Annie in the kitchen, Christmas food in the larder, home-made decorations already up in the living-room – oh, it was good to be home.

"Everything all right, Annie? No problems?"

"We rubbed along, Miss Frances. No need for you to worry."

"Sarah's grown."

"She's spending time with Master Antony – after lessons, I mean. Spoilt he is, no doubt about it even if he is the apple of the Rector's eye, but he's a good enough lad. He gets her nose out of her books and into the fresh air now and again." She hesitated. "I hope I did right, Miss Frances, letting her go."

"Of course you did. She needs to see other people."

Both Frances and Annie knew that the next couple of weeks were likely to be difficult for the family, with memories of past Christmases still vivid, but the festival turned out to be easier than either had thought. Annie made Gwen and Sarah help with the cooking and the baking and they were all expected to help with the distribution of mince pies and parcels for the needy, organised by Mrs. Mackenzie at the Rectory. There was no time for backward glances or for tears.

Geoffrey came home the day after Frances; Gabriel not until Christmas Eve.

Frances could barely wait until she and Gabriel were alone. "I won a prize for drawing at the end of term."

"Did you, indeed? What did Mother and Father have to say to that?"

"I haven't told them yet. I wanted you to be the first to know."

It wasn't so much the money that pleased her, although four pounds would certainly help towards the fees, as the acknowledgement that the sacrifices she was forcing onto her family were justified.

Frances was disconcerted, and the other Purcells upset, when she discovered that she was expected to change at the Rectory before the New Year's Eve dance.

"I wanted to see Boadicea," Sarah said. Her voice wobbled.

"Never mind. I'll dress up again in the morning," Frances promised.

There was a fire burning in Lucy's room when Frances arrived, and rugs on the floor. Frances thought, but only briefly, that it must be pleasant to be comfortably off with no need to worry about money. She was nervous, partly because of the evening ahead, partly because she was still not at ease with Lucy. Although younger than Gabriel, Lucy always seemed older to Frances and frighteningly competent in the way she organised and ran so much of the parish. Tonight, however, she was easy and friendly, helping Frances into her costume and braiding her hair for her.

"It was clever of Sarah to suggest Boadicea," she said. "I can't think what made Mother choose Solomon and the Queen of Sheba for us. Can you imagine anything less like Gabriel and me? Sheba must have been, well, *faintly* dark, I'd have thought – she came from Africa, after all. Whereas look at me." She peered at herself in the mirror, pinched her cheeks and bit her lips. "Lily white."

Frances was surprised to hear Lucy being critical. "It's a very nice costume," she said.

"It doesn't suit me half as well as yours does you. You look wonderful. I'm sure Boadicea must have had red hair."

"My hair isn't red," Frances said. She attributed red hair to the sort of girls, models and students mostly, who clustered round artists like Augustus John and was offended. "It's ... chestnut. Or mahogany."

Lucy smiled at her. "All right. Chestnut then. Are you ready? Let's go downstairs."

Gabriel was waiting in the hall in an elaborate costume of gleaming peacock-coloured brocade. He looked taken aback at the sight of the two girls.

"What's the matter?" Frances said. "Don't I look right?"

"I didn't recognise you for a moment. You look splendid. Much better than I do. Heaven knows how I'm going to dance in this rig."

Dancing had already begun by the time the Rectory party arrived at the Manor. Not all dancers were in fancy dress. Most of the older generation, Frances saw, were, like Mr. and Mrs. Mackenzie, in ordinary evening clothes. Sir James, however, was greeting his guests in satin knee-length breeches and an embroidered jacket, with lace festooned at his throat and ropes of pearls across his chest.

"Clive of India," he explained. "Seemed appropriate with Fergus out there at the moment. Peshawar, his last letter said. Familiar ground, eh, Mrs. Mackenzie? Ah, Frances my dear. Nice to see you. Things going all right?"

The Mackenzies circled the room, greeting friends and introducing Frances. She recognised one or two faces from the Rectory teas in the summer, but was frighteningly aware of a roomful of people about whom she knew nothing.

A beefeater asked Lucy to dance, Mrs. Mackenzie wanted a word with Lady Donne – even grander and more gracious than Mrs. Mackenzie – and Gabriel departed with an exceedingly plump Joan of Arc. Mr. Mackenzie turned to Frances.

"My dear, may I have the pleasure?"

She had only ever danced at school, with schoolgirls. Dancing with Mr. Mackenzie must be like dancing with the King. She was relieved when the music came to an end and Mr. Mackenzie suggested fetching her a drink.

Gabriel came over at last. "There – duty done for a while. Now I can spend some time with you."

She was curious. "Duty? What do you mean?"

"Oh, you know. All the people you have to ask. Your hostess. Hester Donne. Mother and Lucy. And then there are all the females Mother will expect me to partner, either her friends, or their eligible daughters."

"I didn't realise attending a dance was such a complicated business."

"Oh, gracious, yes. In the country anyway. If you step out of line – dance too much with one person or miss dancing with somebody else – word will spread through west Somerset like wildfire. Father has even stricter ideas – you should start with the ugliest girl in the room, for instance."

Frances considered this information. "He asked me for the first dance."

He smiled at her. "There you are then. Come on, let's go."

The two-step was followed by a waltz. No man had held her so close before. Momentary panic made breathing difficult.

"Did you learn to dance at school?"

She nodded.

"Don't tell me – you always took the man's part?"

"How did you know?"

"It's obvious. You're not the man now, let me tell you. Try to relax and follow what I'm doing."

After a time he left her for more duty dances, and presumably pleasurable ones too. She danced with a pirate, a bedraggled Roman citizen, and an elderly man who said that he had heard about her family from Mr. Mackenzie and was glad to know that they were going on all right. She wondered whether she would recognise any one of her partners out of costume. The empty spaces on her programme did not worry her; if she could not be with Gabriel she preferred to sit out and watch, though she wished she had thought to bring her sketchbook with her.

Gabriel came back for another waltz. Joan of Arc's eyes followed him round the room.

"Who's she?" Frances asked.

"Hester Donne." He sounded surprised. "Don't you know her?" He waited until they were out of hearing before murmuring, "I'd always pictured the Maid as rather more undernourished, hadn't you?"

The evening drew on. She was not used to such late nights. When the orchestra retired for refreshment the village band took its place. She recognised the young man from the forge among the trumpets. The instruments were too loud for the confined space of the hall; the beat throbbed inside her head. She wished midnight would come quickly, and go.

Gabriel reappeared. "Are you all right? Here, come with me."

They were in the cooler, moister atmosphere of the conservatory, in darkness except for fairy lights strung between the bay trees. There was fragrance in the air, tropical and mysterious. Stars hung in the sky above the glass roof.

"Better?" Gabriel said.

"I'm sorry. I don't know what happened."

"I expect it was the heat. Take your time. There's no hurry. It'll soon be 1911."

"Yes," Frances said, and thought that it would be a relief to see the end of 1910.

"It's been a very successful year for you, hasn't it? Even a prize."

She said, "This time last year Mother was alive." She spoke without thinking and regretted it immediately; even in the dim light she could see the shock on his face.

"My dear girl. I'm sorry. I didn't think. So much ... It seems so long ago, all that. I was thinking of you and the Slade."

"I know. I shouldn't have said it." She couldn't tell him that she had been remembering last New Year's Eve, when she sat with her mother in the Hillcrest living-room waiting for the grandfather clock on the stairs to chime midnight.

"A special year," Mrs. Purcell had said. "The beginning of a new decade. I remember ten years ago ... oh, so well. The turn of the century, the old Queen still alive, Sarah not born, your father ... We went to a naval ball and danced all night. Oh ... How different life was when your father was alive, everything such fun."

Melancholy seeped into Frances with the memory. Had her mother wanted to talk about the past that evening, tell Frances something of herself? If so Frances had not been listening. Her thoughts had been concentrated on the passing of another year, the knowledge that in a few days' time she would be seventeen; growing old, old, old, and no nearer achieving her ambition to study at art school.

A loud burst of cheering came from the hall, followed by a tattoo on a hunting horn.

"1911," Gabriel said, bent forward and kissed her. "May it be a better year for you all. Come and have some champagne."

Footmen negotiated the edges of the crowd with trays of glasses. The liquid fizzed and bubbled, tickling her nose. She had lost sight of Mr. and Mrs. Mackenzie and Lucy. An old man standing beside her lunged forward and kissed her, his moustache scratching her cheek. The orchestra had returned for Auld Lang Syne. On the other side of the room people linked hands and began to sing, swaying in time to the music.

"Tell me when you want to go home," Gabriel said.

"I think I'd like to now," Frances said. "Would you mind? It's not that I'm tired, just ..." She had had enough of the crowd. She would rather have seen the New Year in at home with her sisters and Annie.

She walked silently up the hill with Gabriel. Sounds of merrymaking came after them, growing fainter. The thin strains of violins pierced the misty air. When they looked back the Manor had become a pattern of blacks and yellows, light from windows falling onto the drive, carriages and broughams silhouetted in the foreground. The melancholy grew worse. Not only the old Queen, but the King, and Mrs. Purcell herself, gone forever, while all these people down there danced and drank and sang ...

[63]

"Will you go back?" she said.

"Yes, of course. Not that my parents will stay much longer; there won't be many of their generation left by one. The rest of us will carry on dancing for some time yet."

She wondered whether Hester Donne would be waiting for him. "I wish I was better at dancing."

"You need practice, that's all. Why don't we come over to Hillcrest some time? Lucy's a splendid dancer – she'll help you. Geoffrey's not bad and even Antony ... It's one of the things Mother's been determined about, our being able to dance. I remember going to classes when I was years younger than Antony is now. We could roll up the carpet in your living-room."

"Or use the kitchen. There's more room, and Annie wouldn't mind."

"That's settled then." He banged the knocker on the front door before he said, suddenly sober, "Frances. I'm ... I am sorry about this evening ... for what I said. I didn't think. I do admire you, you know – all of you – for the way you've carried on."

"It's all right. Don't worry about it."

She could hear the smile in his voice. "If only your mother could see you now. She'd be so proud."

She said bleakly, "She wouldn't. She'd be angry. She didn't want me to go to art school," and as the door opened slipped past Annie and went quickly inside.

1911

Chapter Eight

"I say," the girl said, "do come and look at my room. I've been waiting for hours for someone to admire it."

The room, presumably once as bare as Frances's own, had been transformed into a scene from the Arabian Nights. Swatches of brilliantly coloured silk swathed the walls. Oriental shawls festooned the bedstead and hung over the edge of the dressing-table. A couple of Eastern rugs lay on the floor.

Frances gaped. "It's ... it's fantastic." And very expensive, she thought. "Where did it all come from?"

"The attic at home. Daddy must've brought it all back from Persia. Nice, don't you think? Adds a bit of colour ... you're at the Slade, aren't you?"

Frances nodded. "This is my second term."

"I'm a year ahead of you then. Jamieson, Katherine Jamieson. Why don't we go out this evening? It's always so dismal, the first day back."

"Well ... I've got to unpack and ... you know, all that sort of thing ..." She had glimpsed Jamieson during the previous autumn, rushing out in the evenings expensively, even exotically, dressed, and dreaded to think how much the cost of an evening out with her would eat into her own allowance.

Jamieson looked disappointed. "Oh. Oh well. Another time then."

Gabriel wrote frequently to Frances during the winter but never came to see her. She missed his company, his sometimes barbed comments on life, and the encouragement he gave her, but found to her surprise that she could manage very well on her own. She was beginning to enjoy not only the Slade but London too. The winning of the prize had increased her confidence and the growing friendship with Jamieson helped: she become more at ease with her fellow students and began to make friends. Jamieson amused her and only gradually did Frances realise that Jamieson, despite her partying, was as dedicated to her work as Frances was to hers. They spent many hours together in the Print Room of the British Museum or copying paintings in the National Gallery. Frances even let herself be dragged to the Café Royal.

"You haven't ever been there? Oh, Purcell, you must. It's where artists and writers meet and important people like that. You'll learn a lot just by listening. It isn't expensive either — you can make one coffee last the whole evening if you want."

When Frances returned home at Easter it was with the knowledge of a term well spent and another prize gained.

This time only Gwen and Julia were on the platform.

"Where's Sarah?"

"She couldn't come. She's been ill."

"Ill? What? When? Why didn't you tell me?"

"They wouldn't let us. It's all right, Frances, really. She's better now. She had measles. Mrs. Mackenzie looked after her at the Rectory."

Frances rushed into Hillcrest. "Oh, mouse, mouse," she cried, "what have you been doing to yourself?"

"I didn't mean to be ill, Frances, truly I didn't," Sarah said, white as a little ghost, with shadowed eyes and legs as thin as matchsticks. "I'm sorry. I couldn't help it."

"Why didn't you *tell* me?" Frances said to Annie. "I *said* to write ..."

"We talked it over, Miss Frances," Annie said, "and decided, best not mention it. You'd just worry and there weren't no need. You know Mrs. Mackenzie: she's a wonder with sickness. She looked after Miss Sarah like she was her own child. If Miss Sarah'd been taken bad I'd have written, I promise, whatever Mrs. Mackenzie said."

"Well, I suppose ..." Frances said. She was ashamed to realise that now Sarah had recovered she was relieved to have known nothing. She was anxious nevertheless.

"Spend time with the child these holidays, Miss Frances," Annie suggested. "She looks up to you. It'd give her bit of a fillip if you sat with her."

Frances offered to draw Sarah. It was Monday, the day that Mrs. Mackenzie came over to Hillcrest for drawing-room tea and her inspection of the previous week's accounts. Today, because of Sarah, the fire had been lit early.

"You don't have to be so tense," Frances said. "Don't sit like that, staring at me. Lie back. Read a book. I don't mind what you do, as long as you don't move."

The book slipped onto the floor. Sarah drowsed against the cushions, face flushed by the firelight. Over her head, beyond the sofa and through the French windows, the verandah trellis framed a view across the lawn to the rose garden. Drawing wasn't right for such a scene; watercolour or pastel would be more appropriate.

That afternoon was the beginning of a long partnership. Gwen and Julia were too busy themselves, with affairs of the house or their own drawing and painting, to sit for Frances. Sarah could pose while reading or studying and was happy to do so. They were mostly scenes that Frances did, with Sarah only part of the whole; it was Julia who preferred to concentrate on portraits as such.

Julia was working during Frances's absence. Frances noticed a framed drawing of Mrs. Mackenzie on the mantelpiece of Mr. Mackenzie's study when she went over to the Rectory to discuss family affairs on her return from London.

"I don't doubt Julia will follow you to the Slade in due course," the Rector said, seeing her glance.

Frances noted his indulgent tone and, remembering the

misery and suspense she herself had suffered the previous year, thought how lucky Julia was to have her battles already fought for her.

Gwen expected Frances to fight for her too.

"It's a waste of time, my going to lessons," she said. "Yes, of course I like Mr. Mackenzie but I'm not learning anything useful and I'm needed here. You must talk to him, Frances."

"You're only fourteen," Frances said. "*I* had to go to school until I was seventeen," but she mentioned the subject tentatively to Mr. Mackenzie and was surprised to find that he agreed with Gwen.

"She's extraordinarily knowledgeable about the things that interest her," he said. "Anything else, I don't believe she sees or hears. If she wants to come back to me she knows I shall be delighted to see her. She won't be idle, my dear, never fear. Ask to see her plans for the vegetable garden."

Frances was astonished when Gwen, obviously pleased by Frances's interest, produced diagrams, charts and lists.

"I knew you'd make Mr. Mackenzie see sense," she said happily. "There's so much to do here. I've written down what we need. The things at the top are the important ones, fruit trees, things like that. I know it's extra expense but they'll pay in the end because they're food and anyway some of them won't cost anything. Mr. Whitelaw, you know, Sir James's head gardener, has promised to give me some raspberry cuttings next season, and strawberry runners too. And then there are the things that aren't, well, essential. Father and Mother did a lot in the garden but they concentrated on trees, some of them quite rare, you probably don't realise, but they didn't bother much about flowers and that's what I like painting and Julia does too. So some time, when there's the money ... "

Gwen was putting as much into the Hillcrest purse, with the food she was providing, as Frances was taking out. Frances consoled herself with the thought that Gwen's turn would come, when she too would go to the Slade. She said now, "It all sounds sensible to me. We'll have to go through it and see

... " She remembered the wilderness at the back of Annie's old home under the Blackdown Hills. "You know, Gwen, an overgrown garden can be wonderful to paint. Not neglected, exactly, but kept a bit wild. I think we should get together and decide what we all really want in the garden, from the painting point of view, I mean. Well, not Sarah, but you and Julia and me. Poor Sarah'll never be a painter."

Gwen nodded. "There's one other thing, Frances. Do you think we can afford to buy me some books? I know it's extravagant but I can't always be going down to Mr. Whitelaw."

There was obviously no need to worry about Gwen; Julia and Annie seemed content, and once Sarah had recovered...

It was over a year since Mrs. Purcell's death. Mr. Mackenzie and Frances paid their annual visit to Mr. Baynham in Taunton. Frances looked round his clerk's office as she and Mr. Mackenzie waited to see the lawyer, and studied the posters on the wall that announced sales by auction, farms to let, houses to be had on lease. Had things turned out differently, a description of Hillcrest might have been up there too. The Purcells had been fortunate. The accounts were in order. Hillcrest hadn't fallen down or the stables gone up in flames. There was money in the bank. For the first time she felt confident: Hillcrest was their home and would remain so.

The stable block, where previous, more affluent occupants had kept carriage and horses but which was now used by Willis as his toolshed and for winter storage of fruit and vegetables, ran up the side of Tinker's Lane towards the brow of the hill. The far end was little more than a barn with a door open to the elements where hens clucked and scratched the bare earth and sometimes laid their eggs among the straw of the vegetable clamps. Stairs – half staircase, half ladder – led up to a room under the eaves and here Frances brought Julia for her opinion on its possibilities as a studio. Frances had always known that in time she must have a place of her own in which to work. With the long summer holidays soon to come she had decided she could wait no longer.

Pieces of distemper had flaked from the walls onto the floor. Cobwebs stretched between the bars of the window frame, enclosing within them the remains of unidentifiable corpses. The room smelt musty and old.

"I'd forgotten how big it was," Julia said. She struggled to open the window. Fresh air floated in as she did so. "It's got a good view too. It would make a splendid studio.".

"Help me then," Frances said, "and you can use it when I'm away."

They swept it out, scrubbed every surface, whitewashed walls and ceiling, polished the window. Annie, perturbed, said it was no job for Purcells; she would spare Harriet for as long as it took. Frances refused. She enjoyed the physical activity as well as Julia's company; and was glad of the opportunity to talk on their own. They found a chest-of-drawers in one of Hillcrest's attics which they carried up with the help of a disgruntled Willis, and a bed which they covered with a dragon-embroidered silk bedspread, souvenir of one of their father's journeys in the Far East.

By the time Gabriel came home the room was habitable. Frances took him up to see it with anxious pride.

"Take care of the stairs. They're very steep."

She watched him look round, walk to the window, look out and back.

"Do you like it?"

"Very much."

"It's not finished yet, but you can see how it's going to be."

"I'm impressed."

She indicated the primus. "I can even offer you refreshment. How about a cup of tea?'

"That would be nice."

He wandered round the room, while she waited for the kettle to boil, looking at the pieces she had already gathered, the plaster casts on the shelves, brushes sticking out of the jug, the forsythia in a jar. She hoped he wouldn't recognise the bronze statue of Mercury, lent by Lucy with the assurance that Mrs. Mackenzie would never notice its absence from a Rectory cupboard for a day or two.

"May I look?" he said when he came to a pile of drawings on the chest.

"If you want to."

She busied herself with the tea. He made no comment as he looked through but she sensed surprise, and approval.

"You've changed," he said.

"Oh?"

"A lot more assurance."

"Is that a good thing or a bad one?"

He laughed.

"You didn't come and see me last term," she said.

"You seem to have managed very well without me. Another prize, Father tells me."

"I missed you."

"I wrote."

"That's not the same."

"I was busy. Besides, you can't go through life relying on me. You were all right, weren't you?"

"Yes, of course, but it would have been nice to see you all the same. Will you come down next term now you know I can stand on my own feet?"

"We'll see. Why don't you come up to Cambridge for a weekend? I'll find you somewhere to stay."

"All right." She gave him a rueful smile. "I was afraid you were angry with me and that's why you didn't come."

"Oh?"

"Because of what I said on New Year's Eve. About Mother, and my going to art school."

"I was surprised, I admit. I can see why you didn't tell Father but I think you might have told me. It wouldn't have made any difference. After all, your mother was mixed up with painters, wasn't she – Morris, Rossetti, that lot?"

Frances stared, "Was she?"

"I seem to remember Father saying something of the sort. He always said she was a radical, like me; or had been, before her marriage. He liked her, you know. Original, he said she was."

Frances digested this unexpected information in silence. Odd, to learn such revealing facts about a parent from someone outside the family.

Gabriel looked about him. "Is the light good enough? I thought painters needed a north light . . ."

"Well, yes, they do," Frances said. "I need a skylight really, but I can't afford one at the moment."

"I'm sure if you asked Father . . ."

"No. Don't you say anything to him either. I'm taking more than my share out of the trust fund as it is. I'll wait until I've saved enough from my allowance."

"I could lend you the money."

"Don't be ridiculous."

"I mean it."

"I don't believe in owing anybody anything."

"I'll give it to you then."

"That would be worse."

"You could pay me interest if it would make you happier. Personally I think you'd be mad to be quite so stiff-necked." He smiled mockingly, "You don't realise – it's only self-aggrandisement on my part. I want a mention in the history books as the person who set the English Matisse, or Cézanne, or whoever it should be, on the road to fame."

She burst out laughing. "Oh, Gabriel, really."

"Think about it."

She would not have taken his money for anything other than her work. She agreed finally, after Julia had pointed out that it would be only sensible to get the mess and dirt of alterations out of the way before she settled in. She left Hillcrest at the end of the Easter holidays knowing that the studio was waiting for her on her return and determined to repay Gabriel before that time.

Chapter Nine

Frances was apprehensive during the train journey to Cambridge. Never having spent so long with Gabriel on his own before she feared that he might become bored by her company during the weekend, or she by his.

He met her at the station and took her back to his rooms. The first thing she noticed was her drawing of Mr. Mackenzie on the wall. She made a face.

"It's dreadful, isn't it? I am sorry."

"I like it," he said. He grinned at her. "I forgot. I'm a Philistine. I haven't any taste."

"Oh, I don't know," she said. "You're improving." She looked round the room, opened the window and leant out.

"King's College Chapel," he said. "You can draw that while you're here if we can't find anything better to do. How about that for a challenge? Yes, I think I'd like a drawing of King's on my wall."

She was interested to see how he lived. There was a cheerful disorder about the place very different from the strict arrangement his mother insisted on at home, and an astonishing quantity of books and papers lying casually about. "Do you read all these?" she asked.

He was amused. "We are in Cambridge, you know. I'm hoping to win a fellowship."

He had arranged for her to spend the night with friends of his, a married couple older than he. He dined there with her that evening. The couple treated Frances with an informality and lack of curiosity that pleased her, although her evening was almost spoilt by the discovery, during a heated exchange between Gabriel and the wife about a poem by someone unknown to Frances, that her hostess was a poet herself. Frances had never met a poet before, male or female; she found the information so disconcerting that she scarcely dared venture a remark for the rest of the evening.

Gabriel showed her round town and university, took her into colleges and chapels and dazzled her with his knowledge of history. On the Sunday afternoon he hired a boat; they took a picnic tea and punted up the river, tying up to a willow where he lay back and alternately read and watched her sketch.

He introduced her casually to whoever dropped into his rooms as 'my father's ward'. His friends treated her equally casually, made no special concession, talked to Gabriel, sometimes asked her opinion, but most of the time paid her little attention. She liked it. She preferred watching to joining in and was happy to sit back and listen to the arguments and discussions and to see Gabriel in a different setting.

She had always thought of Gabriel as part of the Rectory. When she talked about 'the Mackenzies', she saw the Rector and his wife in her mind, together with Gabriel and Lucy. Antony came later, Geoffrey was for some reason apart. (It was Sarah who, when being read a fairy story about substitute children, asked wide-eyed, "Is Geoffrey a changeling too?") Now Frances saw that Gabriel had a world of his own and was very much at home in it.

She discovered too, to her surprise, that there were a number of things that Gabriel, whom she had thought essentially light-hearted, cared about, and cared very deeply indeed. Poetry was one; politics another. Several of the friends who dropped in during her stay were Fabians. Discussions centred on socialism; there was mention of 'the settlement'. Out on the river she asked him what had been meant.

She could not take in the finer points of Fabianism on first hearing, and understood only that its followers intended to change the face of English society. She was chagrined to learn, however, that Gabriel had paid several visits to London during the previous term when she had been waiting in vain for him to come and see her.

"You always went to the settlement?"

"Yes."

"What for?"

"I teach there."

"Teach? What?"

"Well ... Ancient History. To some of the boys. Don't look like that. It's very bloodthirsty, Greek history. They love it. I teach German too, to adults. That's not such fun, but they're very keen."

"*German* – in the East End?"

He looked combative. "Why not?"

"Well ..."

"I don't see why people, just because they live in the East End ..."

"No, all right. Don't get so ... I'm sorry."

He said diffidently, "Why don't you come along and have a look? You don't need to help; you'd find plenty to draw."

"It'd be a bit patronising, wouldn't it?"

"I don't see why. Art's universal, surely. There's an art gallery in Whitechapel."

"Yes, I know. But, don't you see, it's all right for people like Gertler and Rosenberg to draw there. That's where they live. It's their home. I couldn't ..."

"Well ... let me know if you change your mind."

She was curious. "What does your mother think about all this?"

"Lord, don't say anything to her. She thinks the world's all right as it is. I can't get her to see that it isn't."

Frances thought the world all right too, though she would never admit to sharing Mrs. Mackenzie's views. She found Gabriel's enthusiasm endearing, all the same.

She returned to Cambridge frequently after that first weekend. The town was preferable to the dust and dirt of London in the summer months, and winter was surely long enough for the work she needed to do in the metropolitan museums and galleries. Gabriel's company and that of his friends became more enjoyable, more instructive too, with each stay. She was sorry when the visits came to an end with Gabriel's departure for Germany.

"Why Germany?"

"Why not?"

"I think I'd rather go to France. Paris, Pont-Aven, Honfleur, places like that. Artists' places."

"Of course you would, but I was seventeen the first time I went abroad and France then was considered to be ... immoral, I suppose. Still is, I daresay. Anyway, I speak German, not French, so ..."

Frances was impressed. It seemed extraordinarily brave for a schoolboy to wander round the Continent for six months, as Gabriel had apparently done before going up to university, even if he did speak the language. She began to understand why, with less than five years between them, Gabriel gave the impression of being so much older than she.

She was intrigued, too. It seemed unlike the Mackenzies to approve such expeditions – Antony never left the Rectory, and there had been no mention of Geoffrey taking time off before university – yet Gabriel said he had not only gone that first year but most years since.

"Father didn't mind. He'd travelled when he was young – the Holy Land, places like that. India, too. That's where he met Mother. She minded, of course ... but I'd been left money by my godmother, so I was more independent than I might have been. She was furious about the money; she thought Aunt Etty should have made me wait until I was twenty-five."

Frances was disappointed at the prospect of his absence from Somerset. "I didn't realise you were going away. You said you'd take me up on the Quantocks this summer."

"I will, don't worry. I'll be home for a couple of weeks in September. I never miss the Dunkery match or the cricket team supper. I'll take you up then."

She had never been up on the Quantocks, although on clear days she saw them often from the churchyard at Huish Priory, rising hump-backed against the skyline. Sometimes, when she walked into Dunkery St. Michael to catch the train to Taunton or visit friends of Lucy's, she looked up at the wooded slopes rising above the village and was tempted to climb and explore, but it was Gabriel who took her up for the first time.

They set off for Dunkery after breakfast one morning with food provided by Annie packed away in Gabriel's rucksack and a map that Gabriel had insisted Frances study before they left. "I thought we'd go up *here*, past Cothelstone, over Lydeard Hill and home through Bagborough and Combe Florey. We don't want to do too much your first time."

She had walked with him in the past, in and around London, but there was a purposeful air about him today that she had not seen before. His boots were hiking boots, his rucksack had a professional look to it and he strode out as if he were prepared to walk the length of England. She was intrigued: this was Gabriel in yet another light.

"Do you like walking?" she said. "Like this, I mean. You've mentioned the Quantocks before."

"Yes, I do. Particularly up here. The Fabians are great walkers, you know, but I'd rather walk on my own than be with people who aren't sympathetic. I'm a solitary soul really."

She thought that she was too and reflected that it was probably one reason why she found him so companionable and undemanding to be with. Subtly her relationship with Gabriel was changing. The older brother was gradually growing younger, imperceptibly revealing depths usually kept hidden.

Dunkery church tower stood tall and square, its red sandstone bright against the greens of the hill behind, as they passed the cricket ground.

"Did you enjoy the match yesterday?" she said.

"I'd have enjoyed it more if old man Roberts hadn't dropped that catch."

She laughed. "And the supper afterwards?"

"Ah, yes. Very entertaining. Bill Roberts got exceedingly

[77]

drunk and couldn't be wrenched from his trumpet. The noise was unbelievable."

She said, "Have you ever been drunk?"

"Yes, of course."

"Have you?" She was astonished. "Really?"

"Well, of course I have. What would you expect?"

"What did your mother say?"

"Oh, Frances. Credit me with a little intelligence. She never knew."

She thought for a moment. "I saw Gertler and Nevinson when I left the Café Royal quite late one night. They were staggering down Regent Street; I'm sure they were drunk."

"I'd think it highly likely from what you've told me of them."

"I was shocked."

He grinned at her. "Oh dear. Poor Frances."

"I can't understand some of the men at the Slade. They don't seem to care. Well, Gertler does, I know, but not some of the others. They hardly work at all. Nash often isn't there and Nicholson spends all his time playing billiards in the Gower Hotel."

"Perhaps they're not driven by whatever devil it is that drives you."

She was not sure how to take that and changed the subject. "You know Bill Roberts quite well, don't you? From cricket?"

"Yes."

"Do you think he'd mind my painting inside the forge? I've always wanted to get in there—it's the firelight, I think, and all those shadows jumping about that fascinate me so. I've often painted it from the road, I don't mind doing that, but I don't like to go in without asking."

"Why don't you ask him yourself?"

"It'd be easier if you had a word first."

"All right. We'll stop on the way back if it's not too late."

In the beechwoods the first leaves were beginning to turn. Sun filtered through the branches, dappling the rich dark humus beneath with paler shapes and patterns.

Something stirred in Frances. "Can we stop?"

"There's a gap in the trees a little further on."

In the sunlit valley below, Cothelstone House basked among the greens of its parkland, the lake beside it shimmering. The fields beyond made a chequerboard of yellows and browns and ochres.

"Phew, it's hot," Gabriel said as they climbed above the trees and stood at last on the ridge. He took deep lungsful of air. "I needed that after last night."

Frances turned slowly round. "I've never seen anything like the view."

"You're supposed to be able to count ten counties from here on a good day and a hundred churches," he said. "I've never managed to check the truth of it myself. It's worth the climb, isn't it?"

They stopped to eat on the ridge above Bagborough. Her sketchbook remained in the rucksack. She preferred to look rather than draw. She was dismayed when Gabriel said. "It's worked out well. We should get you home in time for tea."

"Can't we go on?"

He sounded surprised. "Do you want to? You don't have to please me, you know."

"You know I never care about pleasing people. Of course I want to," and found herself unexpectedly touched by the diffident pleasure he took in her approval.

"I've never really thought . . ." she said slowly, "about, well, places like this. I've never looked further than the village. Mother did, you know. I found some paintings of hers when we went through her things. Scotland, I think they were. They were good. She must have done them before she married Father."

"Didn't she do anything good after her marriage?"

"No. Don't smile like that. I'm serious. She didn't. She didn't paint at all while she was married. And Father . . . she tried afterwards but she couldn't get back. I saw her once crying at her easel . . . I think that was why she was so unhappy, why she cut herself off . . ." She hugged her knees and gazed out across the vale towards Exmoor. "Tonks said something last term which made me understand Mother for the first time. He thinks a lot about women, you know; as artists, I mean. He says they're as good as men between the ages of sixteen and twenty-one and then they start thinking about marriage and their work goes off. And they have babies and all that. Tonks gets very upset about it. He says it's such a waste. When he said that I realised what must have happened to Mother. If she'd really wanted to paint she shouldn't have got married."

"That seems a bit hard," Gabriel said.

"Well, then, she shouldn't have tried again afterwards. You can't do both." She said firmly, "I'm going to paint."

He smiled. "I'll remind you of that when you're happily married with a brood of children round your feet."

She said, "I mean it."

He studied her face and said slowly, "Yes, I think you do." He pulled the rucksack towards him and began packing away the picnic things.

"There's a man who comes in to teach painting at the Slade," Frances said as they set off along the ridge. "Wilson Steer, he's called."

"I thought you did nothing but draw at the Slade."

"That's the most important part," she agreed. "You don't need to paint at all. You could spend all your time in the Life Room if you wanted. Steer's a bit of a joke really. He always falls asleep when he's teaching."

"It doesn't sound as if you'd learn much from him then."

"No." She said after a while, almost to herself, "I like his paintings though. Some people say he's more help than anyone else at the Slade. You have to ask him questions all the time, I think. I suppose it depends on what you're looking for."

She was tired by the time they reached Huish Priory, but happy. "Can we go again before term starts? Please. I feel . . . I think it's important."

1912

Chapter Ten

Antony sat in the Hillcrest kitchen spreading thick layers of fresh raspberry jam on to bread that was still warm.

"The end of the world is at hand, Annie, did you know that?"

"Get on with you, Master Antony," Annie said comfortably. "I've never heard such rubbish. And go easy with the jam, my lad. You'll make yourself sick else. What'll I say to your mother then?"

"I'm never sick." Antony was complacent. "And it's not rubbish. Ask Gabriel. It's the end of his world anyway. He says he won't get the fellowship and he's in the worst black mood I've ever known. It doesn't show any sign of ending either. You don't realise, Annie, it's sanctuary I'm seeking in Hillcrest, like people did in the church of old. If Gabriel comes banging at the door you'll have to pretend to be a monk and turn him away. There's no need to smile either; he's bitten my head off three times already today."

"Your head looks firm enough on to me," Annie said.

Sarah giggled.

The Mackenzies sometimes mentioned Gabriel's black moods and bouts of depression in front of the Purcells, but the Purcells rarely saw them. Gabriel kept himself away on such occasions. Only Frances knew. If at such times she asked him to sit for her or suggested going up on the Quantocks, he would refuse with an abruptness, even rudeness, unusual for him. He would put on his hiking boots, fill his rucksack and set off out of Huish Priory alone.

She always waited untroubled for his return, knowing that when he came to find her, however late, he would be cheerful and relaxed, as well as apologetic. "I'm sorry about this morning. I wasn't feeling very sociable," or perhaps, "You know how I am. I had to be alone." She never minded. She knew what it was to need solitude; knew too that if he could go away and walk far and hard such episodes were short-lived.

This summer was different.

The Purcells saw him rarely: he stayed in his room preparing his dissertation for the Cambridge fellowship that he hoped to win. He never walked and only came over occasionally to Hillcrest.

"He's so stupid," Lucy said, sitting in the sun on Hillcrest's verandah. "Taking things to extremes. He always did. He can't go for a five mile walk; it has to be twenty-five. He didn't work at all for his degree until the Easter before the exams and then it was all hours of the day and night – he made himself ill. He didn't do nearly as well as he should have done. He'll do it again if he's not careful. I suppose you couldn't do anything, could you, Frances? Mother goes on at him so; it only makes him worse. Father and I thought, if you could get him out walking . . . "

Frances went over to the Rectory. Mrs. Mackenzie greeted her with a smile. "Bertha will tell Gabriel you're here. Why don't you wait in the drawing-room?"

Frances scowled at the stag at bay over the mantelpiece. How *could* Mrs. Mackenzie . . . ?

"Hello, Frances."

She thought he looked frighteningly white and tired.

"I want to do some painting up on the Quantocks," she said. "The beeches by Crowcombe Gate. I wondered if you'd come? It's much easier if there are two of us to lug my things, and you can sit and read or write or whatever you want to do while I paint. Would you mind?"

He hesitated.

"Please."

"Well ... all right. If you really need my help."

"Tomorrow then."

The day went better than she had expected. He said little. Her painting things were a nuisance; she considered a fast, long walk would have done him more good but had not been able to think of other means of enticing him out of his room. How much work he did she did not know; she had been too preoccupied with her own to notice.

When they were back in her studio he said, "You haven't nearly finished. Do you want to go back tomorrow?"

"If you like." She said cautiously, "You'd be much better going for a twenty mile walk, Gabriel. Either on your own or with me, I don't mind. You wouldn't consider that?"

"I must work."

"You don't think you might be doing too much? I know it's silly to compare what you're doing with dressmaking but all the same ... If you go on sewing too long you start making stupid mistakes. You can't work indefinitely at a picture either, without spoiling it in the end."

"What do you suggest?"

"Let's take the train to Minehead and climb North Hill. I've always wanted to see the view from there. Or how about the Wellington Monument? I went there once years ago with Mother and Father. I'd like to go back."

From North Hill the Quantocks appeared insignificant and small. Difficult to detect from here the variety that was contained in their tawny-coloured slopes, the streams and combes, beechwoods and heather, the exhilaration of the views from the ridge. Frances looked on them now with a familiarity and affection that would have seemed strange to her a year ago. They had become as much a part of her working life as the tools – the crayons, watercolours, the oils – with which she portrayed them.

"You don't ever get depressed, do you?" Gabriel asked her on their way home. There was a touch of envy in his voice.

"Well ... not like you, no, I don't think I do."

"I'd have thought ... one's always understood, the artistic temperament and all that ..."

"I'm nearly always dissatisfied with what I've done, you know that. Nothing ever turns out as good as I think it will be when I start, but you have to accept that. If you worried about that you'd never start anything in the first place. I suppose you could say I was depressed my first term in London but that's not what you mean, is it?"

He shook his head. "You're enjoying London now, aren't you?"

"It's the Slade really. Particularly since I've been doing so much with Wilson Steer. I wouldn't have got anywhere without his teaching."

She had not expected much of Steer as a teacher and it was only her gradual realisation during the previous summer that landscape was what she really wanted to do that had made her persist under his tuition. A year later she knew that she had learnt a great deal from him, from watching and being with him as much as by listening. The evenings she spent with other students at his home in Cheyne Walk were as valuable to her learning as the lessons at the Slade.

She went out more nowadays. The scholarship meant that she was able to spend more on entertainment, although it was Gabriel who took her to the theatre and the ballet. She spent evening after evening at the ballet, not because she enjoyed the dancing but because she was mesmerized by Bakst's designs.

Her growing confidence meant that she had made more friends, visiting and occasionally staying at their homes. Her visit to Jamieson's family was not a success. She had known Jamieson for months before discovering that Jamieson's father was a member of the aristocracy. Frances was overawed by the splendour of the house. She found Jamieson's father patronising, and the way he talked of his daughter's 'little hobby' made her grit her teeth. She understood for the first time why Jamieson had preferred to live in the discomfort of digs rather than remain in the luxury of her own home. But visits to the homes of other friends were more enjoyable, and often instructive.

"Did you know Nevinson's parents are Radicals?" she asked Gabriel. "His father's a free thinker and Mrs. Nevinson's full of good causes. *Real* good causes, I mean, like Armenian refugees and the natives in Central Africa. That sort of thing. She's had her hair shingled." She looked thoughtfully at Gabriel and said, "I've decided it would make life easier if I had mine shingled too."

She had discovered in the early days of their friendship that the normally even-tempered Gabriel could flare up into sudden rages. His temper was quick, hot, but soon over. Occasionally Frances was tempted to provoke it for the sheer fun of a fight. The possibility that she might shingle her hair was enough to rouse him now. She was triumphant. It was the first sign of life she had seen in him for weeks.

The walk to Minehead brought Gabriel to his senses. He promised Frances that he would break off work for an hour every afternoon to come over and have tea with the Purcells; he went for shorter walks with her once a week and longer ones every ten days or so. "I don't know what we'd do without you," Lucy said and even Mrs. Mackenzie smiled graciously on her. His depression had not entirely disappeared – he confided to Frances that his work seemed pointless, that he knew he would never win the fellowship, and what was he to do with himself then? – but it was at least manageable.

One of their further expeditions was to the Wellington Monument on the Blackdown Hills. The faint pencil-shaped landmark, visible most days from Hillcrest, had long attracted Frances, and there were sentimental reasons too for her wanting to see it from closer range.

"Last time I came it was in a pony and trap," she said as she climbed with Gabriel up through the woods. "Father was on leave. I can't remember how old I was but I must have been very small – Julia wasn't with us."

She stood at the edge of a clearing and looked up at the bayonet shape piercing the sky, before slowly walking forward and round the base.

"What is it?" Gabriel said when she came back to him.

"I don't know. I'm disappointed. It seems so ordinary now, and yet last time I was here I was *terrified*. I remember looking up. All the clouds were racing past it and I was sure – I *knew* – that the whole thing was going to topple over on top of me. I remember my legs wouldn't work. I wanted to get away but I couldn't. Father had to carry me. I couldn't tell him what was wrong, I was too ashamed. They laughed at me. I can still see those clouds, you know. Black and dark grey and the nearest one a sort of maroon colour with a yellow edge to it. I'd never really looked at clouds before."

"So it was a childhood visit to the Wellington Monument that started you out as a painter," Gabriel said. He was smiling.

"I hadn't thought of it like that. Perhaps it was. Clouds still matter, anyway. I paint them out of the stable window every morning, and make a note of the weather and the wind. It's surprising what you learn doing things like that."

He was suddenly serious. "Why *do* you paint, Frances? What makes you paint?"

"I don't know. I have to, I suppose. I remember once – it was that first Christmas – all four of us were in the kitchen. Annie'd closed the shutters and stoked up the range, and it was lovely and warm and cosy. I can't remember what we were doing, making toffee or something, I think, but I do remember knowing that I didn't want to go back to London. It was nothing to do with hating London or being homesick. It was just that life was so much more comfortable and cosy and *easier* somehow, at Hillcrest, and I envied them because they could be there and I couldn't. I thought it very unfair that I was the sort of person that had to go away."

"Do you still think like that?"

"That it's unfair? No. Though I do think sometimes that life would be much easier if I was ... well, like other people. And yet, when you say why do I paint ... Just occasionally, when I'm painting, something magic happens. I can't explain it. It's as if what I'm doing, what I'm *in*, is the real world, and the *real* world, well, that doesn't exist. And then I come out of it and I feel very strange, as if I don't belong. It hasn't happened very often, not more than three or four times, but I'm always waiting and thinking perhaps it'll happen again. I don't care whether my pictures sell, and I don't mind what people think except you, and people like Tonks and Steer. I don't want to exhibit particularly – I hated seeing my canvas on the wall of the last New English Club exhibition – but I paint because of that ... Because I hope it'll be like that again."

"I see," Gabriel said slowly. He made no other comment and was silent for the rest of the journey home.

1913

Chapter Eleven

Jamieson pulled a pillow off Frances's bed and made herself comfortable on the floor. "Extraordinary, really. It's a year since I left but I still feel more at home here than I do back with my family. You'll never gues what, though. Daddy's as fed up with me as I am with him – he's promised to find me a studio or a flat or something so I can move out. Oh ..." She pulled an envelope out of her pocket. "This was in the hall downstairs. It's addressed to you. Isn't it tremendous news, Purcell? Sometimes I almost feel fond of the old man. You will come and stay, won't you? I couldn't bear to lose touch just because you insist on burying yourself somewhere beyond the Styx, and anyway you'll still need to see Wilson Steer sometimes. What's the matter? What's that letter about?"

Frances read it again. "Someone inviting me to call at the Mayfield Gallery for a chat." She gave it to Jamieson. "How odd. Denis Bond. Have you heard of him?"

"No, but I know the Mayfield – it's behind Leicester Square. It hasn't been open long. Why should they write to you? It'll be a plot, Purcell. You're going to be abducted to a Turkish harem. Still, you can't say no, can you, or you'll spend the rest of your life wondering. You'd better let me know when you're going and I'll get Daddy to organise the police and the army and whatever else ... Even Daddy has his uses."

A Matisse still life rested on an easel in the window of the Mayfield Gallery. Frances stood on the pavement, studying it – at the vivid portrayal of coffee pot and fruit in a wooden bowl, firmly placed on the white tablecloth – and tried to analyse how the painter had achieved such vibrant life.

"Nice, isn't it?" said a voice from the gallery door.

She looked up. "Yes. I wish I knew how he gets the light. It looks so easy and then you try it yourself ... "

"And it's a different matter. I know." He held out his hand. "Miss Purcell, isn't it?"

Her surprise must have been obvious. He smiled. "I'm Denis Bond. I'm glad you've come. Come and see what else I've got. What do you think of this? Rather different from the Matisse, I think you'll agree?"

He was not much taller than she was and slight; probably in his early thirties, Frances thought, trying to study him unobtrusively. Dark hair and a smooth, olive complexion gave him a foreign appearance but he sounded English. He showed her round the gallery, keeping up a light conversation until she began to relax. The work on display, some for sale, some lent, varied in both subject and execution. Bond himself was quiet and hesitant, but knowledgeable, as Frances quickly recognised. It was disconcerting to find that his knowledge extended to her, both as regards work and background.

"We can talk in the office," he said when they reached the end, and took Frances into a small, untidy room. "I'm sorry about the mess. We'll get straight one day. The gallery's taking all our time at the moment." He pulled out a chair, removed the specimen picture frames resting on its seat and brushed it down with his handkerchief. "Do sit down. How about a cup of tea, Christine?"

A large, cheerful female smiled at Frances, said, "Milk and sugar?" and disappeared.

"You're one of the fortunate ones, Miss Purcell. I only lasted a term at the Slade."

"Oh?"

He shrugged. "Not good enough. The soul of an artist but not, alas, the talent. A crushing error on the part of the Almighty, I used to think. I'm coming to the conclusion that perhaps He knows best after all. My purpose in life would seem to be encouraging artists and supporting them, rather than being one. Thank you, Christine." He took the tray and offered Frances a large earthenware mug of tea. "One hopes that elegance will come with success. It's a matter of priorities. We're still finding our feet, you know."

He was not only interested in dealing with pictures, he told her, but in running exhibitions as well. "With a theme – French artists maybe, naval paintings, that sort of thing. If you hold exhibitions you get people dropping in casually, people with no intention of buying who might unexpectedly see something they like ... Much more satisfying than only dealing. More profitable too, surprisingly. It's exhibitions that have made the Leicester Galleries successful. That's where I got my experience."

"I went to an exhibition at the Leicester Galleries once," Frances said. "The first I'd ever been to – Holman Hunt, it was."

"Oh yes. I was involved with that one. Dear old man. He came in every day – you must have seen him – sat in front of his pictures and *peered*. He was nearly ninety, you know, and almost blind. Well, well." He smiled at Frances. "Fancy your seeing that. You must have been very young."

"My art mistress brought me up from school specially. That was when I decided I wanted to paint. Professionally, I mean. I hadn't thought about it like that before."

He said, "Tell me more about yourself."

"Well." She stopped. "I don't ... There isn't much ... What do you want to know?"

"You come from the West Country .. ?"

She stared. "How do you know that?"

"From your painting. We go down to Devon most summers; my wife has a cottage on the coast. I spent a lot of my childhood in that part of the world. I suppose that's what attracted me to your work in the beginning – your sense of place. Are your parents still there?"

"They're dead. My sisters are. I'll go back when I've finished at the Slade."

His questions were quiet but probing. Only afterwards did she realise how much he had persuaded her to reveal about herself, her situation and her family. He came at last to the reason for his letter. "I believe I could help you in your career. I like your work; I like what I've heard about you. I believe you have a future, and I'd like to be involved in it."

She was dumbfounded. She said, "You seem much more certain than I am. I'm not sure half the time what I'm trying to do ... And I do dislike exhibiting. I don't think I'm ready for it."

"You've exhibited for two years at the New English."

"Only because Professor Tonks made me. I really don't think ... I don't want to sell either. You won't understand and I don't expect I can explain, but ... I gave a drawing to a friend once ..."

"You should never *give* things away."

"That's what Steer always says. No, but this drawing ... it was a long time ago, before I started at the Slade, and whenever I see it I'm ashamed. I wouldn't like to look back on what I'm doing now – and selling, if you have your way – and be ashamed."

"Forgive me, Miss Purcell, but don't you think that's somewhat arrogant? You're inferring that early works have no merit. At that rate, Shakespeare's schoolboy attempts at playwriting, had we got them, would be of no interest, because he was incapable of writing *King Lear* at the age of fifteen."

She was silent.

"Is your initial reaction to any suggestion always to say no?" he said gently.

"No, of course not. I don't think that I'd be very satisfactory from your point of view, that's all."

"Shouldn't you let me be the judge of that?" He smiled. "We've only been open a year. I'm investing in the future myself. I'll be quite frank with you. I'm looking for people starting out." He mentioned two other painters he was interested in, both of whom had studied at the Slade, one Frances only knew by repute, the other a man who had been in the year ahead of her. "Unlike you, apparently, I'm interested in watching people develop. I would like to be able to provide support while they do so."

He was anxious not to rush her into a decision. "Wait until you've been back in Somerset a while. Talk to your sisters; your guardian, too. Then you can let me know how you feel about the suggestion."

Jamieson was waiting in Frances's room, mentally girding her loins to storm a Turkish harem. Her disappointment when Frances walked in unharmed would have amused Frances had she noticed it.

"What was it all about?" Jamieson said. "What happened? Come on, Purcell, you must tell me. You've been *ages*."

"Another time, Jamie, do you mind? I'm tired." She needed to think over the conversation and Denis Bond's proposition before talking about it; if she were going to discuss it with anyone she would discuss it with Gabriel first.

"What do you want me to say?" Gabriel asked. Water dripped off the pole, leaving a trail of indentations in the water behind them. "That you'd be a fool not to do what he wants? Or a fool to commit yourself? I don't know, and if I did, I couldn't make a decision for you. You must see that."

"You could tell me what you think."

"How can I have an opinion without having met the man? Did you like him? That's the most important thing. It'd be ridiculous to enter into any sort of arrangement if you thought you couldn't get on with him."

She watched the banks slip slowly by. "I felt I trusted him."

"Well, then. I don't see you've got anything to lose."

"He might try to make me paint the sort of pictures I don't want to paint," she said.

Gabriel laughed. "Since when have you ever done anything you didn't want to do, painting or otherwise?"

She was hurt. "Lots of times. I've had to. No, I can't think of anything at the moment, but I know I have."

He stopped punting. The boat drifted slowly over the water. "What I do think you need to consider is the fact of your being on your own in Somerset. You'll miss it, you know, the talk, the gossip, the encouragement, just the stimulus of being with other painters. I think you underestimate the importance of that."

"I shall have Julia and Gwen."

"I thought Julia was starting at the Slade in September."

"So did I. She won't. She refuses. Don't ask me why. I'm furious with her but it's difficult to argue in letters ... I shall have to try to persuade her when I get home."

She had come up to Cambridge for the last time. Next week Gabriel would be in Germany and the week after that she would be back in Somerset, her time at the Slade ended for ever. She lay back with closed eyes, listening to the gentle thlup of water against the side of the punt and the sound of distant voices along the Backs.

"I shall miss coming up here dreadfully."

"You won't stop, will you?" He sounded surprised. "I know it's a tedious journey from Somerset but if you can put up with that ... You'll have to come for longer at a time, that's all. We'll tell Mother you've been commissioned to paint all the colleges, one by one. That'll keep you busy for years."

Later, while she was trying to finish a painting of Gabriel lying under a willow tree with light thrown onto his face from the surface of the water, he suggested drawbacks in the Mayfield proposal that Frances had never considered, the possibility that the gallery might go bankrupt and her canvases taken towards payment of debts being the worst. What sort of experience had the man had, he asked?

"It's only been going a year or so, you said. Where's the finance coming from?"

She was unhappy. "I don't know. I never thought about things like that. I was worried about not being good enough, and not wanting to sell yet anyway."

"That's up to him, surely, as long as he knows how you feel." He said diffidently, "Would it be any help if I went and saw him? I could wander round, have a look at the gallery, talk to him. I'd take care not to mention any connection with you. I expect I could fit it in before I go off to Germany – I'm only going until the end of the month, incidentally. I thought I'd spend the summer at home this year. I don't want to interfere but if you'd like me to ..."

"Oh Gabriel, would you?" She realised that what she really wanted was confirmation of her own opinion of the man. Considerations relating to work itself she knew depended on herself alone. "I'm sure he's all right really, but I'd be much happier if you thought he was too."

Gabriel wrote to her from the train on his way to Germany. He had been to the Mayfield, he told her, and spent an interesting hour there talking to Bond, whom he had liked. He had also made enquiries through people he knew with contacts in the art world and so far had heard nothing unfavourable. His letter was careful: it was obvious that he was anxious not to influence her either way. She did not mind, knowing that if he had felt strongly, whether for or against, he would have told her so. She suspected that in the end she would agree on purely sentimental grounds, because Bond had been involved with the exhibition that had set her on her path – quite the wrong reason, no doubt, for any sort of contract, however tenuous, and one that Gabriel would deplore.

Chapter Twelve

They went up onto the Quantocks as soon as Gabriel came home from Germany, Purcells and Mackenzies together, Sarah included. It was Gabriel who insisted that Sarah should come. Frances thought her too young – Annie knew she was – but did not have the heart to say so when confronted by Sarah's pleading expression.

Lucy, too, had almost been excluded. "It's the Sewing Circle this afternoon," she told Frances. "You know Mother always expects me to be there to pour out afterwards."

"But you hardly ever come out with us," Frances protested. "What made her let you go in the end?"

"Gabriel insisted. They had a row about it last night, all through dinner. They're so alike, Mother and he. Once they've made a stand, they won't back down. They both know they're the only one who's right. I do find it very wearing sometimes. Father's no help – he disappears into his study – and Antony makes it worse by staying and slipping in the odd remark which he knows will aggravate the situation. I'm the one that's left to pour oil on troubled waters."

Frances stared. "Gabriel and your mother alike? How can you say such a thing?"

"It's true."

It had been months before Frances felt she knew Lucy, and even longer before she realised that the life Lucy led was not an easy one. Lucy herself rarely complained. Antony spent much of his time at Hillcrest, with Sarah or teasing Annie in the kitchen. Geoffrey and Gabriel were frequently over during the holidays. Only Lucy was too involved with affairs of household and parish to be able to spend the amount of time both she and the Purcells would have liked at Hillcrest.

"Perhaps it's just as well Gabriel is obstinate," Frances said, "or you wouldn't be here now."

It was Gabriel's idea to take Sarah as far as St. Audries. "She says she can't remember the sea," he said. "A naval officer's daughter too! It's disgraceful. Let's take her to the sea now."

Frances hesitated. Sarah could not possibly walk to the sea in a day and home again afterwards, even if they caught a train for part of the journey. They would have to stay overnight ... She knew she should say no.

They had not seen a soul since leaving the village early that morning. The ridge lay in front of them, wooded combes to the north, steep slopes of tussocky grass, gorse and bracken to the south; beyond it the sea, grey and still. Around them the view stretched out to distant ranges, Exmoor, the Brendons and Mendips, the mountains of Wales. Who could possibly wish to come down from the hills and return to soft beds and enclosed rooms?

She hesitated. Had she been alone with Gabriel ...

"It would be nice, wouldn't it?" Lucy's voice was wistful.

Antony bobbed up and down, begging Frances: "Say yes, please say yes. Don't be a spoilsport."

Frances looked at Sarah's expectant face and across to Lucy and gave in. "Oh, all right. We'll go." She laughed at Gabriel. "You'll have to make peace when we get back."

They took their time over Annie's picnic and lazed about afterwards enjoying the view until the midday heat had diminished. Frances walked along the ridge with Gabriel, silent but happy. The rest of the summer to paint in and Gabriel with her – she had all she needed, all she wanted.

Antony crept up behind Sarah, chanting:

> *"Like one upon a lonesome road*
> *Doth walk in fear and dread*
> *Because he knows a fearsome fiend*

– he pounced, Sarah shrieked –

> *Doth close behind him tread."*

"He never stops," Geoffrey complained to Julia. "He doesn't, you know. If it isn't one poem it's another. Or Shakespeare."

Sarah was tiring. First Geoffrey took her on his back, and then Gabriel. The shadows lengthened, darkening combes and the vale. Soon only the ridge itself would be in sunlight. They came down to a barn that Gabriel remembered from previous walks. He and Frances left the others to make themselves comfortable and rest, while they went to send telegrams to Mrs. Mackenzie and Annie.

"We'd better find the farm, too," Gabriel said, "and make sure that it's all right, our sleeping in the barn. They're usually very good, farmers, as long as you ask permission."

It was the farmer's wife they saw. She regarded them very doubtfully indeed until Gabriel explained that there were eight of them altogether, the youngest only eleven, and they had walked all the way from Huish Priory. She gave permission readily then, insisted on filling a can with milk for Sarah and offered to cook breakfast for them in the morning.

"Don't let's hurry back," Gabriel said, as they passed the pond by the farm gate. "Let's sit and enjoy the evening for a bit."

A drake quacked at the water's edge. Ducks flattened the grass on the island a little way from the shore, settled themselves down, and began preening their feathers. The colours of the evening sky lay over the surface of the pond.

"The trouble with this time of day," Frances said, "is the moisture in the air. It curls the paper. You can't paint."

Gabriel was silent.

"You know Denis Bond?" she said.

"Yes."

"I wrote to him the other day and agreed."

He put an arm round her shoulders. "I'm glad. I'm sure you've done the right thing."

"Unless he goes bankrupt, like you said."

"Unlikely. It's his wife's money. She inherited wealth."

Frances was surprised. "How did you find that out?"

"I told you. We talked. I liked him. His wife regards the gallery as a nice little hobby which keeps him occupied."

"I wouldn't think he'd like that," Frances said.

"I don't believe he does."

"He's giving me an allowance as well," Frances said after a moment.

Gabriel turned his head.

"Not as much as he wanted," she said, "just something to help with the cost of materials. He suggested it. He said he'd been thinking about my situation and thought he should. I don't know that I'd have taken it, all the same, if it hadn't been for your father talking about university for Sarah later on. Did you know about that? He thinks she should go to Oxford. She's bright, he says."

"Yes. We've talked about it. Funny old mouse."

"Do you think I'm funny?" she asked

"What am I supposed to say to that?" He sounded amused.

"I don't know. Sometimes I wonder ... Everyone gets so excited about things in London, you know. They join groups and then cross and change about. There's the Friday group and the Camden Town group and now they're talking about a London Group. I can't understand it. It's such a waste of time. I just want to paint."

"Perhaps it's as well you've come back to Somerset then."

"Perhaps it is."

She was content sitting there with Gabriel, happy to remain, but he stirred as it grew darker.

"We'd better get back. We've got that milk for Sarah." He pulled Frances up on to her feet, held her close and kissed her gently on the mouth.

Sarah was curled up at the back of the barn when they returned, on a bed the others had made for her out of straw. She sat up and obediently drank from the mug Gabriel held to her lips, scarcely aware of her surroundings. They left her to sleep and went to refresh themselves in the stream outside before finishing the remains of Annie's food. Antony, exhilarated by so much fresh air and Coleridge's connections with the Quantocks, was still chanting long stretches of *The Ancient Mariner* and had to be sent to join Sarah as the only means of banishing the Wedding Guest. The others remained in the doorway of the barn, watching the moon rise slowly above the trees and silver the rippled water of the stream. Frances sat with Gabriel's arm round her shoulders, the warmth of his body warming hers, and when at last everyone had settled for the night and the rustling of straw almost ceased she sensed deeper darkness above her and felt his lips brush her eyelids and her nose, and settle on her mouth.

Gracious, she thought and stifled a desire to giggle. Fancy that. Gabriel, of all people . . .

Next morning Sarah had gone. Frances stared in disbelief at the empty hollow of straw beside her, staggered to the barn door and looked out. No Sarah. Her first reaction was annoyance. Bother the child – where could she have gone? Then she remembered the pond.

She shook Gabriel awake. "Sarah's disappeared . . . drowned!"

Gabriel sat up, blinked, brushed away the straw. "Don't be silly. Heavens, Frances, what a state you're in."

Even he became concerned, however, when a hunt round the barn revealed no sign. Leaving Geoffrey with Frances, he went up to the pond while the others fanned out to search further afield. It was Julia who found Sarah and brought her back from the lane where she had wandered in search of the sea. Frances, anger roused by relief, shouted and shook her so hard that Sarah, unaccustomed to such treatment, lost her grip on the hem of her skirt and let mushrooms fall out and shower the ground.

"Calm down, Frances," Gabriel said. His hand was on her shoulder. "The child's not come to any harm." He smiled at Sarah. "Don't look so frightened, mouse."

Sarah's expression was of terror rather than fright. Frances was shocked by it, and ashamed. Her anger went as quickly as it had come; she was breathless and shaking with relief. The thought of life without Sarah ... little mouse, with her quiet ways and funny expressions ... And Annie ... what would she have said to Annie?

The sun was shining on the sea when they came down to it at last, and lighting up the coastline villages on the other side. Antony took Gwen to hunt for fossils. Julia and Geoffrey took Lucy to explore the cliff. Frances walked with Gabriel and Sarah down the beach towards the sea, over pebbles that were mottled with blues and greys and pinks.

Sarah's eyes pleaded with Frances.

"I suppose you want to paddle," Frances said. "Take off your shoes and stockings then and we'll tuck your skirt into your knickers. Do try not to get too wet." She gazed longingly at the sea herself. "Look at it," she said to Gabriel. "Doesn't it make you want to ...?"

"You behave yourself, my girl," Gabriel said. "I'm sure your delightful Slade friends would throw off every stitch they had on and dive headlong into the sea but you're not going to embarrass me like that. Not here. Not in public."

"It's not public." She smiled up at him, daring him. "It's only us."

"Even so. Why don't you take off the child's skirt? Then at least she'd have something dry to put on if she got wet. Come on, mouse, let me help." He crouched beside Sarah and started tugging at the waistband, his fair hair close to her brown.

Frances began to laugh as he fumbled with unaccustomed hooks. She stopped. Some strange emotion moved within her. She felt as if she had never seen him properly before.

He looked up, still crouching, and then stood slowly and came towards her ...

"Gabriel ..."

"My love."

His head bent to meet hers. His mouth was on her mouth. She tasted salt on his lips. His hands moved in her hair, pulling at the pins that kept it up. "Frances, Frances . . . Ever since we first met I've wanted . . . wonderful, wonderful hair . . ."

Pins scattered over the sand. Her hair dropped, flopped onto her shoulders, fell towards her waist; was caught by the breeze that came off the sea and blown up into her eyes, across his face and hers.

"Oh, Frances."

She was like one drugged. She walked over the cliffs to Watchet heedless of the laughter and chatter around her, conscious only of the strength of his hand enclosing hers, of the hardness of his fingers against her palm, and the substance of his body beside her as he matched his stride to hers.

In the train to Dunkery she sat while the familiar slopes of the Quantocks rolled past the open window and looked across at a face that she had thought she knew and now knew not at all, marvelling how for all these years they had walked and talked together without realising the happiness that bound them together.

She came back to the everyday world at the Rectory gate.

"You'd better go home, all of you," Gabriel said. "I'll talk to Mother."

Frances took a deep breath; tried to gather her senses. "We'll come too," she said. "She can't be cross if we're there. Anyway, I don't see why . . . It's not as if we were children."

"I'm not a child; neither's Lucy. In the eyes of the law the rest of you are. Perhaps you're right, though, about being there. Come on then, but you're not to say a word, any of you."

They had kept together, Frances thought, been safe enough in a barn for the night: why should Mrs. Mackenzie be annoyed? But annoyed she was, with a cold anger quite unlike Gabriel's sudden rages. How extraordinary of Lucy to think that Gabriel and his mother were alike.

Mrs. Mackenzie's reprimands might roll off Frances's back. Annie's were a different matter.

"'Twas a foolish carry-on," Annie grumbled. "Not got the

sense you was born with; none of you. Miss Sarah'll be grizzly for weeks, I shouldn't wonder."

"Sarah? *Grizzly*? Oh, Annie."

"Miss Sarah's no walker, you know that."

"Then it's time she learnt to be. I don't see what all the fuss is about. Gabriel and Geoffrey carried her a lot of the way. It was the most wonderful thing that's ever happened to her. Ask her and you'll see."

Annie busied herself at the range. "Don't suppose you thought I might worry."

Frances was instantly repentant. "Oh Annie, I'm sorry."

About Annie; nothing else.

Chapter Thirteen

They spent every possible moment together before Gabriel returned to Cambridge. Heaven knows what Mrs. Mackenzie thought. Frances did not care. She was only thankful that Gabriel had won his fellowship the previous year and was free to spend time with her now. They walked the lanes around Hillcrest looking for new scenes to paint; he sat and read to her while she worked; they spent days up on the Quantocks. When he left Huish Priory they wrote; she went up to Cambridge; they met in London.

In London she stayed with Jamieson, by now installed in a flat round the corner from Soho Square. A studio flat, Jamieson called it. In reality it was not much more than a large attic, but the windows were wide and it boasted a skylight as well, so Jamieson was well pleased.

"I had to strike a bargain with Daddy in the end," she told Frances. "The flat and my allowance, provided I spend Christmas with the family, go to Ascot, that sort of thing." She sighed. "I can't summon up any enthusiasm for horses. I'm not even interested in drawing the beast."

She was delighted to put Frances up whenever Frances came to London and happy to welcome Gabriel, though obviously intrigued – "You, of all people, always so stuffy about men when you were at the Slade. I thought you said they distracted you from your work and weren't serious enough about theirs."

Gwen and Julia, fascinated by Frances's account of Jamieson and the life she led, always insisted on being told every detail of Frances's stay the moment she returned.

"You'll never believe it," Frances told them after one visit. "She's had her hair cut off. All of it . . . well, to just below her ears anyway. As a matter of fact, I rather liked it. I thought it suited her. Gabriel? No, of course he didn't. He thought it was terrible."

She returned from another visit with a pair of baggy red satin trousers. "They're Jamie's. I wanted to paint her in them but there wasn't time so she said I could bring them back. You wouldn't mind sitting, would you, Julia? They look like something from the Russian ballet, I think. Yes, she does wear them out of doors . . . Imagine Mrs. Mackenzie's face if we went down to the village . . ."

Gwen was not sure that she approved of Jamieson. "It seems funny, living like that, when you've got a family. They can't be as bad as all that, surely? *I* wouldn't want to live on *my* own."

Frances found that remark amusing, coming from someone who was happiest working alone on the vegetable patch or spending hours in the solitude of the greenhouse. "Oh, I don't know. If you were all as condescending about my work as her family is about hers I think I'd feel the same."

The disadvantage of staying with Jamieson, Frances found, was Jamieson's indifference to the more practical side of life. Food did not interest her, and she saw no need for housework.

"You'd think she'd get someone in," Frances said. "The place is filthy. I really believe she doesn't notice. I wrote my name in the dust this morning – you should have seen Gabriel's face. He can be awfully fussy sometimes."

Julia stood up. "You know, Frances," she said, "I think you ought to be careful with Gabriel, now you're seeing so much of him. I know he jokes and mocks, but underneath ... He's a very serious sort of person, isn't he?"

Frances stared. "Whatever makes you say that? Of course I'm careful." She was hurt. "I'm serious too. You should know that. Gabriel doesn't joke about things that matter to him and neither do I. You never hear me joking about my work."

"No, I know. All the same ..."

Christmas this year promised to be a historic occasion: Sarah was being allowed to stay up late for the first time. It was Mrs. Mackenzie who had suggested to Frances that Sarah should join the other Purcells for Christmas dinner at the Rectory.

"She's a sensible child and unlikely to become over-excited, I would have thought. It's always seemed sad that she should miss such an occasion ..."

For once Mrs. Mackenzie and Frances were in accord. Frances, touched by the delight on Sarah's face when she was told the news, decided to make her a new dress for the occasion instead of looking through Gwen's old clothes. The burden of responsibility that she had always felt for Sarah's upbringing was beginning to lighten at last with the child's gradual growing up and, with the likelihood of university, the prospect of a more definite future.

She felt a twinge of guilt all the same, thinking about Sarah as Christmas approached. She knew that her visits to London and the strict hours of work she set herself when at home meant she had paid Sarah less attention than she should have done during the past autumn. I'll paint her after Christmas, Frances promised herself. We'll be able to talk together then. A full-length portrait. If she wears my dress and sits on the floor, the skirt'll fall in soft folds and make shadows in the firelight, and her hair loose ... Yes, I shall enjoy painting her like that.

Frances felt like a child herself, waiting for Christmas. To

[104]

have Gabriel home for so long ... She cleared things away in her studio, knowing that she would not use it during the few days of Christmas, and sorted out her work. Gabriel would want to see what she had done during his absence.

She turned out the paraffin stove the morning before Christmas Eve and shivered, with excitement as well as the cold. Gabriel should have arrived at the Rectory by now. How soon would Mrs. Mackenzie let him go? Would she have a thousand Christmas tasks to keep him occupied and away from the Purcells? Or would she say, "They'll be expecting you at Hillcrest. Why not go over...?"

As Frances locked the door and started down the stairs she heard the ring of familiar footsteps on the hard earth outside. He swung into the barn as she reached the bottom step. They almost collided.

"Oh, Gabriel." She felt the familiar rush of happiness at the sight of him. "I didn't expect you so soon. I thought your mother'd keep you ..."

"Frances." He seemed taken aback at the sudden meeting. His breath came and went in clouds in the winter air. "Can we ... why don't we go up?"

"I've finished for the morning. I'm on my way to lunch. Come down with me." She was puzzled by his manner. "What is it? What's the matter?"

"I want to talk to you."

"Not here. It's cold." She started down the path. "Come to the house."

"No." He caught her arm and pulled her back into the barn. "Please, Frances. Don't go. I want to give you your Christmas present. Now, while we're away from the others." He thrust an envelope into her hand, stood back and waited. "Aren't you going to open it?"

She looked down. For some inexplicable reason she felt a sense of foreboding. The envelope contained a small, square box. She recognised the name of the Taunton jeweller on the lid. When she pressed the catch the lid jumped back revealing an emerald ring on a bed of white satin.

She could not believe her eyes.

He was watching her face. "It is ... it is all right, isn't it?" he said. "We'll change it if you don't like it, but I thought ... I know you like emeralds ..."

She said stupidly, "I don't understand. A ring ... Why?"

"I'm asking you to marry me."

It couldn't possibly be true. It was a joke. He was teasing. It *couldn't* be true. Panic surged over her. What do I do? He *knows* how I feel. I've told him. I've never given him reason to think ...

"You do like it, don't you?" His face was flushed, anxious and eager and happy all at the same time. "Oh Frances, say you like it."

"It's ... beautiful." She could not look at him. The emerald sparkled bright green against its white background. She took a deep breath, the air cold in her lungs. "Gabriel, you must understand ... I can't possibly accept it."

"Why not? Oh, I know what you're going to say. Of course I understand. I know all about your work. I know you can't ... I don't expect you to marry me straight away. I'll wait, I don't mind waiting until, well, as long as you want me to wait. Darling, I *know* you need plenty of time to get established and I'm happy to let you have it, really I am, but I thought ... when we love each other so much it seems silly not to get engaged. Doesn't it?"

She began to tremble. Her mind refused to work, as always in moments of crisis. She couldn't think, couldn't find the words. It was ridiculous to be so aware of her surroundings at such a time – the cavernous space of the barn interior, the strong smell of stored vegetables, potatoes, swedes and parsnips in their winter clamps, the noisy clucking of the hens as they scratched at the frozen soil. She should be thinking, thinking ... of words to say, of ways to make him understand.

"You *know*," she said, "I've always told you how I felt about marriage. Haven't I? Haven't I always said?"

"But that was before ... Frances," he said desperately, "you love me, you know you do. You've loved me since that day at St. Audries. I should have asked you then," he said bitterly. "I wanted to. I nearly did. You loved me then. You'd have said yes if I'd asked you down on the beach."

"I wouldn't," she cried. "I'd never have said yes. Never, ever. And what's love got to do with it, anyway? Of *course* I love you. That doesn't mean I'm going to *marry* you." She snapped the lid shut over the ring and thrust the box at him. "Take it. Go on. Take it. I don't want it. I think you must be mad."

He stepped back as if he had been slapped. The silence between them seemed never-ending. "If that's how you feel," he said at last, "there's nothing more to be said. Forgive me. I'm sorry to have taken up so much of your valuable time."

She remained where she was, unable to face her sisters, crouched on the bottom step of the stairs, hugging her arms round her, rocking to and fro, and saw again his face as he had stood there at the last, looking at her.

Julia was serving lunch when Frances reached the dining-room. "We couldn't wait any longer. Where've you been?" She looked up at Frances. "Why, whatever...?"

"It's all right. I didn't mean to be late. Sorry."

Sarah, bubbling over with Christmas excitement, scarcely paused for breath during the meal. Amid her chatter Frances's silence passed if not unnoticed, at least unremarked.

Anger was beginning to replace the shock. Such arrogance. To think that he had only to ask and she would forget the plans laid so long ago, abandon ambition, waste all those years of work ... What's more, she thought, he took it for granted that whatever ring he chose ... He might at least have *asked* me what I'd like ...

Sarah departed to the warmth of the kitchen to sew the last stitches of the spectacle case she was giving Mrs. Mackenzie for Christmas. Gwen and Julia looked at each other. They looked at Frances.

"What's happened?"

To Frances's astonishment their sympathies were with Gabriel.

"You've been going round in a daze all autumn," Julia said. "*Of course* he thought ... Really, Frances. Don't say I didn't warn you."

"But he's always known. I've told him. Lots of times. I told him what Tonks said about marriage and artists. I told him all about Mother giving up when she got married and not being able to get back again. He's always *known* I couldn't get married."

"Well, it's all very unfortunate," Gwen said. "Particularly now, just before Christmas. You'll have to go over to the Rectory this afternoon, Frances, and be nice to him, otherwise it's going be very awkward over Christmas. It's supposed to be special this year, remember, with Sarah staying up. You can't spoil it for her."

Why not, Frances wanted to say. Why not? He's spoilt Christmas for me, hasn't he? He's spoilt everything for me. But Gwen, lips pressed together in an expression of grim disapproval, had left the room before Frances could speak.

"Gwen's right," Julia said. "You'll have to go over and apologise. Tell him you were so surprised you didn't mean what you said."

"Apologise? For what? He's the one who should apologise. Oh, leave me alone. I'm going out."

She could not return to the stables; the memory was too vivid. She set off, walking fast, towards Dunkery St. Michael. Bill Roberts waved as she passed the forge. She did not wave back. She did not see him.

The day was darkening by the time she reached Priory Common. Clouds covered the Quantock ridge that she knew so well. She was suddenly desolate. All those times spent on those hills, all those hours together, all that happy, happy companionship ... lost, gone for ever.

Annie had heard the news by the time Frances returned and wasted no time in giving her opinion. "Time was," she said, "when a girl was flattered to get a proposal. Grateful, she was.

Not like some I could mention, not a hundred miles from here."

In the privacy of her bedroom that night Frances took down her pastel of Gabriel from the wall and wept as she studied the face that gazed up at her, the fair hair and blue eyes, the smile faintly mocking, the face that she had so dearly loved.

Later, as she lay in bed in the dark, incidents long forgotten came to the surface of her mind. She remembered the expression on his face when she told him she had gained a place at the Slade, shock and dismay when she had expected congratulation and delight. She remembered words spoken casually in the past – "I'll remind you of that when you're married," he had once said; "you'll feel differently when the time comes," another time – words that she had dismissed because she had not wanted him to mean them. But he had meant them. He had treated her as he might treat a child, indulging her humours, pretending to believe in what she said, making her believe that he encouraged her talent.

She had thought he loved her. He didn't love her. He didn't know what love was. He had looked at her and in his mind fashioned her into the kind of person he wanted her to be. He loved someone who did not exist except in his own imagination.

The love that she had thought bound them together was no love at all.

Chapter Fourteen

Sarah might be looking forward to Christmas, with all the excited anticipation of an eleven-year-old, but she was the only member of the Hillcrest household who now was.

Gwen kept out of the fuss as usual, merely saying, "Well, I think it's a bit much of you, Frances, I do really, if you can't go over to the Rectory and try to make things up with Gabriel," before retiring to the onion patch to plant out the shallots two days earlier than tradition deemed necessary.

Annie said, "It's not my place to pass judgement, Miss Frances, but you'll know my opinion, I'll be bound," and refused to discuss the matter further.

It was Julia who went on and on, annoying Frances considerably.

"I don't know how you have the nerve to say all that, Julia," she said. "It's my future we're talking about, my work. Are you suggesting that I should give it all up? Perhaps we'd better change places. You don't seem much interested in your future, do you, sitting at home when you should be at the Slade."

She had been hurt by Julia's refusal to study at the Slade, as well as uncomprehending. Julia would give no reason, apart from expense, but that, as everyone knew, was no reason at all. She wouldn't be able to win the prizes and scholarships that had helped Frances, she said. When Frances pointed out that family finances had been much more uncertain when she had started and no-one had known about awards and scholarships then, Julia pressed her lips firmly together and said that was how she felt and would they stop wasting their breath because she'd made up her mind and that was that.

Now, before either of them realised what was happening, Julia's remonstrances over Frances's behaviour towards Gabriel dissolved into a bitter quarrel between the two sisters, a quarrel that upset Frances considerably and probably did Julia too. She had always felt close to Julia whose opinion had always mattered, but even for Julia Frances refused to go over to the Rectory. It was difficult to be private in the Rectory at any time; on Christmas Eve it would be impossible. Parishoners, churchwardens, people with good wishes, problems or presents, would be calling in all day. The Purcells were expected to present themselves to help with the distribution of mince pies and gifts for the needy. Worst of all would be Antony, lurking behind doors carefully left ajar. No. If Gabriel would come over to Hillcrest and be sensible ... But Gabriel stayed at home.

She was nervous when she went up to change on Christmas night. Gabriel had not been at the Communion service, presumably having gone to the earlier one; he had avoided her gaze during Matins, and she, by leaving before the choir emerged, had avoided him afterwards. But as she fixed her mother's favourite earrings in her ears and then stood back to survey her reflection her spirits began to rise. They were both sensible people, they loved each other, they would be able to sort something out. He had been nervous and she taken by surprise that morning: it had all been an unfortunate misunderstanding. When they saw each other ... If they could manage to sit beside each other at dinner, she thought hopefully, and talk ...

Sarah came downstairs to join Frances in the hall. The dress Frances had made her fitted perfectly, its colour emphasising the lights in her hair so that it no longer looked plain mouse. Her face was flushed with excitement, her lips red. Frances was filled with affection tinged with sadness, for a moment reluctant to watch her youngest sister growing up.

It looked as if her hopes over Gabriel might be fulfilled. He came across the Rectory hall, took both her hands in his and kissed her full on the mouth. "There," he murmured in her ear, "now slap my face if you dare."

She couldn't help laughing, but blushed too, feeling Mrs. Mackenzie's eyes on the back of her head.

"Gabriel's arranged the seating this year," Lucy said as Mr. Mackenzie led them into the dining-room with Sarah on his arm. "Sarah, you're in the place of honour, by Father. Frances, you're opposite, next to Gabriel. That's what you said, Gabriel, isn't it?"

"I see so little of you these days," Mrs. Mackenzie said before Gabriel could reply. "Sit by me tonight, Gabriel." She smiled at Frances as she spoke. "Geoffrey won't mind changing places."

Geoffrey looked at his elder brother as if waiting for some command, glanced uneasily at Frances and then said, "I suppose . . . if you want," coming nervously round the table to stand beside Frances.

Mrs. Mackenzie's expression was triumphant.

In that moment Frances understood.

Mrs. Mackenzie knew. She knew about Gabriel, knew about Frances. She knew that they had been meeting in London, despite the Purcells' careful insistence that Frances went to see old friends from the Slade. Mrs. Mackenzie had waited, and in the end Frances had done exactly what Mrs. Mackenzie wanted. Mrs. Mackenzie had never approved of Frances. She would keep her away from Gabriel. Using others as she had used Geoffrey just now, she would poison Gabriel's mind . . .

Mr. Mackenzie said grace. Bertha brought in the soup. General conversation began. Frances turned to Geoffrey. "Why can't you stand up to your mother just once in your life?" she said viciously.

He gave her a startled look, fumbled with his table napkin and dropped the silver ring onto the floor where it rolled under the dining-table. His face was scarlet.

Worse was to come. Discussion turned to women and marriage, to marriage and careers. It was Gabriel who began it, deliberately no doubt, by talk of Sarah and university. Frances, with no intention of losing her temper, was shocked by his hypocrisy. How could he talk about a career for Sarah when he wouldn't tolerate one for Frances herself? Within moments the two of them were exchanging bitter words that only Mr. Mackenzie was able to bring to a halt, by emphasising Frances's debt to Gabriel. "Mrs. Mackenzie and I were very against your going to London. It was Gabriel who persuaded us that we would be wrong not to encourage your talent."

She could not tell Mr. Mackenzie that Gabriel's support had been for the wrong reasons. Instead she said, "Yes, I do know that," and sat with gradually diminishing fury for the rest of the meal, resolutely avoiding Gabriel's gaze.

Christmas presents were always exchanged at the Rectory in the hall after dinner. First of all there were the presents the Purcells had brought for the Rectory servants, and then those from the servants to the Purcells. Even Frances could not remain angry on such an occasion . . .

The servants departed downstairs. Gabriel insisted on acting as master of ceremonies, on being the first . . . He studied the writing on all the presents.

"Hurry *up*, Gabriel," Purcells and Mackenzies cried.

He looked across at Frances and picked up her present to him. She watched him open it . . . the long promised drawing of Mr. Mackenzie, properly posed. His pleasure was evident but during the general excitement of further present opening he came over to Frances's side and murmured, "I like it very much, but I still prefer the other. It means more to me." He put his hand over hers. "I'm sorry you felt as you did. You must know that I'll always support you. I do realise how much your work matters."

"I didn't want to hurt you," she said. "It was just . . . I was . . . shocked, I think."

"Will you take my present as an apology? I know you'll like it. I'm only sorry it has to be shared between the four of you. My bank account couldn't manage more."

She was relieved. She had asked herself, in the night hours of Christmas Eve, what she would do if he produced the ring. What happened to unwanted rings, she wondered now. Did jewellers take them back?

She sensed his suppressed excitement during the rest of the exchange until only his present to the Purcells remained. He held it out to her. "I want you to open it."

Flat, rectangular – a picture obviously. She untied the ribbons, pulled away the paper, the wadding that protected, and looked down on it. She could not believe her eyes. It could not be true ...

"Oh Gabriel."

The Matisse still life that she had last seen in the window of the Mayfield Gallery lay in her lap. The fruit, the oranges and the grapes, rounded, thickly coloured, thrown up by the white of the tablecloth surrounding them, waited for her to pluck them out of the solid wooden bowl in which they lay.

"Oh Gabriel ... the Matisse."

He knelt on the floor beside her. "I couldn't wait to give it to you," he said. "I thought Christmas would never come." He smiled at her. "I had to find some excuse for talking to him, didn't I?"

Mrs. Mackenzie thought the painting terrible. 'A child's daub' was how she described it. Mrs. Mackenzie liked a picture to be a picture; more properly, even, a photograph.

They retired at last to the warmth of the drawing-room, though Frances would have preferred to remain alone in the hall with her present. The brass round the hearth gleamed in the firelight. Cards decorated the mantelpiece, holly the dreadful picture of the stag above the fire, Christmas roses floated in bowls on the low tables. Gabriel and his father were drinking brandy. Mrs. Mackenzie, glacial still, came between Frances and Gabriel, making certain they sat apart, but Mrs. Mackenzie was no match for Frances: she could be too easily provoked. Frances had only to criticise Gabriel, however mildly, deride Mrs. Mackenzie's taste in art ... she could see herself doing it now, knowing that she should not but unable to prevent herself. Even that in the end lost its pleasure. When Lucy suggested charades, Frances knew the time had come to go home, and take Sarah with her.

Sarah's face fell. "Please, Frances ..."

"Let her have one turn," Gabriel begged.

"It is Christmas," Lucy said.

She let herself be persuaded. It was a mistake. She knew it the moment Gwen and Antony reappeared to act out the first syllable of the chosen word. Antony's mischievous face watched Frances's every movement, watched and waited ... She had no idea why, she was never good at guessing charades, until Sarah appeared in veil and train. Of course, of course. Matrimony. What else would Antony choose? His face danced in front of Frances, laughing, exultant, while behind him Sarah parroted words ... stopped, looked at Frances ... burst into tears.

In the confusion Gabriel took charge. "I'll take her back to Annie," he said. "It must be long past her bedtime. Come on, mouse, blow your nose."

"You lot had better go out," Antony said after Gabriel and Sarah had departed, leaving the rest embarrassed, uncertain whether to carry on. "It is your turn. Gabriel can join in when he gets back." He looked sheepish, sounded subdued.

"Geoffrey and I'll start," Julia said in the hall. "You wait out here. Really, Frances. Glaring at the poor child like that. Poor Sarah."

Julia thought the incident Frances's fault. Frances remembered Antony's pert, provocative face, the way he watched her, waiting for her reaction, but was too tired to protest. She sat on the stairs and leant her head against the wall, trying to banish thoughts of Antony, the picture of Sarah's crumpled face, even Gabriel, from her mind.

Gabriel's footsteps sounded on the drive. She opened the door before the bell could summon Bertha. "Is she all right?"

"Yes, of course. It was much too late; I should have taken her home after dinner – and you, too. You behaved very badly this evening."

She wanted to deny it. Honesty prevented her. "I'm sorry," she said at last.

"It's not much good saying that to me, is it? It's my parents you should be apologising to, and that poor infant back at

Hillcrest. I know. You'll say it was my fault in the first place for asking you to marry me — that's what all this goes back to, isn't it? — but you might at least have had the decency to keep it between the two of us." He sighed as he looked down at her. His mouth began to curve. "Oh, Frances, Frances," he said, as he pulled a small packet from his pocket. "I don't know why I put up with you. Here. It isn't much, but I wanted you to have something for yourself in spite of spurning the other ..."

He helped her pull the wrapping paper away, picked up what it contained and slipped it over her head — an antique coin suspended from a twisted chain: the sort of ornament a Florentine sitter might have worn in years gone by. She held the coin in her hand, feeling its weight.

"Coals of fire," she said, and tried to smile.

His own smile was mocking. "Ah, well. That may have been my intention."

"But Gabriel, what about the Matisse ...?"

"That was for all of you. Though I suppose you're right. If I hadn't thought I was already giving you ... And I wish now that I'd given Sarah a present of her own. She's too young to appreciate Matisse." He turned his head as a burst of clapping came from the drawing-room. "We'd better go in before that wretched brother of mine thinks of something else ..."

"He told me you'd hung up mistletoe specially ..."

In Gabriel's arms everything was right once more — Christmas, the two of them, love itself.

"I wish I could make you understand how I feel," she said sadly.

"Perhaps you should try to understand me," Gabriel said.

She made an attempt at an apology when next alone with Mrs. Mackenzie, though she doubted whether Gabriel would ever learn of it. "About the other night, Mrs. Mackenzie. You know, Christmas ..."

"There's no need to say anything," Mrs. Mackenzie said quickly. "Julia explained how you'd been working late on Sarah's dress and were tired. Of course I understand. You must have been pleased with the result. She looked almost pretty, I thought, and so much more confident. She's beginning to come out at last, don't you think?"

"I wish you wouldn't interfere between Mrs. Mackenzie and me," Frances told Julia. "I can fight my own battles, thank you. It was all lies, anyway, what you said. Working late, indeed!"

"Someone has to do something," Julia said, "tact not being one of your virtues, alas."

1914

Chapter Fifteen

Denis Bond wrote to Frances towards the end of that winter, saying that he, his wife and children would be driving down to Devon to open up their cottage at Easter, and would it be possible to call in at Hillcrest? He was always interested in seeing the painter's surroundings, he said, and while he felt he knew her home from her work he would still like to see it 'off the canvas', as it were.

Frances was apprehensive. London was London and Somerset Somerset: she preferred to keep her two lives apart. Jamieson and other Slade friends had visited Hillcrest, and Julia had stayed with Frances at Jamieson's flat, but that was enough.

"It'll be so awkward," she complained to Julia. "I've never met his wife or his children. What do we do with them?"

Julia was shocked. "You are so ungracious. When they're *driving* all that way, too. How long do you think it takes? We'll have to give them a meal, that's certain. Lunch, do you think? There's no need for you to worry, Frances. We'll look after the family and leave you to cope with him."

The Bonds arrived in time for a late lunch, announcing their arrival outside Hillcrest with a raucous blast on the horn. The son insisted on showing the Purcells over the car – a Sunbeam tourer, he told them in a lordly manner – explained its various gadgets at length, and was only prevented by his father from giving a demonstration of wheel changing. By the time the Purcells had shown the proper amount of admiration and awe (even Sir James Donne took the train to London and left his chauffeur to drive the car up on his own) and had taken the Bonds upstairs to remove their protective clothing and rid themselves of the journey's dust, everyone was so friendly that even Frances felt at ease.

The visit was a great success. Denis's wife got on well with Gwen, discussing gardens with her and plants and the best flowers to grow in window-boxes. The children let Sarah take them down Shepherd's Lane and never having been on a farm before were amazed by Mr. Escott's pigs. Denis talked about the Pre-Raphaelites with Julia, showed an interest in her painting and said that he would like to have a look at it sometime. In knickerbockers and Norfolk jacket he looked younger than he had done in London, was much less formal and easier to talk to. Frances decided that she was beginning to like him very much.

Her only regret was her lack of foresight in not moving the Matisse from the dining-room wall to her bedroom for the day. She saw Denis's eyes return to it again and again during the meal and waited for him to ask how it came to be at Hillcrest. Presumably he was too polite to do so, for he did not bring up the subject, nor mention it when he and Frances were alone together in the stables, as she half expected he would.

He looked at her paintings and through her drawings, and talked about her ideas for future work. He was anxious to know about her pattern of working and plans for studying, and was obviously pleased by the discipline they demonstrated. He liked the watercolours, which he had not seen previously and said, as he had said once before, that she should continue to exhibit when the opportunity arose, particularly at the New English, and to bear in mind the possibility of a one-man show some time in the not too distant future.

"I dislike over-confidence enormously," he said, "but I do

have to say that I think you're being unnecessarily diffident. I know what you'll tell me but don't you realise that every artist has to serve an apprenticeship? We've talked about this before, so I won't go on, but you know my thoughts, don't you?"

Frances smiled at him. "Yes. I do." She was content: she knew that he would not push her more than she wished.

There was a haze of green on the trees in the copse beyond the stables and outside her studio the buds on the magnolia were beginning to break. She walked with him down the path past the fig tree and felt enough at ease with him to take him into the house by the back way. He stopped in the little cobbled yard outside the kitchen and looked round, at the outbuildings that surrounded it and the pattern made by the uneven height and slant of their green slated roofs.

"Ah," he said. "I've seen this before. There's been an intriguing feeling of familiarity all day."

"I suppose there might have been."

"What about the Cambridge scenes?" he asked. "Do you go there often?"

"I go with Julia sometimes," she said, reddening slightly. "We know ... people there."

He took a couple of watercolours away with him, packing them carefully between the rugs and blankets in the back of the car, and said that he looked forward to seeing her when she was next in London.

"Meanwhile," he said, as he helped the children climb up into their seats, "if there's anything I can do ..."

"No. I can't think of anything. Everything's splendid at the moment."

Life could not be better. She was as satisfied as she could ever be with her work; she had Denis's support and encouragement; the family were free of all but normal, everyday problems; and she and Gabriel were happy together. The incident at Christmas had disappeared into the past. Gabriel had not mentioned marriage again, nor referred to his proposal. She could almost forget that he had spoken.

She went up to London to meet Gabriel on his return from Germany. It was July; the weather hot and heavy. He looked preoccupied and glum as he came through the barrier.

"Is anything happening?" he said in the taxi, after only the briefest enquiry about his parents and the Purcells.

"What do you mean?"

"What's the government doing about the Sarajevo business? All the ultimatums." And as she looked at him blankly, "The Archduke's murder, Frances, surely you've heard about that?"

"Oh. Oh, that." She vaguely remembered Antony talking about some assassination in Sarajevo. Antony always revelled in gory details. What had it been this time – the wife killed as well?

"There'll be war," Gabriel said. "Mark my words. This summer."

"Oh, surely not," Frances said. "Your father says there's been trouble in Ireland for hundreds of years but they've never had civil war yet."

"Not Ireland. Germany. God, I hate the Prussians."

She looked at him in surprise. "I thought you liked them."

"I like the Germans. Not the Prussians. If you'd come across the Junkers lot that I have in the universities over there – beer-swilling louts, who think they own the world because they've got blue blood."

Frances felt her heart sink. If they were going to have a summer of politics, of gloom and depression ... She had longed for his return, bought tickets for the Russian ballet, planned expeditions over the Quantocks and the Brendons ... Was it all to be like this?

The declaration of war brought excitement rather than gloom. The village band played tunes of martial glory on the village green. People talked of teaching the Kaiser a thing or two. Men enlisted, Gabriel and Geoffrey among the first. Others in the village followed in quick succession, anxious not to miss the fun. Everyone knew time was short, that the war would be over by Christmas. Willis, the Purcells' gardener, joined up too, to Gwen's delight. She had always complained of his unwillingness to try anything new and was looking forward to more freedom, undeterred by the prospect of managing two-and-a-half acres with only her sisters and an occasional schoolboy from the village to help.

Bill Roberts's departure was regarded with dismay by local farmers, who were less than enthusiastic at losing a blacksmith – or any of their labourers for that matter – during the harvest. Sir James Donne's popularity, normally high in the area, sank to unprecedented depths after he had sent his men round the countryside fixing recruiting posters to the trees.

Frances, too, was dismayed by Bill Roberts's departure. She enjoyed painting in and around the forge and had grown to like Bill Roberts and admire his skill. Old man Roberts, who had replaced his son while he was away, was bad-tempered and awkward and didn't take kindly to having women about.

No-one expected Antony to enlist. He was no more than a boy, precocious still, but a boy. Now, in the space of a morning, he had become a man, having gone secretly into Taunton and come back a soldier. The Purcells were shaken. Annie shed tears in the kitchen. Mr. and Mrs. Mackenzie aged visibly overnight.

"I don't understand the Mackenzies," Frances said to Annie as they cut up green tomatoes for chutney. "He's under age – years under age. Why doesn't Mr. Mackenzie do something about it? He must be able to appeal, write to someone, do *something* to get him back."

Perhaps Mr. Mackenzie had accepted Antony's decision and did not wish to interfere. Pride mingled with sorrow in his voice as he spoke to Frances.

"He tried to enlist before, you know. One can't help admiring his persistence, even if he did have to fib about his age." He sat in the study, gazing at the photograph of Antony on his desk. He tried to smile at Frances. "Forgive me, my dear. I didn't ask you over to talk about Antony except so far as his departure affects Sarah."

It was Sarah's education that Mr. Mackenzie wanted to discuss with Frances. He considered she should go away to school. He had already chosen the school he thought most suitable – in Bristol, not far from the Purcells' two great-aunts. "I visited them last week, after I had talked to the headmistress. Sarah would be able to stay with them."

"But when Mother died," Frances said, finding her voice, "you said they were too old."

"To take in the four of you. One child, and only during the term, is quite a different matter. They said they would be pleased to have her and I'm sure they meant it."

Her initial reaction was dismay. "I don't know. I hadn't ever thought ..."

"I worry about Sarah with Antony gone. He provided competition. Without him I fear she may become lazy."

"How does Sarah feel?"

"I thought that you, as head of the family, should talk to her first. Think about it, my dear. Discuss it with Julia and Gwen if you wish. There's no hurry. She wouldn't be able to start before the beginning of next term, in January."

"All right. I'll ... I'll let you know."

"We both agree, do we not," he said, smiling, "on the importance of making the most of the gifts God gave us? Sarah has a good brain. It would be a pity to waste it."

Oh, he was clever, Frances thought, walking back to Hillcrest through the churchyard. He had produced the one argument she could not gainsay, the argument she had used in her own fight to get to the Slade. How could she deny Sarah a similar opportunity?

"I wouldn't want to leave Hillcrest myself," Gwen said, "but if that's what Mr. Mackenzie thinks best ..."

"She's always wanted to go away to school," Julia said, "ever since I can remember. So, yes, I suppose ..."

Frances stared. "She's never said anything to me about boarding-school."

"Don't you remember how she used to pester us when she was little, always wanting to know what it was like and what we did?"

"So she did. I didn't realise that's what it meant." Frances sighed. "I'd better see what Annie thinks."

"Don't ask Annie," Julia said. "She won't want to lose Sarah. Soon enough to tell her if we decide."

Sarah showed no delight when Frances broached the subject but did not turn the idea down either. "I don't mind," was all she said.

"The headmistress suggested you should spend a day at school first, to see if you liked it and to see if they thought you'd fit in," Frances said, watching for her reaction. "We thought if you spent the day there you could stay with the aunts the night before and after."

"All right. When can I go?"

What an extraordinary girl she is, Frances thought. No doubts, no fears; or no sign of them at least. I was terrified when I went for that interview at the Slade and I was seventeen.

Sarah had never been a noisy child. She spent her time with her books, tucked away in odd corners of the house or garden. It was strange that Hillcrest should seem so quiet without her.

"I don't know, I'm sure," Annie said, heating milk for the bedtime cocoa. "Things don't seem right without Miss Sarah around, for all she's so quiet. How's she going on with the old aunts, I wonder?"

Frances wondered too, and next morning worried more, picturing Sarah in the strange surroundings of an unknown school, among more strangers than she had met in her life.

Julia was helping Annie with the baking, Gwen attending a meeting in the parish room about the benefits of beekeeping. Lucy never came over before lunch. Frances had no-one to talk to as she sat in the kitchen garden painting the border of cutting dahlias. Her thoughts circled round Sarah. She knew that she would have to let her go.

Sarah had grown during her two nights away, in height – or so it seemed – and in confidence. She was amusing about the aunts, their disagreeable maid, the house they lived in – "you'd have loved Aunt Maud's room, Frances. It was full of mirrors, it looked like lots and lots of rooms, with hundreds of Aunt Mauds lying in bed like old pigeons."

Annie was shocked. "I never did, miss. 'Tis disrespectful, talking that way about your aunt."

"But that's how she looked, Annie. Her hands were exactly like pigeons' claws gripping the sheets. What's the matter with her, Frances? Aunt Bessie wouldn't say."

"I don't know. She's been an invalid for years – long before Mother died, I think."

"Aunt Bessie promised to take me to the zoological gardens but we didn't have time. You could hear animals roaring from their house – lions, Aunt Bessie said they were."

She said very little about her day at school, and her sisters were taken aback and shocked when she said firmly that she had no intention of going to Bristol. She would give no reason for her determination to remain at Hillcrest. Frances was baffled.

The aunts had been charmed by their newly met great-niece. Aunt Bessie told Frances so, in a letter in which she and Aunt Maud offered to be responsible for all term-time costs – board, fees and uniform.

"It does seem a pity to throw away an opportunity like that," Frances said to Sarah. "Are you sure, mouse? Why don't you try it for a year?"

"No." She was adamant. "I'm staying here."

"She doesn't want to go," Frances told Mr. Mackenzie at last. "I've tried to persuade her but she's quite determined. I'm sorry, after all the trouble you've taken, but I'm not going to force her."

She felt helpless – first Julia with the Slade, and now Sarah – and was nervous of Mr. Mackenzie's reaction. Suppose he insisted? But he smiled. "It's a pity, no doubt, but if that's how she feels, and you too, there's nothing more to be said. I can't say that I'm sorry. I would have missed the child. She keeps me young."

The objections, strangely enough, came from Gabriel. It was absurd, he wrote to Frances, to let a child of Sarah's age dictate whether or not she should go to school, and Frances was irresponsible to allow it.

He came home on leave at the end of the year and spent the greater part of his time arguing with Frances. "Just because you made such a mess of school yourself . . . "

She was indignant. "That's got nothing to do with it. I'm sorry if you don't agree, but it's too late now. It's over. In the past. Forgotten. And don't you dare try to change her mind. She's getting extra French from Madame Defosse at Clay Court, and mathematics from Mr. Dunn at Dunkery. If your father's happy about her education you should be too."

She was more upset by Gabriel's opposition than she let him see. Fear that she had allowed her own experience to affect her decision on Sarah's future remained with her long after Gabriel had returned to his battalion.

The real reason for her agreement lay deeper, barely realised. There was still guilt at having gone against her mother's wishes by going to the Slade. Sarah was a hostage for her own redemption. If there were an afterworld, if she ever had to face her mother, she could produce Sarah in expiation. To send Sarah away would be to free herself of responsibility for the duty which her mother had by dying laid on her. She could not do it.

Perhaps there was yet another reason – the memory of the terror on Sarah's face outside the barn that morning on the Quantocks. Frances did not want Sarah to look at her like that ever again.

1915

Chapter Sixteen

In Huish Priory engagements tended to last years rather than months. Bill Roberts and Mary Hancock had been walking out for three years before they married, but Lizzie, Bill's pretty sister, was marrying her young man only weeks after they had first met. The reason was obvious: Lizzie's fiancé was about to be sent to the front.

Frances watched and was silent. She had seen Lizzie and her young man holding hands as they came out of the Rectory after their talk with Mr. Mackenzie, had caught sight of them kissing in the Sunday twilight down Shepherd's Lane. Of course they wanted to marry before he went overseas – but how would they feel on his return?

Gabriel too was going overseas. He wrote saying that his next leave would be his 'last leave', the final time at home before departing for France.

Frances was haunted by the thought of Lizzie, the memory of Lizzie's face with her young man. Lizzie was a simple village girl. Was Frances so very different?

Marriage had never been mentioned by Gabriel again. Frances never doubted that he had understood her reasons for refusing and had accepted them. But ... the situation had changed. She knew from his letters that the thought of leaving England to fight had brought feelings to the surface, of family, of life and love, of the future. In the poems he wrote her she sensed passion underlying the words. He could be persuasive, even forceful, when he wished. He was going away to face danger, possibly death. She loved him. Was she really any stronger than Lizzie Roberts?

During the day she listened to Mrs. Mackenzie's plans to give Gabriel a memorable leave; at night she lay awake, arguments tossing about in her head. Marriage would be impossible, disastrous, absolutely wrong, but ... She could not trust herself to be sensible if she stayed.

She considered going to Jamieson first of all but decided against it. Jamieson was fascinated by Frances's relationship with Gabriel, would ask after him, put two and two together and then probe. Frances refused to explore her emotions with anyone, even Jamieson.

She went instead to the Johns at Alderney. In that extra-ordinary household another visitor never mattered. People came and went as they pleased. On this occasion Augustus was away, having gone over to Ireland to paint Bernard Shaw for Lady Gregory. Frances was relieved. Her admiration for John as draughtsman and painter was tempered by nervousness of him as a man. She hated his wandering hands and always took good care not to be alone with him in a room.

Dorelia had recently given birth to a second daughter and was slowly getting back to normal. She and Frances sat in the garden in the April sunshine and, while Frances worked, talked about gardens and plants, exhibitions and paintings, and people they both knew. The most surprising men were in uniform. Professor Tonks himself had left the Slade to join the Royal Army Medical Corps and was now somewhere in France. He had been a surgeon, of course, before becoming an artist, but would surgical skills acquired so long ago be of as much value as his skill as a teacher?

Frances had not left Hillcrest since the outbreak of war. It was refreshing to be back in her other world, among people who knew her work and understood how she felt. During her time away she managed to keep thoughts of Huish Priory at bay. Not until she was sitting in the train on the way back to Taunton did she let herself consider Gabriel and wonder what kind of welcome she might receive on her return.

"Humph," said Annie, when she walked into the kitchen at Hillcrest. "So you're back."

"How was he?"

"Not best pleased."

"Annie, I had to do it."

"It's not for me to pass judgement."

But you have, Frances thought, as she went to find Julia. It was, strangely, Annie's opinion that mattered most. Annie had had to make sacrifices in her own life; Frances had hoped that despite disapproval she would understand. Apparently not.

"How did he take it?" she asked Julia.

"You know Gabriel. He hid his feelings well enough. It confirmed everything Mrs. Mackenzie already thought about you, of course — 'Frances behaving badly, as usual'. You always let us down with Mrs. Mackenzie."

Yes, it would be that aspect that would annoy Julia.

"Did he leave an address? I must write."

Her letter crossed with one from Gabriel, a brief note thanking her for letting him choose a drawing to take to France. She read it and was mystified.

"That'll be Sarah's doing," Julia said, when Frances reluctantly sought information. "I know she took him up to the stables the first morning he was home."

Sarah had avoided Frances since the latter's return. In Frances's presence her eyes became large with reproach. Frances could not ask Sarah what Gabriel's letter meant. It was clear from a second reading that Gabriel's thanks were formal only. He knew, whether by supposition or from something Sarah had said, that the present of a drawing had been nothing to do with Frances.

She wondered whether he understood the reason for her absence. To tell him might give him false hope. She could only write as if nothing had altered between them. She knew it had been a terrible thing to do, but she was sure that in a little while he'd see the sense of her action and forgive her.

She had not considered the possibility of Antony's death.

The shock was worse for being unexpected. Anyone who had a man fighting in France knew of the growing casualty lists and dreaded the knock on the door, the arrival of a telegram, but Antony had not been in France. He had been cruising at the far end of the Mediterranean, sending back ecstatic descriptions of the Greek islands, sounding as if he were on some latter-day expedition to Troy. Mackenzies and Purcells alike feared for Gabriel and Geoffrey, but because of the nonchalant letters they received from Antony were under the impression that the youngest Mackenzie was enjoying a tour of classical sites and would reach Constantinople without hearing the sound of a shot. Ridiculous as it might seem, looking back afterwards, it did not occur to any of those reading the first newspaper reports of the successful landings on Gallipoli that Antony might be involved.

His was the first death in the village. The horror of it was accentuated by his youth. People rallied round. Mr. Tasker, from Clay Court, intoned evensong every night until Mr. Mackenzie felt able to do so once more, and Sir James Donne conducted all the church services the Sunday following the telegram's arrival. Dr. Milne called to see Mrs. Mackenzie. The Sewing Circle paid for a wreath to be laid, in Antony's name, under the list of those serving their country that hung in the church porch.

Later came the memorial service with Antony's favourite hymns, 'Fight the Good Fight' and 'To Be a Pilgrim', the Dead March from Saul played, with difficulty, by Miss Podimor, who had replaced her brother as organist after his enlistment, and at the end the muffled peal of bells echoing over the churchyard.

Frances struggled with a letter to Gabriel. What could you

say to someone who had lost a brother? Of the four Mackenzie children Gabriel and Antony, despite the difference in age, were the closest, in thought and interests and talent. Gabriel had always considered Antony to have great promise. The loss of such promise would be, to Gabriel, an almost mortal blow. He had lost others too, in the Eastern Mediterranean, close friends and companions from the Fabian days. There was no consolation that Frances could give. Her absence, at a time when her presence had been most needed, diminished any sympathy that she could offer.

She herself could not believe Antony to be dead. Every day she expected to see his impudent face come round the side of the house or find him teasing Annie in the kitchen. She had always regarded him with a mixture of affection and irritation but would now have willingly put up with endless annoyance to have him back, and with him the spring in Sarah's step, the colour in Sarah's cheeks.

She could not banish from her mind that final picture of Antony's departure at the end of his last leave, hanging halfway out of the taxi window as it turned out of the Rectory drive on its way to Taunton station and the train, waving frantically like the child he was, a schoolboy wearing fancy dress, the uniform of a soldier.

The weeks passed. Hill 60 replaced Gallipoli in the headlines. It was summer when Julia announced one afternoon that she was thinking of joining the Voluntary Aid Department. She was sitting on the verandah at the time, hemming flannel nightshirts for the Red Cross, while Frances painted the view into the greenhouse. Her voice was casual. She might have been admiring Frances's portrayal of the swelling grapes on the vine or commenting on the profusion of Gwen's orchids. She added, "Well, not thinking. I've joined. I'm going to nurse."

Frances stared. "What on earth for?"

Julia gave her an astringent look. "Nurses are in demand these days, surprisingly enough. I know you don't read the newspapers but even you must know that."

Panic seized Frances at the thought of losing Julia as well as Gabriel. "You can't."

"Why not? You wanted me to go to the Slade. You went on and on about that. What's the difference? Except this time I'll be helping other people instead of myself."

"Julia, you *can't*." A thought struck her. "You won't be able to. You're under age. The Mackenzies won't let you."

"Being under age didn't stop Antony, did it? Sixteen, when he joined up. I shall be twenty-one next year. Besides, can you see the Mackenzies stopping me?"

No, she couldn't. The Mackenzies would admire Julia, support her, see her off with affection and pride ... and talk afterwards of Julia doing her bit.

"Why the V.A.D.?" she said. "If you're so eager to nurse, why don't you do it in Taunton?"

"I want to go abroad. I'm going to London first – I'm waiting to hear which hospital – and then I'll volunteer. For France, if one's allowed to choose."

"I suppose you have some ridiculous notion of nursing Geoffrey on the battlefield," Frances said, trying to hurt as she herself was hurt. "Things like that don't happen, let me tell you, except in books."

"Oh, don't be silly, Frances," Julia said. Not bitterly, or with anger, but as if Frances were a foolish child.

Frances was desolate. Hillcrest would not have been the same without Sarah, but Hillcrest without Julia was unimaginable – Julia who had so adamantly refused to go to the Slade but was now contemplating not only London but the Continent too. There was nothing Frances could do if Julia was determined, she knew that. She slipped through the gate in the wall by her studio into the copse beyond, and sat there all day looking out on the pale-coloured wheat of Tinker's Meadow. The world she had known had disappeared without her realising what was happening. Antony, Gabriel, Geoffrey and Julia – all gone or going; Sarah like a little ghost. Even Gwen had changed. ("And if you don't know what's the matter with Miss Gwen," Annie said when

Frances brought the subject up, "then I'm not the one to tell you.") Only Lucy remained.

"I hope you're not thinking of going off to nurse or drive an ambulance or anything like that," Frances said the next time Lucy came over, bringing the Sunday School attendance registers with her for help in working out the end-of-term prize winners.

"How about munitions?" Lucy said. She smiled. "No, I'm not serious. How could I leave Mother and Father now, after Antony?" She said in a tone of voice that surprised Frances, "Sometimes I wonder if I'll ever leave."

Frances was astonished. "What do you mean?"

"You don't know how lucky you are," Lucy said. "All of you. You can do what you want – Julia going to nurse, Gwen growing vegetables for the hospital. What do I do to help the war effort?"

"More than me."

"Yes, well. You're different. Your work will last long after the war's over and forgotten."

"I wish I could think so." She sighed and began counting the ticks in the register again. "Hannah Gould doesn't seem to have attended very often."

"Her mother never picked up after that last baby. Hannah has to look after the children and there are eight of them. No, it'll be Jess Hancock who wins again. We'll have to send the prize over to Nether Stowey."

Frances kept her eyes on the list of names. Her voice was casual. "How's Gabriel these days?"

"It's hard to tell. He says life's like Cambridge walking parties before the war. He's never had so much time to read. He'll like that, of course, though I suppose it won't last." She glanced at Frances. "Has he forgiven you yet?"

"I don't know. He won't write. Well, a couple of times but that's all. And a postcard or two."

"I tried to make him understand about your going away but I don't think I did any good. It was Lizzie Roberts getting married that frightened you, wasn't it?"

Frances was surprised at her perception. "Yes. Yes, I'm sure that was it. I don't regret going, you know. It was the right thing to do. I just wish it hadn't meant hurting Gabriel."

"Do you write to him?"

"Yes, of course."

"Oh well, I expect he'll come round in the end. He's always made a meal of being a martyr ever since I can remember."

Frances laughed, for the first time for weeks. Lucy, so kindly, so gentle, could sometimes be refreshingly frank about her family.

1916

Chapter Seventeen

There was an emptiness at Hillcrest where Julia had once been. At first she came home whenever she was able, but once she had sailed for France there was no knowing when the Purcells would see her again. Gabriel had always come and gone. Julia had been like Hillcrest: always present, ever dependable.

Frances had not realised how much she relied on Julia – for the smooth, efficient running of the household, for her comments on Frances's work, and her suggestions; more than anything else for her companionship. She would even have welcomed the occasional acid remark that Julia was inclined to deliver if she could have had Julia's company once more.

Julia's going had to be endured. The absence of a loved one was, after all, a cross borne by most of the country's population. What was almost unendurable was the long wait through those hot, dry days of June. The push had been long expected. When Gabriel wrote – casually, in a postscript – that she could not expect to hear from him for a while Frances knew immediately what was meant. She carried on – they all did – as if life were no different. She painted. She helped Annie. She worked in the garden with Gwen. All the time she wondered. Had it begun? Where was he? What was happening in France?

News came on the first Sunday of July. 'Attack launched 7.30 a.m. north of Somme,' announced the official bulletin. The British, so it said, had advanced along a sixteen mile front. The French attack had been equally satisfactory. British raiding parties had been successful along the remaining front. Victory at last. But Frances was silent as the Purcells joined other villagers to read the paper posted up outside the Post Office. It was too soon to rejoice. Even success brought casualties.

They waited. Frances could scarcely bear to visit the Rectory and see the strained faces of the Mackenzies, the anxious expressions of the servants. It was two weeks before a scribbled field-card from Gabriel reached the Rectory telling them that he was alive and unhurt.

Later came the award of the Military Cross – 'overcoming the Hun by my command of his language,' he wrote to Frances. According to his cursory account he had taken a trench and its six occupants merely by shouting at them in German. 'A waste of time, as it turned out. We lost the trench half an hour later, though not, I'm glad to say, the Huns.'

Fears were over, however briefly. In September he came home on leave.

Frances's relief at having him home once more was so great that she could scarcely contain it, the welcome he gave her finally putting to rest any fear that she might still be unforgiven for her absence the previous year. She sat beside him at dinner the first evening, shiveringly aware of the pressure of his hand on her thigh under the dining-table, smiling at Purcells, Mackenzies and servants alike, too full of emotion to speak.

Only later, sitting in the Rectory drawing-room as light died, did unease creep over her. Gabriel sat silent while Mrs. Mackenzie recounted every incident of parish life that had taken place since his last leave, and Lucy played a quiet accompaniment on the piano. He smiled across the room at Frances. Dusk made it impossible to read the expression in his eyes.

He walked back to Hillcrest at the end of the evening. He sounded cheerful, gave no hint of anything wrong, but after Gwen and Sarah had slipped discreetly indoors, leaving Frances on the doorstep, he said, "Will you come up to the Quantocks tomorrow?" with a desperation in his voice that stirred memories Frances could not place. Not until she reached her bedroom did she remember – the summer of 1912, when he had been working on his dissertation for the fellowship.

She walked with him; for the first days of his leave almost without rest. She had never walked so far or so fast. In the beginning he scarcely spoke, except during that first morning when he said, "What about your work? I don't want to get in the way ..."

She would have given up work altogether for the short time he was home if it would have helped. She said, "It's all right. I'm taking things in all the time. Looking's as important as sketching. You know that. What about your parents, though? Won't they mind your being away all day?"

"Father'll understand. If Mother doesn't, Lucy'll explain."

Frances scarcely understood herself. She only knew that he was going through a crisis of some sort and that she could help him by being with him, encouraging him to reach physical exhaustion, listening when he wanted to talk.

This was nothing like his usual black moods, nor the depression of earlier years. It went deeper than that. It was as if he had discovered that the precepts by which he had ordered his life until now had never existed, as if he had somehow to find the resources to come to terms with life as he now conceived it to be.

Gradually he came back from whatever abyss had held him. The walks became leisurely, enjoyable again. He smiled more easily. By the end of the first week it was almost possible to believe that he had never been away.

He wanted to know how Frances's work was progressing, to see what she was doing. He was so anxious that he should not hinder her that it never occurred to Frances that he might still entertain ideas of marriage. When, haltingly, he brought up the subject in the garden of Hillcrest on the last afternoon of his leave she was so taken aback, so shocked, that she handled it badly; looking back afterwards she could not believe how badly. Her astonishment that he should be mentioning marriage yet again, his reasonableness at first masking the shock of what he was proposing, made her slow to understand. When she did, her wretched temper – and his too – took the quarrel beyond the subject of marriage. Her refusal to send Sarah to school, his idolised position in the Rectory household, her selfishness, his arrogance – all were thrown to and fro with a bitterness that left her weak and trembling long after he had stormed away.

She felt herself betrayed. She thought of those hours spent in each other's arms up in the stables. Had he been planning it then, the offer – blackmail, bribery, call it what you will – to marry him, with the two hundred and fifty pound pension due to a captain's widow held out as bait? Did he really think that she was the kind to marry on those terms? To marry for money when she would not for love – was that what he expected of her?

Afterwards, in the solitude of the stables, when her anger had died, she thought that perhaps he had not meant it as she had imagined. Perhaps he had really thought he would be helping her work by marrying her. The possibility of a pension after his death ('when' he was killed, was what he said, not 'if') was what he offered, but could he not see how terrible it would be to marry him for that? Did he expect her, married, to wish him dead? It was surely what he was implying. And if not, then everything she had said to him over the years about marriage had meant nothing to him, nothing at all.

Gwen had taken the place of mentor in Julia's absence. She looked at Frances when Frances returned to the house and said, "How *could* you? It is his last day."

Frances was too weary to argue. She only said, "I don't expect you to understand, Gwen, but I wish you'd mind your own business. I'd give anything for a bit of privacy. You can

[138]

be at the bottom of the garden in this place and people still know what's happened within two minutes of it happening."

"If Gabriel comes striding across the lawn in a rage," Gwen said, "and won't say why or what's happened, well then, it's obvious. It must be something you've said or done."

"It never occurred to you that it might be his fault, I suppose?"

"No," Gwen said drily, "it didn't."

The hours moved inexorably forward towards Gabriel's departure. She knew that she could not bear an estrangement like the last. She would have to go to him. She prayed that it would be the more easy-going Bertha who opened the Rectory front door, but it was Hilda who stood before her.

"Miss Frances." No hint of surprise at Frances's unexpected arrival at such a late hour showed on her face.

"I'd like to speak to Mr. Gabriel, please, Hilda."

"The family are still at dinner, Miss Frances."

"Would you tell him there's someone to see him."

He came out into the hall, napkin in hand, saw Frances and stopped. "What is it?"

"I must talk to you," Frances said, uncomfortably aware of Hilda's disapproving presence at the dining-room door.

"I can't walk out in the middle of dinner."

"Please."

He hesitated. "All right. Later. For a few minutes. It is my last evening, in case you'd forgotten."

She flushed. "I'll wait in the Rectory field."

She sat on the seat, watching the shadows advance over the grass towards her, and the light climb up the trees until there was nothing left but grey and black beneath a colourless sky. The air smelt of wet grass and damp earth. Memories of past times hung over her, of cricket dances and church fêtes, of band concerts and rounders matches. The field was full of ghosts. She remembered Antony dancing with Gwen, Geoffrey and Julia, and Gabriel's arms around her as they danced to the music of Bill Roberts's trumpet the night before war was declared.

He came at last, when the evening star was already visible in the sky, and sat down in silence. Frances searched for the right words to say and failed to find them.

He gave a deep sigh. "You do seem to have the perfect knack for ruining a man's leave, don't you?"

The unfairness of it assailed her. If he hadn't mentioned marriage, when he'd known for years how she felt . . .

"I'm sorry," she said.

"What did you want to see me about?"

"Just that. To say I'm sorry. For shouting at you this afternoon. For not being able to do what you want."

He got to his feet. "That's it, then?"

She said desperately, "Gabriel, please . . ."

"What is it?"

"May I go in to Taunton with you tomorrow?"

He shrugged. "If you want."

All the Mackenzies disliked station farewells. Goodbyes were said at the Rectory – in the hall to the servants, outside to family and friends. With the memory of Antony's departure still vivid in her mind, Frances would not risk her last view of Gabriel being through the glass of a taxi window. Whatever the Mackenzies thought she would go with Gabriel into the station.

He greeted her perfunctorily at the Rectory gate and helped her into the taxi. He looked quite different in uniform, stern and remote. A stranger. Frances felt bereft.

The village was left behind. On the common a gaggle of geese hissed under the signpost that pointed to the Quantocks. Gabriel sat upright looking out of the window away from the hills.

"What are you thinking?" Frances said.

"That the wind's getting up and it might be rough."

She realised then that she should never have come. His mind had already detached itself from its surroundings and was preparing him for his return to France. She was in the way, her presence unwanted.

A newly arrived express was disgorging passengers onto an adjoining platform. The London train was expected at any moment. The station seethed with people. At least, Frances thought, there was privacy in a crowd, where there was none on an empty platform.

"We'd better say goodbye," Gabriel said, and looked at her as if seeing her for the first time that day. "Good lord, Frances! You look terrible. What's the matter?"

She didn't know whether to laugh or cry. "Oh, Gabriel, you are absurd. What do you think's the matter?"

He held her to him, so tightly she could scarcely breathe, while she cried onto his jacket and said over and over again, "I'm sorry, I'm sorry, I'm sorry."

"No, no. It was all my fault. I'm the one ... " He wiped her face with his handkerchief and blew her nose for her, as if she were a child. "Go home now," he said. "You've just got time to catch the Dunkery train. There's no point in waiting ... I'm no good at station farewells."

"You will take care, won't you?" she begged.

His eyebrows went up. "Take care?"

She tried to smile. "What an idiotic thing to say. It's just ... I'd rather have you home safe than a hundred Victoria Crosses."

"You might not believe it," he said, "but that's how I feel." He bent and gave her a final kiss. "Off you go. Please."

She let the Dunkery train leave without her and walked back to Huish Priory, probably for the first time in her life unaware of her surroundings so that when at last she reached the stables at Hillcrest she could not have said whether she had come the long way round by the road or taken the short cut across the fields, but only knew that her studio was the one place in the world able to give her shelter at such a time.

1917

Chapter Eighteen

There was snow over the Easter weekend. Snow – in April. Frances went up to the stables, lit the paraffin stove and looked out over the thin white layer covering grass and tree branches with more pleasure than the Mackenzies would have done. She preferred the whites and blues and browns of winter landscapes to the bleached colours of high summer, liked the economy of bare-leafed trees. She would be glad when spring came, all the same. This winter had seemed neverending. She was never free from fear for Gabriel, fear that ranged from terror when she knew him to be in the front line, to general unease when he was in the rear. Stray shells could kill a man anywhere in Flanders, according to Julia.

She was thinking of Gabriel now as she went through her canvases, wondering about his chances of getting leave in the summer, wanting him home for her first exhibition but knowing that it would take a miracle for leave and exhibition to coincide.

It was Sir James Donne, visiting his nephew in a Bristol hospital, who discovered Gabriel to be lying wounded in an adjoining ward. It was fortunate that it was Sir James who made the discovery. He decided at once that Bristol was too far away for the Mackenzies to visit and, being Sir James, made plans to bring Gabriel home for Mrs. Mackenzie to nurse at the Rectory.

"It's difficult to know what to do," Mr. Mackenzie confessed to Frances. "It would be, well, unorthodox. The War Office won't allow officers even to convalesce at home these days, I understand. It would be ... wrong, I feel, for us, and yet ... Sir James is being very kind."

Frances watched him with affection. She did not share his scruples and knew that no other Purcell or Mackenzie did either. Mrs. Mackenzie was upstairs supervising the transformation of Gabriel's bedroom into a sickroom at this moment. What did it matter if officers were supposed to be nursed only in military hospitals? If Sir James could arrange otherwise, Frances would say thank you and be grateful.

"After all, Mr. Mackenzie," she said, "Sir James is a Justice of the Peace. He wouldn't do anything *illegal*, surely? And I believe military hospitals get very crowded. Lucy said there were stretchers all down the corridors at Taunton after the Somme. Southmead'll probably be glad to have a bit more room."

"Do you think so?" He gave Frances his diffident, kindly smile. "It is sometimes difficult, when the end is so desirable, to tell whether one is being tempted or not."

"It's all right," Frances reported back to Gwen and Sarah, tearing up her letter to the aunts asking for bed and board and the use of their attic to paint in while Gabriel was at Bristol. "Mr. Mackenzie's agreed. Thank heavens – I really thought for one terrible minute he was going to refuse."

Because Gabriel had been wounded in the leg, Frances assumed he would look much as usual when the Purcells went over to the Rectory to visit, so was both shocked and frightened by his haggard appearance. It was the journey from Bristol that had tired him, Mrs. Mackenzie said, making that an excuse to dismiss the Purcells after only a short time. "He'll be feeling more himself in the morning. Come over then."

Gabriel caught Frances's hand as she moved towards the door. "Not you," he said. "Please stay."

She expected objections but Mrs. Mackenzie only said, "I'll see that Bertha puts another cup on the tray when she brings up the tea."

Frances sat by the bed, her hand still held in Gabriel's. The liveliness that he had put on for the Purcells' benefit disappeared with the departure of Gwen and Sarah.

"You can't get any sense out of people in hospital," he said. "They treat you like a child. No-one would tell me anything, Frances." His hand gripped hers. "It is going to be all right, isn't it? Life wouldn't be worth living if I couldn't walk."

She understood his meaning at once — his long walks, the expeditions, rather than the day-to-day getting about. Such a possibility had never occurred to her: she felt panic grip her stomach at the thought. She said, "I'll see what I can find out."

He closed his eyes. There was faint amusement in his voice. "I'd have felt quite differently sitting in that damned shellhole if I'd known I'd be seeing you in a couple of weeks."

She had not been in his bedroom before. The photographs, of teams and classes, reminded her of his father's study. She looked up at the portrait on the wall facing his bed. "I'd forgotten you'd got that," she said. "Not one of Julia's best."

"You say that because you're the subject. I think it's good. There you are — about to say something which would have been much better left unsaid. It's very like."

"Do get Bertha to take it down. Please. I'm surprised your mother lets you have it up."

"Mother knows when it's wise to keep quiet." He gritted his teeth. "You'd think they'd have learnt how to do something about pain by now, wouldn't you?"

Lucy came out of the morning-room as Frances reached the hall. "All right?" she said.

"He's dozing. Lucy, he's worried about whether he'll be able to walk properly again ..."

"Really?" She sounded surprised. "The sister at the hospital didn't say anything to Father, and Dr. Milne's quite cheerful about it, though he did say it would take a long time. Four to five months, he thought, before the muscle's healed."

"As long as that?" Frances said, and went home as if walking on air. She had realised that Gabriel would be in England for her exhibition, perhaps even be able to stagger to London to see it. Miracles sometimes happened after all.

Denis came down to Huish Priory not long after Gabriel's return, to see Frances and discuss her forthcoming exhibition. The Purcells had naturally talked about his visit in front of the Mackenzies, never dreaming that Mrs. Mackenzie would object to their having a man to stay. They were astonished when she decreed that Denis should spend the night at the Rectory rather than at Hillcrest.

To Frances's surprise, Annie supported Mrs. Mackenzie. "We don't want to annoy them over at the Rectory at a time like this, Miss Frances. Let Mrs. Mackenzie have her way. I daresay there's something in what she says."

Worse was to come. Mrs. Mackenzie considered it sensible to entertain Denis in the evening without the Purcells. "You would only be tempted to spend the evening discussing art. You can do that during the day." She smiled at Frances, challenging her to protest. "We'd like to get to know Mr. Bond ourselves. Mr. Mackenzie does, after all, have a certain responsibility."

Frances did not reply. She was prudent these days: she did not want to be banned from the sickroom. She went instead to Gabriel.

"Can't you persuade your mother? Poor Denis. He doesn't know any of your family. Imagine being surrounded by strangers. It'd be much better if I were there too."

Gabriel was unhelpful. "Much simpler if you're not. They're going to put him through it – make sure he's not exploiting you. Or planning a seduction. They do have your interests at heart, Frances, remember that."

So she went into Taunton to meet Denis and on the train to Dunkery St. Michael prepared him for the Mackenzies. "Mr.

Mackenzie's a dear, almost a saint really, and very easy to talk to. It's Mrs. who's a bit ... Don't mention art to her, or painting or anything like that."

Denis looked at her in astonishment. "What else is there to talk about?"

"Well ... you can talk about Landseer. He's all right. She thinks Lord Leighton's wonderful too. Whatever you do, don't mention John, or any of those ... She'd die if she thought I knew him."

"My dear Frances, you fill me with apprehension. I shan't dare open my mouth during the entire visit."

She smiled. "No, but seriously ... it's just that I don't want to offend Mrs. Mackenzie at the moment. You'll like Mr. Mackenzie, though, and Lucy. She's quiet, but well worth getting to know."

She said nothing about Gabriel, thankful that he was still confined to his room. She was disconcerted therefore when, after she and Denis had gone through her work next day and were discussing it over a cup of tea, Denis said, "That portrait in Mackenzie's bedroom — it's not an early self-portrait surely?"

She said sharply, "How did you see that?"

He seemed amused by her reaction. "When we were introduced. You didn't mention him, incidentally, when you gave me your little résumé of the family."

"I didn't think you'd meet."

"Naturally we would meet. I was taken up to see him ... and he insisted on coming down to dinner — for the first time, I understand. You know him well, presumably?"

She hesitated. "Quite well."

His eyes were shrewd. "Like a brother?"

She was uncomfortable. "Well ... I suppose so."

"And the portrait?"

"Julia painted it, years ago."

She would liked to have known what Denis thought of Gabriel but was reluctant to ask and Denis did not volunteer an opinion. Gabriel, later, was more forthcoming.

"Very charming," he said. "Tactful, too. I take it you'd primed him beforehand. He certainly knew how to handle Mother. She couldn't understand why she should have had such an inaccurate notion of the art world after he'd finished. He's a good chap, Frances; you're lucky to have him behind you. Though I gained the distinct impression that he regarded me with a certain amount of suspicion."

"I don't know why," Frances said.

"Don't you?" His smile was mocking.

Ever since their first meeting Denis had talked of a probable exhibition, talk that Frances had ignored as being too far in the future to worry about. Now that dates had been arranged she was surprised to find that the prospect of an exhibition gave an enormous impetus to her work. She painted all that summer with an energy and a commitment that was unusual even for her.

She began in Gabriel's room, painting the view from his window. She had always been able to paint the same scene over and over again. It was what those hours of copying in the National Gallery and the South Kensington museums had taught her in her student days – to look and, looking, find something different, something new. She painted the church as it appeared beyond the shrubs and trees that bounded the Rectory lawn, watching light change at different times of the day and in different weather, and as the weeks went by seeing winter disappear and spring give way to summer, until the trees had filled out with green and only the pink sandstone tower of the church was visible against the sky.

When at last Gabriel was able to leave his bedroom, the scenes changed. Frances had never given much thought to her domestic pictures, referring to them disparagingly as conversation pieces and considering the drawings and paintings she made of her sisters, Lucy, Annie, at work and leisure round the house and garden, as little more than exercises. She was surprised that Denis should be so taken by them.

"Yes, yes," he said, "I know it's the landscapes that are

making your name, but you need to widen your scope in the public's eyes. These are charming." He was looking at a watercolour painted the winter before Julia's departure, of Julia and Gwen discussing the layout of a dressmaking pattern on the living-room table. Light from the table lamp in the foreground shone up onto their faces and threw elongated shadows onto the wall behind them. "It's the way you have with light, of course. Why don't you do some more of this sort of thing for me?"

She had enough for him to choose from already but was happy to do more, and once Gabriel began to come downstairs regularly she painted him, and Lucy too, in the drawing-room. She painted him reading the newspaper, leg supported on the couch, preparing Sarah's lessons ("she's very bright, isn't she?"), holding wool for Lucy to wind, turning pages for Lucy at the piano. They were not portraits but scenes, where the light coming through the French windows was as important as the figures themselves: the heavy darkness of an impending thunderstorm, the golden glow of late evening, the colour-draining light of a hot day.

"I thought," Gabriel teased, "that we weren't going to allow ourselves to be dictated to about subject matter."

"I'm not," Frances said with dignity. "It's what I want to do. And, anyway, it's only sensible while you can't move about. It'll be different when we get you over to Hillcrest."

He came over to the Purcells as soon as Lucy was able to borrow crutches from the Red Cross, and long before Dr. Milne considered it sensible – "though I suppose, if you lie with your leg up once you're there ..." Mornings, when Gabriel gave Sarah her lessons, and the evenings belonged to the Rectory. Afternoons Gabriel spent at Hillcrest, hobbling slowly and painfully the short distance up the hill and round the house to the garden, remaining there until Mr. Mackenzie came to help him home after evensong.

His presence brought new happiness to life at Hillcrest and not only to Frances. Sarah flourished as she had not done since before Antony's death. Gwen spent more time out of the vegetable garden, sitting on lawn or verandah according to the weather, and becoming, for Gwen, almost loquacious. People dropped in to visit and chat — even, a couple of times, Lady Donne at her most charming.

"I don't know where people think we get things from, I'm sure," Annie said after a disastrous experiment with margarine-made cakes. "I'm ashamed, really I am." But when Frances pointed out that as ingredients were so difficult to get these days no-one expected to be offered anything at all, she bridled and said, "I'm not having Mr. Gabriel let down, Miss Frances, and that's flat." But even cooking difficulties could not keep the smile from Annie's face when Gabriel was around.

Frances did not look further ahead than her exhibition. Perhaps ... by autumn ... peace would have come. She would not hope or fear. Her work was going well. She had Gabriel with her. It was enough.

Chapter Nineteen

Gabriel had come a long way since that first Post-Impressionist exhibition seven years ago. His appalled reactions then seemed unbelievable now. Over the intervening years he had read and talked and studied. His understanding and knowledge in the field of art was such that Frances never hesitated to ask his advice and always respected his opinion. She did not know what she would have done without his help and comments and encouragement in the weeks before her exhibition. She felt that his place should have been at her side in London and was distressed that she had to leave him at home.

"If only you hadn't got yourself so badly wounded," she grumbled when she went over to the Rectory to say goodbye, "you could have come too."

"If I were fit enough to go to London," he said, "I'm afraid

I'd be fit enough to go back to the front. You'll do better on your own." His eyes searched her face. "Frightened?"

She would have admitted it to no-one else. "A bit."

"I'm sure you don't need to be. Denis was very confident; I'd trust his judgement."

Jamieson was out when she arrived. There was a strong smell of rotting vegetation in the flat, which Frances eventually discovered came from the discarded fruit of a still life gathering dust behind the couch. The stew on the draining board in the cupboard-like kitchen was beginning to sprout fine blue hairs.

The physical labour it took to get the place cleaner if not clean was a relief, distracting Frances's mind from thoughts of the next few days. "I don't know how you can live like this," she said when Jamieson came in, elegantly dressed as for a social event but with yellow ochre on her chin.

"Oh, Purcell, you are so dreadfully bourgeois. I can't understand it when you paint so well." She pulled her dress over her head, revealing expensive silk underwear, and put on an ancient paint-daubed smock. "I don't have an efficient family round me like you do, remember. Would that I did!"

"You could perfectly well afford to pay someone. Think how it'll look in the papers – 'Lord's daughter kills herself with poison stew'."

"Oh well, there's always the silver lining. Daddy'd think it was good riddance."

Jamieson had never made a secret of her difficult relationship with her father but such remarks still tended to take Frances aback, although she tried to treat them as lightly as Jamieson did herself. "And how is Daddy?" she said now.

"Flourishing like the proverbial weed in the field. He's in the Government, did I tell you? Doesn't give one much confidence in the way the war's run, I'd have thought, but who am I to judge?"

"There isn't any chance of it finishing in the next month or two, I suppose?" Frances said wistfully.

"Heavens, Purcell, you know me. I haven't the faintest idea about the war. I'm sick of the air-raids, though, I can tell you that. I was caught in one the other day. On a Saturday morning, would you believe it, and the planes so low you could actually count them. Gothas, somebody said they were. Even the name sounds nasty, doesn't it?"

There was a raid that night; over Essex, Jamieson said, and insisted that Frances climb out of the window to watch from the roof. Frances expected to be frightened and was almost ashamed to feel exhilaration instead. Shadows cast by the full moon made abstract patterns of roofs and chimney-pots around them. The towers and domes of the city horizon were silhouetted against a sky raked by searchlights. Clusters of light burst without warning high above them to an accompaniment of distant gunfire.

"Fantastic, isn't it?" Jamieson said. "I keep on saying I'm going to paint a raid one of these nights. My sister was there when that Zeppelin was shot down in Essex last year. Very dramatic, she said it was. They gave the crew a military funeral, did you know? Disgraceful, I call it. The crew'd been dropping bombs on people. That's not war, is it? It's murder."

They gossiped endlessly. "Nash was in France the last I heard. Cookham's gone out to Salonika. Oh, and Tonks is back at University College three days a week. He'll be able to come to your exhibition. The rest of the time he's down in Kent. Drawing faces of wounded soldiers, I believe, so plastic surgeons can make them new ones. Very appropriate, really, when you think he's a surgeon *and* an artist." Hiles was Barbara Hiles no longer, Jamieson said, but Barbara Bagenal. "And it's no good looking like that, Purcell. Your Archangel'll carry you off one of these days, you see if he doesn't." Worst of all, another of Frances's year at the Slade, Carrington, had fallen in love with a dreadful old man, years older than she, and was looking for a place in the country to housekeep for him. "Only don't say anything about it at John's party tomorrow, for heavens' sake. She made me swear not to tell a soul."

Frances could not have stayed with anyone more suitable at such a time. Jamieson's conversation might be light-hearted but it was sympathetic and provided welcome distraction from thoughts of Denis and the Mayfield Gallery. 'A watershed.' That was how Denis had described the rôle of the first exhibition in the life of a painter. 'The moment of truth.' Such remarks only increased Frances's reluctance to exhibit, despite her faith in Denis's judgement.

There was a more serious side to Jamieson. Her dedication to her work was almost as great as Frances's own, but she had had to come to terms with the knowledge that she would never be outstanding as an artist. "I tell myself that if it weren't for people like me, people like you wouldn't shine as brightly as you do," she told Frances. "One has to find some reason for one's existence."

It was obvious that she considered the present reason was to support Frances. Having recently shared an exhibition with three other ex-Slade students, she knew exactly how Frances felt and how she could be helped. Jamieson spent hours in the gallery during those first days when Frances was most nervous, rounded up her more aristocratic friends and dragged them in to look at the pictures, repeated all the favourable comments she had overheard, and in the evenings whisked Frances off to meet old fellow students at exotic Chelsea parties.

Denis was well pleased. The exhibition received good reviews; people whom he considered important came in and looked and talked even if they did not buy; several municipal galleries showed an interest, one buying a watercolour as well as two oils and a drawing; collectors he knew and was fostering also bought.

"I know it's pleasing when someone comes in off the street and buys," he told Frances, "but it's the collectors we want, especially those beginning to form a collection. They buy one of yours now, live with it for a while and like it. They'll think about another, in a year's time perhaps, and come back. It takes a long time to build an artist's reputation, but from now on they'll be watching you and following your progress. There'll be a market there for years to come."

"I hadn't thought about it like that," Frances said.

She had been greatly impressed by Denis's flair and organisational abilities. He might consider himself an artist manqué but it seemed to Frances that his talents lay in more practical directions. He had insisted on supervising the picture hanging himself. When she demurred about the position of one particular landscape he was quite amenable to changing it. Only after they had experimented with various other positions did she decide that he had been right in the first place. There were little touches about the gallery that showed obvious care and thought – a bowl of roses that repeated the shape and colour of those in the still life on the wall above, a swatch of material on the table below her only abstract that picked out and thus reinforced the main colour of the painting itself. Then, too, he was good with people. Frances watched his success with the envy of one who is never totally at ease with strangers. He was charming, easy, and if there was, as she sometimes suspected, a touch of ruthlessness beneath the charm, he kept it hidden.

She was thankful for his sake that so much had sold. For herself, the favourable opinion of fellow artists was more important. "You seem to be muddling along all right," Wilson Steer told her; Tonks even smiled. Not that she was indifferent to the financial side of the exhibition. At a time when prices were rising so rapidly and Sarah's probable time at Oxford only three or four years ahead, it was pleasant to know that she could augment the family income so substantially. She had no illusions. Selling paintings was an intermittent and unreliable business, public favour came and went, outside events – the war itself – affected would-be buyers in ways no-one could foretell, but this time she had done well and she was returning to Somerset with increased confidence and renewed energy.

She had thought that Denis might expect her to stay on after the end of the exhibition to help supervise the despatch of unsold canvases to Somerset, but she discovered that he preferred to keep them in London. People came back to have another look, he said; had second thoughts about whether or not to buy. Others would have heard of the exhibition too late. There was still interest generating ... "I'd rather I kept them for the time being. If you agree."

"Yes, of course."

She had told them at home not to expect her before Friday. If she went tomorrow she could surprise them all ... "Would you mind if I went back to Somerset? I've had a very entertaining time but I really don't like London much and if there's nothing I can do ... "

"No, off you go. I shall have to fetch Pauline and the children from the cottage some time – I might call in. You should come and stay with us, you know. Try painting wild seas for a change."

She smiled. "I'd like to. Not this year though."

"I'll keep you to that," he said. "Next year, perhaps." He added, "How's young Mackenzie these days? Still at home?"

"Yes. I think it'll be some time before he goes back."

"I don't suppose he's in any hurry. I must say, I never thought I'd be grateful for rheumatic fever. Category E removes all doubts."

"I didn't know about that," she said.

"Long ago, when I was a child," he said. "I spent a year with my aunt in Exeter, convalescing. The start of my long love affair with the West Country." He was silent for a moment. "You're not thinking of doing anything foolish, are you, Frances?"

"Foolish? What do you mean?"

"Getting married, or anything like that?"

She was annoyed to feel her colour rising. "Of course not. You know what I've always said. Fine wife I'd make, anyway."

There was no answering smile. "It wouldn't be sensible."

Sensible. She had always been sensible where her work was concerned; she had no intention of changing now. The mere thought of marriage was ridiculous.

She had expected to feel flat after the exhibition, to suffer from a sense of anticlimax. She did not. She sat in the train taking her back to Somerset, and the smile she saw reflected in front of the passing scenery was the same smile that she had seen in the Slade days when she was returning to Hillcrest. Today she was returning to Gabriel, and the picture she drew in her mind of the expression on his face when she walked in a day early made the three hour journey to Taunton seem like three minutes.

Chapter Twenty

The euphoria lasted until the Mackenzies' return from holiday. Gabriel had tried to persuade Frances to join them. "I know ten days at Budleigh Salterton with my mother wouldn't be your choice but it would be nice for me to have you there."

She refused to go, despite his pleas, and those of Sarah too, not because of Mrs. Mackenzie but on grounds of cost. Purcell savings might be building up but if prices rose as fast during the next three years as they had in the last, sending Sarah to Oxford would be a drain on the family finances. It had not worried Frances, being short of money at the Slade, but she was determined that Sarah would not have to economise as she had.

She regretted her decision after the Mackenzies' return, though whether her presence at Budleigh Salterton would have made any difference to Gabriel's attitude she did not know. She realised afterwards that since Easter Gabriel had been living in a little world of his own. Colonel Sherwood might come over from Dunkery St. Michael to discuss campaigns and battles, but Colonel Sherwood had not progressed further than the South African campaign. It was true that there had been occasional days when the outside world impinged – the terrible morning when newspaper casualty lists announced the death of most of Gabriel's fellow officers in the latest push, the day news came through of Bill Roberts's blinding at Sanctuary Wood – but most of the time the war seemed very distant and barely penetrated the happiness that enveloped Hillcrest and the Rectory.

In Budleigh Salterton, crowded with those who normally holidayed abroad and the blue-flannelled wrecks of men who had once been young and active and were no longer, war was all around.

"It was the people really," Lucy said. "It was their attitude that did it. You wouldn't believe the women, Frances, really you wouldn't – the way they boasted about how much they'd 'given' to the war. People, I mean. As if relations were things. 'And *I've* given four dozen comforters and ten pairs of khaki socks, three sons and a brother,' that sort of thing. It turned my stomach over. And then there were the black marketeers and people like that. Of course I know they exist, we all do, we just don't have anything to do with them. Mother *hates* margarine but she eats her bread dry rather than buy butter on the black market. But Gabriel ... he had only to see the thick cigars and gold watchchains and he'd explode. So now he's determined ... He won't listen to Father, they're arguing about Ireland all the time – you know, that business in Dublin at Easter last year – so Mother and I thought ... well, you're the only one of us he listens to, really listens, I mean. Couldn't you make him see sense?"

Frances hadn't believed Gabriel was serious when he'd told her he intended returning to France before the end of the month. "How can you?" she said. "You can't walk properly yet. No doctor would pass you fit."

"Don't be so sure. That fellow I see at the hospital – you could go to him with only one leg, shaking like an aspen in a thunderstorm, and he'd still put you on the next train. They're desperate for men out there."

She was angry as well as frightened. "You might as well shoot yourself as go out in your present state."

"Then I'll have to improve my state."

Attempts to change his mind soon made her realise that argument was useless. She could only insist on accompanying him on his walks. He had drawn up a timetable, increasing the mileage day by day. It seemed to Frances that he was pushing himself beyond endurance, and there were times when she wondered whether he might not do permanent damage to his leg by such a rigid routine.

It seemed to her that the stay in Budleigh Salterton had altered his outlook on the war. Extraordinary as it might seem she felt that he had switched sides. He no longer opposed the Germans. English troops and German troops on either side of the front line were united, in his mind, against a common foe – England and Germany, their citizens and their governments, the men who ran the war machine.

He was not against Frances: her attitude in the early days of the war towards the jingoistic patriotism then rife redeemed her in his eyes. Besides, unlike the music world with its ban on German music and German pianos, the art world still regarded German art favourably. The *Burlington Magazine* continued to print excerpts from German magazines. No, in Gabriel's eyes Frances occupied a strange no-man's land, but even she could not persuade him to remain longer in England.

Gabriel might not pay attention to what Frances said on his account but he still sought her advice on other matters.

"A present?" Frances said. "For Sarah? Oh, Gabriel, you've given her enough already this summer. Her room's full of books that have come from you. They drive Annie frantic. It's very kind of you but there's no need . . ."

"I wasn't thinking of books. I was thinking of something more expensive. Something permanent. A necklace, perhaps. Jewellery anyway."

"She's only a child. She doesn't need jewellery."

"You don't understand. I want to give her something now, before I go back, something that will last. The sort of thing that . . . well, that one might give for a twenty-first."

She glanced sharply at him. He would not meet her eyes.

Her heart thumped with dread, but she tried to sound cheerful and practical, as if it were commonplace to choose a twenty-first present six years early.

"Oh. Oh, I see. Yes, if that's ... what you want, yes, a necklace would be very suitable. It's the sort of thing she'd love. She'd treasure it always."

His smile was bleak. "That's what I thought."

He went on to the jewellers in Taunton after he had seen the army medical officer. He refused Frances's offer to accompany him, saying that her preferences would only interfere with his own, but came over to show her his purchase on his return, seeking her approval. He had chosen an intricate piece, a spray of flowers and leaves formed out of silver and clustered pearls. It was too delicate for Frances's taste but it would suit Sarah admirably and was exactly the sort of thing, Frances knew, that Sarah would have chosen for herself. She held the necklace between her hands, admiring it, and silently prayed that it would never occur to Sarah to wonder why Gabriel should give her so expensive a present before returning to the front.

He still limped – quite badly, Frances considered. She wondered whether the medical officer had bothered to watch him walk across the room; wondered how he would be able to keep up in the marches across France, how much his lack of agility might hinder him in the trenches.

"Really, Frances," Gabriel said. "You'll be telling me I'm not fit to take you dancing next."

She tried to smile. "Never that."

They went out together on his last evening, taking up Sir James Donne's offer of the loan of his car to do so. The sobering effect of Sir James's gloom – he had just heard of the death of a former bailiff in Mesopotamia, and his own son was involved in the worst fighting round Ypres – lasted as far as Dunkery St. Michael before the natural delight in their own company, the pleasure in being alone together with no member of the two families present, however discreet, bubbled up and overwhelmed them. In each other's arms on the dance floor, with the old, nostalgic tunes washing over them, they could wish themselves back into those distant heady summers of a golden past.

The war was never mentioned. They talked of past times and past places, discussed Sarah's future, Frances's work.

"If I ever do work again, that is," Frances said. "I suppose I'll get back to it some time."

"You don't seem unduly worried," Gabriel said. "I'm astonished at your lack of concern – quite out of character, I'd have thought."

"Denis says it's to be expected – not working, I mean. He's quite happy about it. He says that painters can drain themselves without realising what's happening. Not just painters, either – any creative worker. When that happens they've got to fill themselves up again, which may take weeks, he said, or even months. I'll walk this autumn. I need to do that anyway, doing landscape ... That's the only regret I have, that we haven't been able to walk as much as usual or go up on the Quantocks. If it had been your arm ..."

"I'd have been sent back weeks ago." He was silent, suddenly sober. "I think we'd better talk," he said. "Come and sit down."

He sat playing with the stem of his wineglass, avoiding her eyes. "I don't want to seem morbid," he said at last, "but I think you should know. If anything happens to me ..."

"Nothing will happen." She was filled with inner conviction. She knew that he would come back. "You must believe that."

"Well, yes, but if it does ... everything comes to you. It's not much – from my godmother mostly – but I'd like to think it would help with your work. He smiled wryly. "No strings attached. No pension either, I'm afraid, but that was your decision."

Her cheeks burned. "Gabriel, if only I'd been ... kinder, that time. If I could take back the things I said then ... I misunderstood. I took things the wrong way ..."

"I know. I don't suppose it was your fault ... I expect I handled it badly. Don't let's go over that now – I've forgotten about it. What I wanted to say was, I'd like Sarah to have my books. You can take what you want first. And I suppose Father'd better have a look. All right?"

She nodded. Must we talk like this, she wanted to say. I can't bear it. I know you're coming back, I'm as certain of it as I am of anything, but if you're not, why can't we pretend ...?

"If Sarah goes to Oxford – when she does – I wondered whether you'd give her an extra allowance out of the income you'll get, just for the years she's there. It needn't be much but I'd like her to have something extra to spend on clothes or little luxuries – you know what Sarah's like. It's up to you, though. I haven't said anything about it so don't feel you have to ..."

"I'll do it. Of course I'll do it." She clutched his hand over the table. I never really believed he'd have to go back, she thought. All these months at home ... I was so sure peace would come first.

"I'm coming round to the idea that you may have been right to keep Sarah at home," Gabriel said. "I think she would have lost her originality if she'd gone to school, been too anxious to conform, which would have been a pity."

"I can't thank you enough for all you've done for her – I don't mean just in the way of lessons, though there's that too of course, but helping her grow up, and over Antony, as well." That was a mistake. She mustn't mention Antony, not tonight; nor wonder what Sarah would do if anything happened to Gabriel. "She's going to miss you terribly."

"And you?" he said. "Will you miss me?"

"You know ..." She could not say more. "Let's dance."

His body was hard against hers. Bittersweet memories flooded over her, of all the times they had danced together since those first lessons in the kitchen at Hillcrest, of evenings spent in Cambridge and London, at the Manor, on the Rectory field ...

> *"When day is done you'll hear me call,*
> *Ramona ..."*

She remembered Bill Roberts laughing at Mary Hancock over
the top of his trumpet as he played, swaying in time to the
music; his favourite piece played drunk or sober on every
occasion, suitable and unsuitable – *Ramona ...*

> *"I press you, caress you ..."*

She mustn't think of Bill Roberts, lying blinded in a London
hospital, one hand missing. Think of now. Remember, let me
remember every moment of now ... how it feels, Gabriel's
arms, his face, flesh against my flesh ...

> *"I dread the dawn when I awake to find you gone,*
> *Ramona ..."*

Night air floated in through the open car windows as they
drove home along the empty road, cool and refreshing after
the heat of the evening. Gravel crunched under the wheels as
Gabriel drove into the Manor grounds. The engine coughed
and died. No light showed in the house but a full moon hung
in the sky above, the colour of clotted cream, casting silver
light on the lawn that stretched away from the drive to the
boundary trees. It was very quiet. Not even a peacock stirred.
They sat without speaking in the comforting darkness of the
car interior.

"Life's strange, isn't it?" Gabriel said at last.

"How do you mean?"

"I was thinking ... if your mother hadn't died when she did
and if Father hadn't become your guardian we'd probably
never have got to know each other. I tried to make him refuse
your mother, you know. Did he ever tell you that?"

"No. But I do remember ..." The hostile face, the unsmiling
countenance watching from the Rectory drawing-room.

"I was on a walking holiday when Mother wrote and told
me what was happening. She was against it too – nothing to
do with you four personally, but she felt the responsibility

would be too much for Father. I came back the moment I read the letter, I can tell you."

"You didn't persuade him, though," Frances said.

"No. I used every argument I could think of, but you know Father – he considered it his duty. I suppose it was – there wasn't anyone else who could do it. Lucy supported him, surprisingly enough."

"Lucy would. If Lucy thought something was her duty she'd do it. She and Julia are much the nicest of all of us, you know."

"Perhaps," he said, and added, "I must see if I can meet up with Julia in France. Father didn't believe your mother was going to die, of course. He thought he'd be able to discuss the whole matter with her once she'd recovered and they could come to some sensible arrangement."

"Do you think he's ever regretted it?"

"He had no choice, being the sort of person he is. And anyway, as far as Father's concerned it would have been worth it for Sarah alone ..."

"Do you still think he should have said no?"

He shook his head. "He wouldn't have been able to live with his conscience if he had. And then ... it's easy to list the disadvantages when you're arguing against something, as I was. It's not so easy to consider the advantages, because you don't know what they'd be. I don't think it occurred to any of us that you would all become so close; part of the family, really. I can't imagine, now, what life would be like without Purcells up at Hillcrest."

"Or you at the Rectory." She smiled at the memory. "What really frightened me those first few weeks was the possibility of our having to *live* at the Rectory."

"Oh, yes. That terrified me too. Antony and I had a long discussion about it, as I recall, late at night, when he should have been asleep. Four little girls running wild in the house, getting all the attention rightfully due to us – horror of horrors! I couldn't advance it as an argument to Father, though, however strongly I felt about it: it would have sounded pure selfishness. As it was. Funny how one's attitudes change. Now I think it might have been rather fun."

"You wouldn't have thought so at the time," Frances said. "Imagine — your mother and me arguing all the time."

"You're better these days. Quite civilised, this summer." His voice teased. "You must be growing up."

Their arms were round each other as they walked slowly up the hill. They paused at the end of the Rectory drive. Light glimmered through the trees.

"It's the study window."

"Father'll be waiting up."

If anything happens to Gabriel, Frances thought, it will kill Mr. Mackenzie.

"You will help Lucy with Mother and Father, won't you," Gabriel said, "if, well, anything happens?"

"Yes, yes, of course. You know you don't have to ask. Only ..." Don't talk about it, she wanted to say. If you don't talk about it it won't happen.

"You know what I said in the car — about disadvantages being obvious where advantages are not? I think marriage must be like that. No, don't panic, I'm not going to ask you again. All I want to say is, if you ever change your mind, or even if you only think that one day you might, will you write and tell me?"

It was the first time she had ever been tempted to say yes. She wanted so much to make him happy. Not enough. "I'll let you know, I promise."

She hesitated on the doorstep. "Your father'd understand if you came in, wouldn't he, just for a minute?"

The house was still, the household already gone to bed. The steady *tock*, *tock* of the grandfather clock on the half-landing filled the hall. She picked up the lamp that Annie had left on the chest and took Gabriel into the kitchen. "Tea? Or would you rather have cocoa?"

"Tea would be very welcome."

He sat back in Annie's chair, rocking himself gently to and fro. "It's amazing, the quantity of tea one drinks over there," he said, more to himself than her.

Boiling water splashed over the teapot as she poured from the kettle with sudden shaking hand. Drops sizzled and jumped. He was withdrawing already, easing himself away from Huish Priory, preparing himself for France. She felt a great sadness, wanting to wrap him round with her love but knowing that love was no protection for the dangers ahead.

"I'd have thought you'd be drinking something stronger," she said lightly.

"Plenty of that too."

They sat for a long time in Annie's chair without speaking. He sighed at last. "Father'll be waiting . . ." The chair rocked behind them as they stood up. "It's been a good summer, hasn't it? For both of us."

She could not trust herself to speak.

He said, "I don't think I could go on if I didn't believe things would work out in the end."

In the hall they came together for the last time.

"Come upstairs," Frances whispered urgently. "Please."

Tock, *tock*, went the grandfather clock. *Tock*, *tock*. So loud . . .

A stair creaked. The third stair – she should have warned him. Upstairs someone cried out.

He stopped.

"What was that?"

"Sarah. She talks in her sleep . . ."

The spell was broken. Perhaps, had it been anyone other than Sarah . . . but it was not.

The heavy front door supported her after he had gone. She waited without moving, hearing the faint ting of the gate as it closed, the footsteps fading down the hill. Her body ached with longing. Please God, let him return.

Chapter Twenty One

Geoffrey had changed. It was not only his appearance, the flattened hair and ridiculous moustache that made him look middle-aged, but the character beneath. His anxiety to please, his diffidence, the way he could never say boo to a goose despite Frances's attempts to make him stand up for himself, had all disappeared. Now he seemed to take pleasure in upsetting people, being rude to family and villagers alike, sarcastic about the local war effort, belligerent towards Sir James and Colonel Sherwood. He upset Mrs. Mackenzie before setting foot in the village by spending the first days of his leave with friends near London.

"Wouldn't you think," Mrs. Mackenzie said sadly, "that he'd have come straight home? It's two years since we've seen him."

Frances thought Mrs. Mackenzie was making a great fuss. "Why shouldn't he go up to town and have some fun?" she said to Lucy, but was herself put out by the discovery that Geoffrey had spent leaves with Julia in France. It was not the leaves themselves that upset Frances – she was glad that Julia should have some pleasure – but the fact that Julia had never mentioned them in letters home.

"I know she did talk about seeing Geoffrey in Paris," she said to Gwen, after Geoffrey had been over for tea, "but from what she said I thought they'd bumped into each other by chance. And as for a walking holiday in Normandy – why didn't she tell us about that?"

"Perhaps she wants some privacy," Gwen said. "You don't think she and Geoffrey...? Mrs. Mackenzie would love to have Julia as a daughter-in-law."

Frances feared that Julia was growing away from Hillcrest.

It was an intolerable thought, but what could she do to prevent it except write?

She wrote to Gabriel too, almost every day. He was regretting his impulsive return to France. His old battalion had been decimated in the pushes of the summer; he had been sent instead to a Regular Army unit. In the past he had been among men like himself, intellectuals in the main, who would have found nothing strange in reading Euripides, as he himself had done while waiting to be rescued from a shell-hole. His present companions could recite regimental history back to the day of the regiment's formation but Euripides meant nothing to them. The fact that the reading matter Gabriel carried was Latin or Greek, and his most prized possession Frances's painting of the church viewed from his bedroom window had, as he said, marked him out as a very odd fellow indeed. 'I daresay we shall come to terms with each other in time,' he wrote philosophically, and Frances did not doubt that he would. He was, after all, much better at getting on with people than she was.

For herself, she was thankful. The battalion he had joined had recently suffered heavy losses, was reforming and retraining. It would be some time before it could be thrown back into battle. There was no need to worry about Gabriel yet.

To Frances's surprise, Geoffrey asked to see her paintings. "I think you're marvellous, really I do. The whole world goes up in flames but never mind, Frances Purcell paints on. Bit like Nero, isn't it?"

She took him up to the stables. She was always careful not to force her work on anyone but Geoffrey was insistent.

"There isn't much at the moment," she said. "Denis has quite a few still, and of course there were all the ones that were sold."

"Ah, yes. A big success, Gabriel said. Well, he would." He smiled at her mirthlessly. "You amuse me, you know, Frances. You've always been the same, ever since I've known you.

Single-minded. It must be nice, being you. No doubts, no worries. Your work all that matters. Frances Purcell. Painter. Lucky you."

She said nothing. What could she say?

He prowled round the studio, picking up plaster casts, putting them down. She waited for one to slip from his fingers. He looked across at her. "How's Gabriel, these days? Still dangling on your apron strings?"

"He's all right. He had a good summer. We're happy."

" 'To him that hath' . . . " he said bitterly. "While Julia and I . . . "

She said on impulse, "Let me paint you."

He raised his eyebrows. "You've never shown any interest in painting me before."

"You always took care that I didn't."

"For posterity, is it? So that Julia . . . in case I finish up on the barbed wire . . . is that what you're thinking?"

It was one reason. "Don't be silly, of course it isn't. I'd like to, that's all, but if you don't want . . . "

To her surprise, he came. He sat by the window, so that the light fell across his face, accentuating the bony highlights and darkening the hollows. He sat in silence but his eyes darted to and fro and his fingers never stopped moving, tugging at the buttons of his jacket, twisting a handkerchief corner, scraping his fingernails. She had hoped that by having him with her she might be able to help him, but very few minutes of his company told her that that had been a vain hope. She painted his head without background, realising halfway through that she could not bring herself to finish. When she looked at what she had done she was appalled.

Geoffrey made little comment. "That's how you see me, is it? Lieutenant Geoffrey Mackenzie. It's nice to know." He turned on her. "Do you ever think of Antony, that gallant child, dying a hero's death?"

She was shocked by his tone. "I don't think you should talk like that."

"Oh no, of course not. I'd forgotten – we mustn't offend the artistic susceptibilities, must we?"

"It's nothing to do with artistic susceptibilities. I'd just rather you didn't ..."

"Do you remember that time we all went to St. Audries? Antony wouldn't stop quoting that awful poem. It was always one of his favourites, heaven knows why. *The Ancient Mariner*. I feel like that sometimes. Not a mariner, of course, but ancient. You're the wedding guests, all of you, everyone in England. You listen but you don't understand. You haven't the faintest idea what's happening, any of you."

'Let him be.' Let him cry, let him talk, let him be – that was Annie's way of dealing with things. Perhaps that was all that was needed, to let Geoffrey talk. If only she knew what to do, what to say. If only Julia were here ...

"Do you remember it?" he said. " 'It was an ancient mariner' – you remember, don't you?"

"Yes, of course."

"They're still banging round my head, the words. I can't get rid of them. Like the pictures in my mind.

> *The many men, so beautiful!*
> *And they all dead did lie:*
> *And a thousand thousand slimy things*
> *Lived on; and so did I.*

There you are, Frances. Why don't you paint that sort of thing, instead of your comfortable landscapes? Of course they're pretty, your landscapes – but do you know what *really* goes on beneath the nice green grass you paint so well? Do you, Frances? Do you ever think about that? Do you ever wonder? Well, I'll tell you what goes on. Death, that's what. Blood and claw and guts, spread out through the earth ... Do you know what the Somme's like now – has Gabriel told you? Covered with flowers – daisies, poppies, stretching for miles and miles. And the air thick with butterflies, white butterflies, and the sky very blue. It's fairyland. You'd love it – you'd get out your paints at once – but do you know why it's so special this year? What's underneath it all, have you thought of that?"

"Geoffrey, please, *stop it*."

He leant back against the door, supported by one shoulder only, eyes half shut.

> "I closed my lids, and kept them close,
> And the balls like pulses beat;
> But the sky and the sea, and the sea and the sky,
> Lay like a load on my weary eye,
> And the dead were at my feet."

He could see dead men, she was sure of it.

> "An orphan's curse would drag to hell
> A spirit from on high;
> But oh! more horrible than that
> Is the curse in a dead man's eye!
> Seven days, seven nights, I saw that curse,
> And yet I could not die."

"*Geoffrey.*" She was trembling. She did not know what to do, only that she must stop him talking. "Listen to me. Please. Go and see a doctor. There's an army one at the hospital in Taunton – you could see him. Gabriel liked him." She hesitated. What help would such a man give to mental distress when he had given none to Gabriel's more obvious physical disability? "Or go and talk to Dr. Milne. You're *ill*, Geoffrey. You can't possibly go back. You mustn't go back."

He studied her for several moments. "I've always thought you were slightly mad," he said. There was a smile under the moustache. He was not being rude. It was a statement of fact; that was what he thought. "Imagine Mother ..." he said. "One son dead, another an M.C. and then ... me. It was kind of you to paint me, anyway. Thank you."

There must be something she could do. She talked to Annie and Gwen in the kitchen after Sarah had gone to bed.

"I don't know, I'm sure," Annie said. "He seems all right to me. A bit twitchy perhaps, but he was never the easiest, was

Master Geoffrey. He was in here with Miss Sarah this afternoon, trying to get me to bake biscuits as if I was made out of butter and sugar. Jolly, they were, the pair of them."

Yes, Frances reflected. Geoffrey was his old self with Sarah. She had come across them shuffling through the leaves in the lane outside in their hunt for chestnuts for the national chestnut collection, laughing and teasing each other like a couple of schoolchildren. Was that sufficient reason for Frances to do nothing? Suppose Geoffrey went back to the front and put a bullet through his foot? How would Julia feel then? She must do something, for Julia's sake.

"I think you're making a big to-do," Gwen said, getting up to go. "Antony was all right, after all. *He* didn't make a fuss."

Frances was taken aback. Antony's experience of war had lasted twenty minutes, an hour at most. How could Gwen compare him to Geoffrey? It was impossible to say anything to Gwen. Frances was distressed by the realisation that neither Gwen nor Annie were sympathetic. "Do you think if I went and talked to Dr. Milne.. ? What else can I do?"

"You must do what you think best, love," Annie said. "Just keep it quiet from Mrs. Mackenzie, that's all I'd say."

So Frances sat in Dr. Milne's consulting-room in Dunkery St. Michael and tried to explain ... how Geoffrey had been over two years in France and for several months now at Ypres, that he was jumpy, not his usual self at all, and she feared that he was going mad. She listened to herself as she spoke and thought how ridiculous the words sounded. Reciting poetry could hardly be regarded as madness even if the reciter had previously derided and despised all verse. The familiar smell of methylated spirits from the tray of instruments on the table in front of her should have put her at ease but sickened her instead. Only the thought of Julia kept her in her chair.

Dr. Milne was silver-haired. A little goatee beard stuck to his chin and moved as he talked. He reminded her of Professor Brown but Professor Brown's eyes had been kind. Frances noticed the broken blood vessels on nose and cheek, marked the florid complexion. The view through the window behind his head looked up towards the beech woods of Cothelstone. Dr. Milne would spend every minute he could on horseback, riding with the staghounds on the hills behind his home. What could he know of war, or the effects of war on human mind and body?

He peered at her over half-rimmed spectacles. "I must confess, Miss Purcell, that I'm not certain of your motives for consulting me."

"I don't think he should be allowed to go back. I think he's ill. I thought you might be able to do something . . . "

"Correct me if I'm wrong. He's no relation of yours?"

"No, but . . . He wouldn't come and see you himself though, so I thought . . . well . . . someone should . . . "

"Ah. He's asked you to speak on his behalf?"

"No, no. He doesn't know anything about it. He'd be furious."

She was making a mess of the whole interview. Julia would have been able to make Dr. Milne see sense but Julia was in France. Desperately she tried to recall what Gabriel had said about nerves, shell-shock, medical officers' opinions.

"It's all the bombardments and the attacks and that sort of thing – they give some men, well, shell-shock, it's called. It's the noise as much as anything, and when it goes on and on for months . . . They shouldn't be at the front when they're like that. They're a danger to other people as well as to themselves."

"I'm grateful for your instruction, Miss Purcell. I'm not without experience myself, however surprising that may seem to you. If Lieutenant Mackenzie wishes to consult me I shall naturally be obliged to see him, though I would point out, in case you are thinking of persuading him to do so, that some men are better able to cope with the difficulties of military life than others and while some are, to put it kindly, less brave than the rest, that is no reason for their escaping their duty. Now, I am a busy man so if you will excuse me . . . I shall forget you called. I shall certainly not mention your visit to either Mr. or Mrs. Mackenzie."

She stood in the road outside the gate. A light wind came down from the Quantocks, scattering the last of the autumn leaves along the hedges. She had tried. Julia would never know, just as she would never learn the details of Geoffrey's leave nor be shown his portrait, but Frances knew. She had done her best and failed.

1918

Chapter Twenty Two

Antony's death had been unexpected, a tragedy for which none of them had been prepared. There was a sad inevitability about Geoffrey's end.

Frances's immediate reaction was thankfulness that it had been Geoffrey who had been killed rather than Gabriel. She was ashamed of such feelings, but could not deny them. Later came the realisation that however dreadful Geoffrey's end, it could have been worse. Gabriel had talked of shell-shock, about men who shot themselves in an attempt to get a Blighty one, and men being themselves shot, for cowardice or desertion. In the state he had been in there was no telling what Geoffrey might or might not have done. 'Missing' meant that he had at least met an honourable death – Julia could take comfort from that. It did not comfort Frances who was filled with rage at the thought. Honourable, indeed. What was honourable about sending a shell-shocked boy back into the battlefield? And who was to tell Julia? Frances could not do it. She sent a desperate plea to Gabriel. Not until Gabriel wrote and said that he had seen Julia, who had already heard, did Frances feel able to write herself.

Mrs. Mackenzie refused to believe that Geoffrey was dead. The telegram had only said that he was missing. Anything could have happened. Young James Hancock from Northridge had been missing for three months before the Red Cross sent word that he was in a German prisoner-of-war camp.

Mr. Mackenzie shut himself away in his study while Mrs. Mackenzie sat smiling bravely in the drawing-room with Lucy. "We have to be patient, Frances. He may be in some French hospital, for all we know. We can't expect the French to be as efficient about notifying us as the War Office ... He may be on his way to Germany. If he's a prisoner-of-war we may not know for weeks ..."

She dismissed as unimportant the letter of sympathy that eventually came from Geoffrey's commanding officer. "He doesn't say anywhere that he *saw* anything happen to Geoffrey. He's taken it for granted that just because Geoffrey didn't report after the action ..."

Frances read the major's words and wondered grimly whether Gabriel's letters of condolence were filled with as many dreadful clichés. 'A gallant officer ... plucky behaviour ... always ready with a quip ... gladly made the Supreme Sacrifice ... Duty to God, King and Country.' He didn't seem to be referring to the Geoffrey they knew.

At Lucy's request Frances went up to Harrington House in London, the headquarters for information about the wounded and missing, in an attempt to find out more.

"I know he's dead," Lucy told her, "and so do you. The sooner Mother faces up to it the better. Father knows too, but he won't say so to Mother. He thinks it'd be easier for her if we let her give up hope gradually. I'm sure he's wrong. If you could find out something definite ..."

There was nothing definite to discover.

"I have to say," said the official who interviewed Frances, brusque but not unsympathetic, "that if you've had a letter from his commanding officer it seems unlikely your friend's still alive. There's nothing we can do. Thousands of men are missing round Ypres at the moment."

"How can thousands be missing?" Frances asked Denis. "Men don't disappear off the face of the earth, just like that. Not thousands."

"Modern artillery's a dreadful thing," Denis said. "When you think we can hear it in London . . . How many miles away is that?"

She was thankful Denis had time to spare for her. She had gone to the gallery rather than take the first train home, because she needed to talk to someone and preferably someone detached from the unhappiness that hung over Hillcrest and the Rectory.

"I'm sorry to be so dismal," she said at last, "but you can't imagine what a relief it is to get away for a bit and be able to talk."

"Frances," he said, "you know that you can come and talk to me, at any time, on any subject. That's what I'm here for. What happened to the son and heir, by the way? Is he back in France?"

She was annoyed at the way she always blushed when he mentioned Gabriel. "He's been back a while now." She tilted her chin. "You don't need to worry, you know."

He laughed. "I hope not. I don't want to lose you after all these years, just when things are going well."

She was surprised at how much had been going on without her knowledge and was grateful to Denis, as always, for the work he put in on her behalf. A curator of a northern art gallery was interested in her work, he said, and several people had begun to collect it seriously.

She was amused. "Patrons – it sounds delightfully medieval, don't you think? Florentine."

He gave a little bow. "You may call me Lorenzo whenever you wish."

"You remind me of an Italian," she said thoughtfully. "Yes. One of the Medicis. I must paint you one of these days."

The fallow period that had followed her exhibition and Gabriel's return to France had come to an end. She was painting a great deal and walking too.

The walks had begun as a means of helping Sarah, who, unexpectedly, seemed to have been much more badly affected by Geoffrey's death than she had by Antony's. It was Annie who suggested walking with Frances as a cure for Sarah's distress. 'A good blow in the fresh air' was Annie's remedy for a multitude of ills, and in Sarah's case she seemed to have been right. Over the weeks colour came back to Sarah's cheeks. She began to smile once more, and to laugh. Her natural enthusiasm returned.

She and Frances had never known each other well. The ten years' difference in age had been a barrier between them. It had been years before the weight of responsibility that Frances felt for Sarah began to lift. There was, too, the difference in their talents. Frances felt herself to be badly educated, largely – she admitted – through her own indolence at school. Nothing that she had learnt or taught herself in the years since could eradicate that feeling. Sarah, on the other hand, was clever, had been well educated by Mr. Mackenzie and by Gabriel, and was widely read. Frances knew, because Gabriel had told her so, that Sarah hoped to write; Gabriel considered that she had very fair talent. When Sarah sat in the family circle, silent but watchful, Frances was always conscious of the child's penetrating gaze and of her own ignorance and inferior education.

Now she discovered that her sister was a child no longer, but an amusing companion, one who was a delight to be with but thankfully not one who expected Frances to provide intellectual stimulation. The walks would have been worthwhile if only because they provided the means of getting to know Sarah better, but they were more than that. Sarah had worshipped Gabriel since their first meeting. Frances found to her surprise that she was able to gain relief and great happiness by talking about Gabriel to someone who loved him too.

The war had gone on so long that the Armistice when it came seemed scarcely believable. In Huish Priory one Union Jack flew from the church tower, a second from the Manor flagpole. Miniature flags hung out of village windows and bunting stretched across the street. The school closed so that pupils could collect wood for a celebratory bonfire. The bell-ringers rang a triumphant peal and in the evening Mr. Mackenzie held a service of thanksgiving in the church. Thanksgiving there was, certainly, but it was hard to rejoice when the sad face of their Rector reminded the congregation not only of the two sons he himself had lost but of all the others in the parish who would never return.

The day after the Armistice Frances left Sarah at home and went up alone to the Quantocks where she walked for miles, remembering Antony and Geoffrey, Bert Hawkins and others she had once known. She thought of what the war had done to Bill Roberts and Mary, to Gabriel and the Mackenzies. There was little reason to celebrate. She could not even be sure yet that Gabriel had survived. Celebration would have to wait until he and Julia came home.

Gabriel's return was far in the future. He remained in uniform and went with the Army of Occupation into Germany. Mrs. Mackenzie's anguish was obvious, although she said little. "We should have realised that he would be too valuable to release, knowing the language as he does . . . One can't expect the army to consider the feelings of parents."

Frances suspected that Gabriel himself might have had some say in the matter. He had always had a strong sense of attachment to Germany and its people and she sensed that in some way he thought that by staying on in Cologne he was making reparation to the ordinary German people for his own part in the war. She did not reproach him as she guessed his mother did, nor did she ask the likely date of his return but she longed for it all the same. She was but half a person without him, and her pleasure – and astonishment – at her growing success was diminished by being unable to share it with him other than in letters.

Julia came home in time for Christmas, thin, wan and apathetic. She had already had one bout of flu; the New Year had scarcely come in before she went down with a second.

"I'll be all right," she said. "Don't call the doctor. Aspirin and quinine. That's all I need."

Frances insisted on getting Dr. Milne, despite Julia's wishes and her own embarrassment. It was over a year since she had consulted him about Geoffrey, however, and Dr. Milne made no reference to their previous meeting.

"She'll pull through," he said, coming downstairs to where Frances hovered in the hall. "Not that it'll be easy for someone as run down as she is. It's pneumonia we've got to watch for."

Frances turned cold with fear. It was pneumonia that had killed her mother; Dr. Milne had forecast recovery on that occasion too.

This time he was right. Julia recovered, though it took many weeks. By the time spring came she was able to sit out on the verandah with a rug over her knees, reading, helping Annie with the vegetables or doing the mending, but no-one ever saw her pick up a pencil or paintbrush and she never asked what had happened to her paints during her absence.

"Let her be, Miss Frances," Annie said, when Frances expressed concern. "We don't know what she's gone through out there in France. I daresay it'll take her time to get back to the way she was."

It was taking a very long time, Frances reflected. Her happiness at having Julia home once more was turning into disappointment. Julia had changed. She had become hard and uncaring in her three years away. She shocked the Purcells by her lack of sympathy for the Mackenzies. "Photographs of Geoffrey everywhere," she said, after her first visit to the Rectory. "I don't remember seeing one in the old days. It's a pity no-one appreciated him until he was dead."

Frances took her up to the stables when she was stronger. Julia sat on the bed, studying without comment the paintings that Frances produced, while Frances talked about Denis, the work she was doing and her plans for the future. When she came to an end Julia said, "Yes, well. I can see you've come a long way since I went away. You must be pleased."

Frances was crushed. She had always valued Julia's opinion, listened and paid attention to what Julia said. To have almost no comment at all ... She told herself that she must try to understand, be patient, jolly Julia along. "So will you, once you get going again. You must, now you're better. Tell me what you want, and I'll bring everything down to the house. You could work on the verandah now it's warmer."

"It's no good. It's all finished. I shan't paint again."

Frances felt a spurt of irritation. "Don't be silly, Julia. All that talent going to waste – you'd be mad. Of course you'll paint again. I know you're depressed still but if you start gradually ... "

Julia dragged herself to her feet. "You always were the born organiser, weren't you? Well, it won't work any more, not with me anyway." She went carefully down the steps from the studio, one stair at a time, gripping the banister with both hands. She looked like an old woman.

1919

Chapter Twenty Three

Frances always feared disappointment when she came back to her pictures, even those where there had been magic in the painting of them.

There was no disappointment today.

In the painting, the sun's rays were beginning to break through the early morning mist that lay over the brow of the hill. The leaves of the walnut tree and magnolia were beginning to turn, the first few to fall resting lightly on the long grass beneath. In the foreground hens pecked at the rough path that led up to Frances's studio and thrust their heads between the grasses, their bodies outlined in a nimbus of light from the sun behind them.

It was a scene that Gabriel loved, symbolising all that he held dear, countryside, home, peace and England. She had painted it for him, to welcome him home and as thanksgiving for his safe return. She looked on the canvas now and was happy.

Her eagerness to give it to him had to be contained.

"You do understand, don't you?" Lucy said, breaking the news to the Purcells that they were not invited to dinner on Gabriel's first day home. "They're very . . . well, tearful, really, at the thought of having him back. They think it'd be easier if it was just the four of us the first night. You don't mind, do you? Mother'd hate you to feel hurt. We'll have a proper celebration the day after, she said, all of us." She smiled at Frances. "Don't worry. He'll come over and see you some time during the evening. I know Gabriel."

The Purcells were sitting on the verandah in the half light when they heard the clang of the churchyard gate. Frances was round the corner of the house before the familiar figure had reached the bottom step.

"Oh, Gabriel."

In the darkest days towards the war's end she had wondered whether she would ever hold him in her arms again. Now, in the middle of the road and not caring who might see them, they came together once more . . .

He raised his head at last. "Where are the others?"

"Being tactful, I expect." She scarcely knew whether tears were the closest, or laughter. She held him away from her and searched his face. No shadow lay over it. The clear blue eyes were untroubled. She breathed a deep sigh, of relief and happiness.

"I can't stop," he said. "You'll come up to the Quantocks with me tomorrow, won't you? First thing? Mother's asked Cook to see to the food. We'll talk then. Oh, Frances, I love you so much."

She stood at her bedroom window next morning and looked out on a grey sky. Heavy storm clouds gathered over the distant Blackdown Hills. So cruel, after the weeks of sun . . .

But Gabriel was unperturbed. "You're not suggesting we let a spot of rain keep us at home, are you? Good heavens, Frances, it's *fun* walking in the wet. Swimming's even better — you should try it some time. I remember once at Budleigh Salterton, when I was a boy . . ."

She laughed at him. "I don't think you've ever grown up."

They walked in comfortable silence, savouring each other's company again after so long a separation. Time had changed the village. The forge had been sold when old man Roberts's arthritis finally overcame him, and Nanny Mackenzie no longer occupied the cottage by the spinney, but the fields were the same, and the curves of the road. In the cricket field the grass was close-cut and the crease marked out for Saturday's match. The annual match against Dunkery St. Michael had already taken place and been forgotten, the dreadful defeat quickly banished from Huish Priory memory. Perhaps next year, when Gabriel was free to play ...

"When are you coming back for good?" Frances asked.

"As soon as I can get out of the army. I went up to Cambridge the day before yesterday to sort things out at that end."

She was surprised and disappointed. She had thought from his letters that he wanted her to accompany him to Cambridge and had been looking forward to having time alone with him. She said nothing. There would be time enough to visit familiar places once he was permanently back in England.

"Your leg seems to have recovered, anyway," she said.

He grinned. "Too fast? We'll slow down when we get nearer. You know what I'm like. I can never get onto the Quantocks quickly enough the first time I'm home."

Mr. Mackenzie had brought him up to date with local affairs after dinner the previous evening and shown him the articles and cuttings about Frances which had appeared over the past two years.

"I feel quite intimidated. I don't know that I dare talk to such an august person."

"Don't be silly," she said. "It is nice, though. It means we don't have to worry quite so much about Sarah. Not that you can rely on being able to sell whenever you want – people might decide they don't like my style, or I could go out of fashion. You don't know."

"Father seems to think Sarah might win a scholarship."

"We don't want to rely on that either. We should be all right. It's just that ... well, Sarah's different somehow. I don't want her to be short of money. I'd like her to be able to do whatever she wants."

"You can't protect her from life, Frances. If money's tight she must learn to adjust. You did."

"Yes, but don't you see ... it's not the money. I want her to be happy. She was only seven when Mother died. I feel she's missed so much ever since ... The rest of us have had each other. Life was such fun before the war, too. You know it was. Everything's always been so serious for Sarah — Mother, the war, Antony, all that. I want to make it up to her."

"Well ..." Gabriel said. He sounded doubtful.

"You'll see the change in her. She's grown up. It's nice, but sad, too."

"And Julia — is she really better? She does sound so, from her letters."

"She still won't paint."

"Don't force her."

"But, Gabriel, with her talent ..."

"You can't make everyone do what you want them to do," he said. "Or even what you think they should. I'm sorry, but that's the way it is."

They took the steep way up to Will's Neck. As they climbed out of the woods the sun came out briefly. It gilded his hair as he laughed down at her, holding out his hand to haul her up the last few steep feet. For a moment he looked younger than she had ever known him, a boy, triumphant on a mountain peak ...

He had planned to eat at the highest point, with the view spread out around them, but the wind was cold, and the dark clouds scudding across the sky threatened imminent rain, so they walked along the ridge until they came to the Triscombe Stone and picnicked in the shelter of the beeches. Gabriel had asked Cook to put the food together, but regretted it as soon as he unpacked the rucksack.

"I should have asked Annie. Annie knows the amount walkers eat. I'm famished and here's Cook thinking walkers have ladies' appetites."

"You certainly look as if you could do with fattening up," Frances said.

[183]

"Yes, well, we all had to tighten our belts. They were starving in Cologne; you couldn't let kids die. Not even German kids though I doubt whether you'd find anyone in England who'd agree. It's the Army giving up their rations that keeps them alive ..."

His bitterness was evident. Traces of his feelings after the Budleigh Salterton holiday still remained. Frances knew that he had been deeply depressed for weeks after the signing of the Peace Treaty, as he considered that the terms made another war inevitable. She wondered whether he would take up politics again once he was back permanently in England, but she would not spoil the day by mentioning the subject.

"I wondered whether we might go up to London, the two of us," Gabriel said when hunger was satisfied, despite Cook's parsimony. "Hugh and Mary are there. We could do a show, go on dancing somewhere, the four of us. It would be fun."

"When I think of the miserable letters you wrote last time you went out," she said, "and how you complained about the other officers, I can't believe you're suggesting we should actually go out with one of them ..."

"Ah well, I was mistaken. I obviously don't have your facility for reading character. And there was nothing like the retreat last year for engendering a healthy respect for one's fellow officers. Hugh decided I wasn't the Oscar Wilde figure he'd first supposed either. You'll like Hugh. No intellectual, but nice ..."

"What's he doing in London?"

"He's at the War Office. He's being seconded to Army Intelligence in Ireland. He tried to persuade me to join him."

"I trust you won't," Frances said.

"Lord, no. I know where my place is. Yours too, and it's nearer to me than you are at present, let me tell you." He pulled her down towards him. "This is better than walking," he said.

"We ought to get back." She was laughing. "It's going to pour any moment now."

"You don't really mean that. What if it does? We'll wait till it's over and go home in the dark."

"Think what your family'd say. They're probably killing the fatted calf at this moment."

"We could always make a dash for the stables." He showed no sign of moving. "I must see what you've got in the way of paintings when we get back. I haven't given Hugh and Mary a present yet and they were married in the spring. I decided it was better to wait until I could choose what I wanted rather than give them something I felt was second-best. Mary's been an army wife for years – she was married to Hugh's best friend until he was killed just before I joined the battalion – but she still gets homesick for the West Country. I thought one of your landscapes would remind her of home."

"It might make the homesickness worse."

"I don't think so. Not with Mary. She's a very practical sort of person. You'd like her at Hillcrest; she and Julia would get on famously."

"Not me?"

"Well, perhaps. She's very domestic. Housewifely, you could say. The sort of girl Mother would have liked me to marry."

She lay back in his arms, her eyes closed, enjoying the warmth of his body against hers, savouring the strength in the arm that held her, matching her breathing to his. Peace, comfort, contentment. If only I'd known, she thought, if only I could have known through all those dreadful years of war that this moment would come, how much easier life would have been.

"I was wondering ..." He sounded hesitant, almost shy. "I suppose ... you wouldn't consider getting married before I go back?" And as she said nothing, he went on, gathering speed, "I know it doesn't give you much time but you wouldn't want all the works, would you? I'll be able to get special leave. We could have a week away, a walking honeymoon. What would you say to Switzerland? The Bernese Oberland, I thought, but it's up to you. I don't mind where we go as long as we're together. I know it's rushing you and if you'd rather wait, well, all right, I understand. I wouldn't expect you to come back to Germany with me, anyway, you could stay here until I get out of the Army, but I thought ... oh Frances, I've waited so long. I can't wait much longer."

She drew away. "What are you saying?"

"That we should get married, now, while I'm home. I know it would be sensible to wait until I'm free but I don't feel sensible. I thought if you felt the same ..."

She said incredulously, "You know how I feel about marriage."

He stared. "Yes, but ... you agreed. You said – you *promised* – you'd marry me."

"*I* did? I never did anything of the sort. You're crazy. When did I ...?"

"Your last letter. You said you'd come to Cambridge with me. You did, Frances, you know you did."

She faltered. "Well, yes, but ... I thought you meant now. To go for a day or two, while you were home, so that you could see about going back ..."

"I meant forever. I was asking you to marry me."

She scrambled to her feet. "You didn't say that. You never mentioned marriage, I swear you didn't, and if you did you must have known what I'd say. I can't believe it ... going over the same old ground, year after year ... don't you *ever* learn?"

She could not stay. She left him by the stone and walked away under the avenue of beeches. Leaves had already begun to fall; thin, curled and grey, they lay in pockets between the twisted roots of the trees along the side of the track. Rain pattered on those that still clung to the branches above. Her heart beat suffocatingly fast. Dismay, disbelief, apprehension overwhelmed her. What could she do, what should she say?

When she returned he was sitting where she had left him, head buried in his arms.

"Gabriel ..."

"Don't touch me."

"I'm not . . . I wasn't going to. I'm so *sorry*. What can I do?"

"Go away. Go home."

"I can't leave you like this."

He lifted his head. "I'll go to Ireland. I'll stay on in the army and go to Ireland. I'll get myself killed, and then you'll be sorry."

She was exasperated. "Don't be so childish, Gabriel. Go to Ireland – *really*!"

"I mean it, don't think I don't. I told you, Hugh's been trying to get me there for weeks. He'd grab me, if I said . . ."

A cold chill went through her. He was obstinate enough – stupid enough when angry – to do something ridiculous . . . something irreversible. He had always felt strongly about Irish politics, for years had supported Home Rule. If Hugh had already tried to persuade him . . . Dear God, how was she going to face the Mackenzies?

"You can't go to Ireland. I won't let you."

"How would you stop me?"

She was silent.

"You could if you really wanted to." He was talking quickly, feverishly. "All you have to do is marry me and we'll go to Cambridge and forget about Ireland, and I promise you you can come back here as often as you like for as long as you like, and I won't make a fuss. I know you've got to work. I understand about that, I always have. Well, almost always. I'm proud of you and I love you and I'll do anything to make you happy. I know we'll be happy – of course we'll be happy. We can make anything work if we both want it enough."

The wind was growing stronger, flattening the grass beyond the beeches. There was a stinging behind her eyes. She could not bring herself to look at him. "Then perhaps," she said slowly, "I don't want it enough."

There was a long silence. She packed the picnic things into the two rucksacks. He did nothing to help but sat without moving, looking out over the valley.

"I think we should be off," she said. "We'll get wet as it is, but it'll be worse still in an hour or two."

"Tell me," he said. "That summer I was home – 1917. What if I'd asked you then? What would you have said?"

"Oh, Gabriel, it's so long ago. It's in the past. Gone. Why torture yourself?"

"Would you have married me?" he persisted.

"I don't know."

"You must know."

"I was ... I can't remember. I think I was relieved you hadn't said anything. I thought you'd come round to my way of thinking."

"And that last night ... if I'd asked you then you'd have said yes, wouldn't you?"

"Not marriage ... perhaps ... I don't know. If only ... oh, Gabriel, if only I'd taken you up to the stables that night. I never thought of the stables until after you'd gone. We could have been alone there."

He said after a while, "It was deliberate, you know, my not saying anything. I'd thought it all out. I thought there were two possibilities. There was the chance I might get killed – a certainty I thought it then. You'd made it quite clear what you thought about marriage in those circumstances. But if I did come back I knew that it was likely to be in years rather than months and I thought that would ... give you time to establish yourself, I suppose, without any ties. Your exhibition had been a success, you were beginning to do well. I knew you had to be free to concentrate on your work. That was the main reason why I stayed on with the Army of Occupation, to give you more time. Oh, I know it's been interesting in Cologne and my German's been useful but I could have got out of the army and come home last winter if I'd really wanted to." There was a long pause before he said, "I suppose you're right. It doesn't do to go over things." He got to his feet and picked up his rucksack. "Let's get back."

The rain hit them as they emerged from the shelter of the beeches. Driven by the wind it lashed them mercilessly as they came down from the open slopes into the valley, stinging their flesh with icy barbs, penetrating hair and clothing, piling misery onto silent misery.

Chapter Twenty Four

He came over the following afternoon to apologise. "I'm ashamed," he said. "To have taken it so badly ... it's unforgiveable. Particularly when you've always made it clear ..."

He looked terrible, with deep shadows under his eyes as if he had not slept for days. Frances had lain awake for most of the night herself.

"It was my fault," she said. "I misunderstood ..."

There was a silence between them. She had never felt awkward in his presence before. At last she said, "You know what you said yesterday – about Ireland. You weren't serious, were you? You'll go back to Cambridge?"

"Of course I was serious. I went down to the Post Office this morning and telephoned Hugh Meredith. He's delighted to have me. Well, of course – he's been trying to persuade me for weeks. I'm going up to London on Monday to sort things out."

"For the day?"

He shook his head. "For good. You know the state Ireland's in at the moment. They need men at once. With my experience of intelligence work in Germany ... There's a War Office course in London that Hugh thinks I should do first. I'll go over after that."

She felt faint with shock and dismay. "Do your parents know?"

"I told them yesterday. After you'd gone."

"Did they guess why?"

"They're not stupid. They've got eyes in their heads. After last night ..."

"I thought you carried it off rather well. I didn't think they suspected anything. Lucy knew, though, didn't she? Did you tell her?"

"Yes. And no. In that order."

The grass outside was still wet from the previous day's rain. Fallen leaves lay in sodden heaps where the wind had blown them against the trunks of trees. Summer was over. Frances shivered. "Your parents must hate me."

He did not deny it. She wondered whether his love had turned to hate too.

"Please don't go to Ireland, Gabriel. You know I care about you. It's because I care that I won't marry you. I don't want to hurt you – "

"Oh, that's splendid," he said bitterly.

"How do you think your parents feel?" she said. "And Lucy? Have you thought about them? You're the only one they've got left – or had you forgotten?"

"Frances," he said, "you've made it quite clear that you want to have no part in my life. I accept that. Now you must accept that you've no right to tell me what to do with it."

She flushed. "Just because you made a stupid threat when you were angry and upset you're childish enough and obstinate enough . . . " It was fear that made her go on, and on, fear of the effect his action would have on the Mackenzies who had been waiting for so long . . . and anger that he should let hot temper and spite, spite against her, spoil other people's lives and ruin his own.

He stood aloof and silent until she stopped. He said, "We agreed that I could choose a painting for the Merediths. I don't know what, exactly. A Quantocks scene, perhaps. Or Exmoor. Mary's family farms towards Winsford."

He saw the morning mist canvas immediately, propped up against the far wall. "Oh, Frances." There was warmth in his voice for the first time that afternoon. "I don't have to look any further. That's the one."

She shook her head. "No. Not that."

"But it's . . . I haven't seen anything I like so much . . . please, Frances."

She had looked forward with such pleasure to presenting it to him. To give it to him now after yesterday was impossible. It was ridiculous to be so upset at his wanting to give it away. He could not know that she had painted it for him alone. "I'm sorry. No."

"Why not? You said I could choose."

"Any other one. Not that."

In the end, though under protest, he chose a view from North Hill above Minehead, looking inland, with storm clouds building up over distant hills. "If you change your mind about the other before I leave . . ." he said, "but knowing you you won't. How much do I owe you?"

She stared. "I've never charged you for anything in my life. Don't be ridiculous – I'm not going to start now. You can have anything you want of mine, you know that."

"Then I'll take the other one."

"I've told you. No."

His mouth set in an obstinate line. "If I have to have this then I'm going to pay for it."

"Oh, for heaven's sake, Gabriel!"

She had to give way in the end, however, if only to stop an argument that was becoming unpleasant. Reluctantly she named a price, less than Denis would have given her for the painting and very considerably less than the gallery price. Gabriel's obvious stupefaction made her realise how little idea he had of how far she had come, despite the articles his father had shown him, or of the value of her work. "I told you," she said, wearily. "I don't want to take your money, but if you insist, then that's the price. If you think it's too much you'd better go and talk to Denis. Ask him what he'd charge."

"You've become very touchy all of a sudden," Gabriel said. "I don't know why you should think . . . I'll let you have a cheque."

Bertha brought it over that evening. No note was enclosed. Frances looked down at the signature, stiff, upright, like its writer, and for a moment contemplated tearing the paper into a hundred little pieces. Knowing that such an action would only cause more trouble between them she put it away at the back of a drawer with a sigh.

She stayed away from the Rectory. It was a busy time of year at Hillcrest – fruit to bottle, jams and chutneys to make, wine to get started. She tried to keep her thoughts occupied with domestic chores, the household preparations for winter that she usually left to her sisters and Annie.

She sat with Annie on the verandah in the autumn sunshine, and helped string beans for salting down.

"Mr. and Mrs. Mackenzie must rue the day Purcells ever set foot in this village," Annie remarked to no-one in particular.

Surprising how soon movement becomes automatic. Pick a bean, trim one side, turn, trim the other. One pile grew as the other diminished. Frances said nothing. There was nothing to say.

"You look proper peaky, I'll say that for you."

He came over the evening before his departure to say goodbye. Frances had retreated to the stables, her only place of escape from the reproachful glances of her sisters, and was sitting idly in front of a still life on the easel.

He leant against the door as if reluctant to come into the room. A memory stirred in Frances's mind, faint, elusive, somehow disquieting.

She offered him a cup of tea. He refused. There was silence. A pigeon sitting on the skylight scratched and cooed.

"You'll come back before you go to Dublin, won't you?" she said.

"I doubt it."

"It's so stupid, going to Ireland. Such a waste of your talents. Why won't you go back to Cambridge?"

"I consider I'll be more usefully employed doing intelligence work in Ireland, helping restore the country to some sort of order, than I would be at Cambridge. It's as simple as that.

What do you think I'd be doing at Cambridge? Writing esoteric poetry? Trying to teach dead languages to a generation whose brains have been shattered by four years' artillery bombardment? Is that what you want?"

"You're trying to punish me," she said, "because I won't marry you. Can't you see — you're punishing everyone else too? Your parents. Lucy. Yourself most of all."

He looked across at the painting on the easel as if she had not spoken. "The current masterpiece, I take it. By Frances Purcell. Painter. They'll have to carve that on your headstone, won't they? There's nothing else they can put. No beloved wife or loving mother. Does that thought make you happy?"

She wished she could retrieve the memory that lingered at the back of her mind. "It'll have to," she said. "I don't have any choice."

"Well," he said, "if there's nothing else ... I suppose I'd better be going. I haven't said goodbye to Sarah yet."

"She'll be reading down in the lower garden."

He made no move to go. "Nine years. It's a long time, isn't it?"

"What do you mean?"

"Nine years since I knew I wanted to marry you."

"You're wrong," she said. "It was 1913 when we went to St. Audries. Six years."

"Nine. St. Audries was where you fell in love with me. I was in love with you long before that. Your first New Year's Eve ball at the Manor. 1910. Do you remember? You were Boadicea, with your hair braided down your back. You'd never been to a social occasion like that before but you were damned if you were going to let anyone else know it. I wouldn't have guessed myself, if I hadn't seen so much of you that autumn and got to know you rather well. There you were, head tilted back, ready to fight anyone, that lawyer, my father, Sir James, everyone ... I thought I'd never seen anyone so brave. Fighting to keep the family together, to keep Hillcrest, get to the Slade ... only a child and so much against you."

Her voice was shaking. "It doesn't do any good ... all this ..."

"And then suddenly there, on the dance floor, I looked at you and I knew. It sounds ridiculous but it was true. I knew you were the only girl I'd want to marry. Ever."

"Gabriel, don't. Please don't."

"I didn't want to fall in love. Perhaps I realised then what it would be like; I don't know. I told myself that it was absurd. I kept away from you all that term, do you remember? I thought that when I saw you again I'd realise you were really quite plain and ordinary and what I felt for you had been, well, a brainstorm, I suppose. The effect of alcohol and dancing and the romantic evening ... I came home at Easter telling myself that, and you brought me up here – it was the first time I'd been up here – and I looked at you and I knew..."

"Stop it. Don't tell me. I don't want to know. I can't bear it." In the silence between them she heard a hen's triumphant clucking in the barn below, and her own sobs going on and on.

"Has it ever occurred to you," Gabriel said at last, his voice quiet, conversational, as if discussing something as ordinary as a parish clothing sale, "that you've never been able to bear anything? That you've never *had* to bear anything? That you've always been able to use your work as an excuse and escape up here to your own little world where no-one's allowed to intrude. Anything nasty and you shut it out, pretend it's not there, that it doesn't exist. It amazes me how much you've managed to get away with over the years. Bill Roberts, for instance. It's Julia and Gwen who visit him, isn't it, and Lucy who sits in to relieve poor Mary. How often do you go and see him? Oh, I know it's upsetting, looking at him now and remembering how he was, but you were the one who was friendly with him before the war and spent so much time down in the forge. Everyone has to be so careful not to offend your susceptibilities – even I'm not allowed to say what I feel for fear of upsetting you. Oh yes, I know your work's important but have you ever wondered about that? Inspiration isn't a bottomless well. You can't go on for ever, drawing stuff out. It's got to be replaced some time, somehow.

There's a dark side to life, Frances, and one of these days you're going to have to face up to it or you'll find yourself turning out bland, picture-box stuff that will only sell to the sort of people you despise. No doubt you'll say I'm only going on like this because you've turned me down yet again. Maybe I am. Think about what I've said, all the same. I won't stay; there's Sarah to see, and Julia. I'd wish you good luck with your work, except that you'd say luck has nothing to do with it, so I'll just say goodbye. And thank you, for all the times we've shared."

He went out. He did not kiss her or shake hands. He did not touch her. They might have been strangers. He bent his head in the merest nod, and left her.

He stopped outside the stables and remained immobile for several minutes, looking out on the scene of her painting, while she watched from the upstairs window, tears scalding her cheeks. He pulled himself together at last, took a deep breath and set off across the brow of the hill towards the lower garden.

As he disappeared through the gate into the vegetable garden, the memory that had eluded her during his visit slipped back into place. It was of Geoffrey, castigating her and her landscapes during his last leave.

Chapter Twenty Five

Lucy was in her bedroom when Frances went over to the Rectory, folding undergarments over layers of tissue paper into a suitcase while Bertha knelt on the floor and filled cotton bags with Lucy's shoes.

"That'll do for now, Bertha," Lucy said when she saw Frances. "I'll call you back later. Careful of my hat, Frances. Put it on the dressing-table."

"I can't imagine Alexandria being old enough to get married," Frances said. "It makes me feel positively aged."

"You can imagine what it does to me, then," Lucy said. "You're younger than I am. Alexandria's not much older than Sarah, and the man she's marrying may be in the Guards but he's too young to have fought in the war." She sat on her bed, hands in her lap. Her voice was pensive. "I'm beginning to feel very maiden auntish, to tell you the truth."

Frances was sometimes filled with such impotent rage on Lucy's behalf, at the way Lucy was taken for granted and the tacit assumption that her place was at home as companion to her parents, that she felt physical pain. There was little comfort she could give Lucy. She could only change the subject.

"Will Gabriel be at the wedding?"

"He says so. He could easily get out of it, I'd have thought, by saying he can't take time off the War Office course he's doing, but you know Gabriel ... and I suppose it would be difficult, when he's staying with the Strongs. All the same ..."

They looked at each other. Both knew what the other was thinking – Gabriel having to endure another man's wedding when he had hoped to be celebrating his own.

"I've written him a letter," Frances said. "I don't want anyone else to see it, or know about it, so if you could manage to give it to him in private ..."

"Yes, of course." She glanced at Frances as she took it.

"I haven't changed my mind," Frances said, "in case that's what you're hoping."

"No. I didn't think you had. I'm glad you've come, though. We never seem to see each other by ourselves these days and I did want to say ... well, how much I admire you. I'm sure you've done the right thing, but it can't have been easy."

Frances was taken aback. "Don't you want ... I thought you'd be pleased to have me as a sister-in-law."

"Of course, but it wouldn't make any difference between us, would it? No, I think you're right. It wouldn't work. Gabriel's much too selfish for you."

Frances stared. "Selfish – *Gabriel*?"

"Don't say it like that. Of course he is. He likes his creature comforts and Mother's always spoilt him. Cream on his porridge, that sort of thing, every whim catered for. She even stirs his tea for him, haven't you noticed? He says he could cope with you but I doubt it. Oh, he'd be fine with all the big things – your work, exhibitions, things like that. It would be the little things you didn't have time for or were too preoccupied to notice that would get him down and make him nasty-tempered. So, I just wanted to say ... I don't know what's gone on between you, but I'm quite sure you never gave him any reason to expect ... I'm sorry, that's all, the way it's turned out."

Frances walked soberly home. Sympathy from Lucy was unexpected – and unwelcome, she was surprised to discover. She did not want to hear criticism of Gabriel: it was she who was selfish, not he.

Lucy came over to Hillcrest on her return from London. Julia was arranging the church flowers, Gwen and Sarah picking apples in the orchard. Frances was alone on the verandah, supposedly roping onions together for winter hanging in the outhouse but in reality gazing out over a garden that she barely saw.

Lucy pulled up the wicker chair and began to sort the onions by size. "How are you?" she said.

Frances shrugged. "How was the wedding?"

"Grim. Oh, all froth and champagne and everyone frightfully jolly and half the bridegroom's friends rip-roaring drunk by the end, and then those two children in the middle who haven't the faintest idea what life's about ... None of the young have. All they're interested in is having a good time. Being old these days hasn't anything to do with reaching the age of thirty or forty, I've decided. It's how old you were during the war."

"Oh, Lucy."

Lucy looked sheepish. "You know what I mean."

"Yes. I do." She hesitated. "How was Gabriel?"

"All right. Poker-faced, of course." She sighed. "It was

awful, really. Do you know, Frances, I've come to the conclusion that if one didn't care about other people at all life would be easier and very much more comfortable."

"I know how you feel," Frances said. She waited for Lucy to say something and when she did not, asked, "Did you give him my letter?"

"Yes."

"And?"

"He said there was no answer."

"But there must have been. Didn't he say . . . he must have said *something*. Lucy? Didn't he?"

Lucy looked away. "He did say . . . he thought you must be mad."

Mrs. Mackenzie considered the wedding to have been a great success and gave the Purcells details over Rectory dinner on her return. "With most of the family on the Indian continent reunions are so rare – and all the more enjoyable for that, I always think. I was pleasantly surprised by Alexandria, I'm glad to say. I thought her somewhat *wild* when I met her before the war, but she's grown into a charming young woman. The chief bridesmaid was a very fetching little thing, too. Gabriel was very struck, wasn't he, Lucy?"

"She was much too young for him, Mother."

"And such a beautiful dancer," Mrs. Mackenzie said, as if Lucy had not spoken. "She and Gabriel . . . you would have thought they had been partners for years, they danced so well together."

The hurt, reviving as it did so many memories . . . As for the rest, Frances could not believe that Gabriel had been attracted. It was Mrs. Mackenzie, defending her son in the way she thought best. Frances admired her for it. Her attitude to Mrs. Mackenzie had changed, almost overnight. Mrs. Mackenzie, desperate to keep Gabriel in England and knowing, as did Mackenzies and Purcells alike, that Frances was the only person who could change his mind, came and begged Frances to marry him – not, it was true, in so many words but her meaning was clear, both to Frances and to the other Purcells who were there at the time. Frances was humbled. That Mrs. Mackenzie, to whom the possibility of her son's marriage to Frances had been anathema for so many years, should beg . . . It was something that Frances, shaken, knew she herself could never have done.

It was only by chance that Frances saw the exhibition of war paintings at the Royal Academy. She went up to London at the beginning of December to talk to Denis and visit the Matisse exhibition, and was walking along Piccadilly when it began to rain. The exhibition would while away a couple of hours as well as provide refuge from the storm. She paid her shilling for a catalogue and went in.

It was years since she had thought of Geoffrey's words during his last leave. She had buried them in the recesses of her mind, just as she had Gabriel's diatribe before he left for Ireland, persuading herself that both had been so swayed by emotion at the time of speaking that the words bore no relation to truth. This afternoon, as she went through the galleries looking at paintings that portrayed in visual images the landscapes that Gabriel had tried to reproduce in words, she remembered.

She looked on the many works by men she had known well, the companions of her student days, and remembered how she had decried their idleness at the Slade and their lack of application. Now she saw that they had gone on to portray the world of the twentieth century, while she had sat at home content to paint the countryside around her with as much depth as the Victorian story-book artists that she so despised. Where was the blood, tooth and claw that Geoffrey had talked about, if not here, looking down on her from the walls of room after room after room?

She remembered how Gabriel, in letters denouncing the inhumanity of those in power, the ignorance of people at home who did not know what their men were enduring in France and did not care so long as England won the war, had cursed his own helplessness to bring about change. The painters of these landscapes had been more fortunate. By being able to portray in images more terrible than any that could be conjured up by mere words they were able to show to the world the full horror of war, and in so doing discover both the purpose and fulfilment of their gifts.

A cold, unwelcoming emptiness greeted her when she let herself into Jamieson's flat. Jamieson, the only daughter still unmarried, had been summoned by her family for help in a domestic crisis. She had been annoyed and disappointed at missing Frances but Frances was thankful now to be on her own. She could not have coped in her present state with Jamieson's good humour and cheerful gossip. She sat, clutching her coat close to her and shivering with something more than cold, as she watched the rain lash against the uncurtained windows and waited for Denis to arrive.

He came at last. She heard his steps, bounding up the stairs. "Dear Frances," he said, coming in and giving her a bear hug. "How lovely to see you again. It seems months. Any preference in eating-place? No? Then we'll go to a little place I use, near the gallery. It's quiet, we can talk."

He was in high spirits, laughing, enthusiastic, full of plans for the future and eager to communicate them to her. There was no need for her to say anything at all, though when he asked her what she had been doing since her arrival in town she did mention the Imperial War Museum exhibition.

He showed little interest. "There weren't many people there, I imagine. It's finished, Frances, all that. It's a year since the war ended – more. People aren't interested in looking back. It's the future that matters."

There are some who can't help looking back, she thought. What sort of future could people like the Mackenzies envisage? What about the painters themselves, the Nashes and Nevinsons, the Spencers and Lewises? What were their thoughts on the future? What effect had the sight of those twisted, desolate landscapes, what effect had the painting of those huge, desolate canvases had on them?

"You don't realise how the world has changed," Denis said. "People were so insular before the war. It was the middle-aged and the wealthy, who *invested* in art. Now the people who buy are years younger, widely travelled – a result of the war, of course – and *interested*. They want pieces of art around them – paintings, sculpture – that they like, that they can admire. People drop into the gallery to look and talk as well as buy. Intellectuals, writers, poets, artists themselves – I tell you, Frances, it's an exciting world we live in."

He leant back in his chair and smiled at her. The smile faded. "Is something wrong?"

She tried to tell him. She tried to put into words impressions and emotions that she had difficulty defining even to herself, to make him understand what it was like to look back to her student days and remember the scorn she had felt for painters who, she now knew, had gone on to discover the world that existed and their purpose in it, while she had wasted the years in mere tinkering, too self-satisfied to try to dig deeper. "It's so superficial, the sort of thing I paint, and I ... oh, Denis, what am I going to do?"

Even then she could not tell him everything: not Geoffrey's scorn, nor Gabriel's criticism, nor make clear to him the dawning realisation that her own work was hollow, hollow with nothing at its heart.

Denis did not take her seriously. He laughed. He asked whether she thought she would be as well regarded if her work were as superficial as she seemed to think. "I'm planning another exhibition. Next summer or autumn. And this time, well, you'll see ... I'll be aiming for the general public. The art world knows all about you. We want to spread your name further afield ..."

He poured her more wine. He said that all creative artists had doubts, they wouldn't be any good if they didn't, that no-one could expect to sail through life without problems, that bad patches hit everyone from time to time ... Her present feelings were a result of the war, he told her, a delayed reaction to the strains and stresses she had undergone during those years.

"But don't you understand?" she said desperately. "I didn't have any strains and stresses. That's part of the trouble. I sat at home and painted and did exactly what I wanted all the time. It was everyone else ..."

"Oh, come now, Frances. I remember your sitting in my office the day you came up to London to find out about – I forget his name, the Mackenzie boy, the one that went missing. And when I think of the worry you've had with Julia ... I don't know how you can say such things."

There was no need to worry, according to Denis. It was possible to work through and out of any depression. Painting little, but daily, an hour or two at a time, not more, without worrying about the end result, was what he advised. "It'll take time," he said, smiling at her, "of course it will, but you'll come out of it at the other end, I promise you, and probably be a better painter, too, in the long run."

He turned the conversation to other, innocuous, subjects and did not comment either on her silence or her lack of appetite. He called for the bill, asked for her coat, helped her to her feet. "How's the son of the manse these days?" he said. The expression in his eyes belied the casual tone.

"All right, I think. He stayed in the Army, you know. He's in Ireland."

"I can imagine better places to be."

"Yes, well ... It was his own choice."

Mist hovered over the stream and filled the space between the cottages of Huish Priory. The church was barely visible from the road outside Hillcrest and the garden round the side of the house disappeared into cloud. The air was damp and chill against her face.

A deep weariness enveloped her as she stood on the doorstep trying to summon up the courage to go in. For the first time in their relationship Denis had let her down. Only

Gabriel remained. Perhaps, at last, there would be a letter from Ireland waiting for her on the oak chest in the hall.

Julia came out from the living-room to greet her, Annie from the kitchen, Sarah down the stairs. The blackness of the oak chest was unrelieved. There was no letter, no card. There was nothing.

Chapter Twenty Six

Age was never discussed at the Rectory. Frances had no idea how old Mr. Mackenzie was, but looking at him now, sitting silent in the crowded café, she was saddened. She stretched out her hand.

"She'll come back to you, Mr. Mackenzie. You know she will."

He gave her a faint, wintry smile. "I'm afraid, my dear, that with the passing of the years it becomes more difficult to accept change. I look back to all those mornings with Sarah sitting at the table, so eager, so attentive, knowing that they have gone for ever and I am ... sad."

The waitress arrived with their coffee. Mr. Mackenzie, making a visible effort to be cheerful, offered Frances sugar and biscuits. The moment passed.

Sarah's departure for Oxford, though only for two nights, had left Frances surprisingly tearful herself. It was hard to believe that the small child she had held in her arms and tried to comfort so many years ago was now older than Frances had been then, and in a few months' time would have left home for university.

"I'm filled with admiration," Frances said. "I really am. To go off like that, without a backward glance ... I was terrified when I went up for the Slade interview, and I had Gabriel to hold my hand."

"I'm sure that Sarah was rather more nervous than she let you see. She's always taken care to keep her emotions under control. You must remember, too, that she already knows she has a place at Oxford. The interviews will determine whether she wins an award or not, and if so, which. When you went up to London you weren't certain whether the Slade would accept you. Or," he smiled at her, "if we'd let you take the place should you gain one."

Frances watched the swirling patterns set up in the coffee by her teaspoon. Oh, to be seventeen again, to be young and happy and confident. To be able to start afresh ...

"Forgive me, Frances," Mr. Mackenzie said. "You know that I would never willingly interfere, but it is hard to see such unhappiness ... Is there nothing I can do to help?"

She shook her head. "If only he'd write," she said.

He wrote to Julia and Gwen. And to Sarah. Every few days there was a letter sitting on Sarah's plate. In the past Sarah had been unable to wait, had torn letters open and read them at once at the breakfast table. Now she left them unopened on the tablecloth and took them away with her to read secretly, alone. Terrible, to be jealous of your youngest sister.

Frances had written to Gabriel on her return from London before Christmas. Forgetting the cheerful, everyday letters that she had been so careful to send after his departure for Ireland she had written desperately and at length, about the exhibition and its effect on her, telling him of her despair and begging for his help and support. She had heard nothing.

"I believe Gabriel feels," Mr. Mackenzie said now, "that only by separating himself from you can he be free. Try to look at it from his point of view, Frances. He wants a home of his own and a family. If you let him go now in time you may be able to come together in a new kind of friendship."

"But I'm so lonely without him."

Mr. Mackenzie was silent, gazing down into his empty cup. "Do you think," he said at last, "that if you talked together –

if you went over to Ireland and talked to him perhaps you might . . .? It was so quickly over, his last leave. Neither of you had time to think things through."

"I don't know. I don't seem to know anything any more. Julia keeps saying I should go to Spain. Well, not Spain, exactly. Anywhere, she says, as long as it's abroad. She thinks I've become stale, stuck here for so long, and if I went away I'd get a new perspective on things."

"And you thought of Spain?"

"I know people there, through friends from the Slade. They've already said . . . I could stay with them for a couple of months. I suppose it would be sensible. I can't decide, that's all. When we know about Sarah, I might think again. I'll decide then."

There was an unspoken agreement between Mackenzies and Purcells that Mr. Mackenzie should be burdened as little as possible. He had aged greatly during the years of the war. The loss of his sons as well as the countrywide turning away from the church, both during the war and after, had grieved and depressed him. Frances did not feel able to tell him now that there was more to her unhappiness than Gabriel's defection. She could not work. She was haunted by memories of her mother, who had tried to return to painting after Commander Purcell's death and failed. Was that to be her future? Sometimes she thought that Gabriel had put a curse on her and her work in that last speech of his. She did not think she would ever paint again.

The result of the Oxford entrance came one morning in a telegram. Sarah took the news that she had been awarded an exhibition so calmly that for a dreadful moment Frances feared she was going to turn it down as she had turned down Bristol. But the smile that slowly dawned on Sarah's face was beatific. "I can't believe it," she said.

After the exclamations and congratulations were over, Frances went up to the stables, as she had done every morning that winter however little work she knew she would accomplish. The daffodils on the brow, always the last to bloom at Hillcrest, were about to transform the grass into a golden carpet. There was a green haze on the trees and the rambler rose along the stable wall was already sending out long maroon shoots. Soon Easter would come and with Easter the fine weather. It's the winter that's made me feel so dreadful, Frances told herself. Now spring is here, and Sarah's future settled . . .

The relief was unbelievable. Until it lifted she had not realised the weight of the burden that lay on her shoulders. Whatever mess she had made of her own life – and Gabriel's too, for that matter – Sarah had not suffered. Whatever had been her motive for keeping Sarah at home (and sometimes she wondered whether Gabriel had been right in ascribing it to the misery of her own experience at school), she had not spoilt Sarah's chances. How delighted, how happy Gabriel would be.

She had an irresistible yearning to see his face again, to watch it light up as she told him the news, and to hear the mocking tones with which he would mask his pride. "Just fancy – old mouse an exhibitioner. Three artists and a bluestocking – what a family. Shall I dare open my mouth at Hillcrest ever again, I wonder?"

I could go to Ireland, Frances thought. Why don't I go and tell him myself? Just for a couple of days. After all, I need to know if there's anything I should be doing for Sarah before she goes in the autumn. There wouldn't be any harm in a visit – Mr. Mackenzie suggested it himself. And I must thank Gabriel. If it hadn't been for his teaching and help and interest Sarah might never have succeeded. I'd never be able to make him understand how grateful I am in a letter, but face to face . . .

She picked up her brush, dipped it in colour. She felt happier than she'd felt for months. While we're together, she thought, we'll be able to talk sensibly, about us.

A hen squawked below the studio window. Footsteps sounded on the stairs outside. There was a knock on the door.

"It's me, Miss Frances. Lily. Annie said I was to say, you're wanted in the living-room."

"Lily, you know I never . . ."

"It's Miss Mackenzie from the Rectory, Miss Frances. She wants to talk to you. Urgent, she says it is."

Frances sighed as she went out, going down the stairs ahead of Lily who stood aside to let her pass. Strange that Lucy, who knew as well as anyone that Frances's mornings were sacrosanct . . .

As she came down the steps into the cobbled yard she heard Annie in the kitchen, sobbing . . . dreadful, gasping sobs.

Frances swivelled round to look at Lily and for the first time saw the girl's ashen countenance.

"Not . . . Mr. Mackenzie?"

Lily shook her head.

"No," Frances said. "*No!*"

Lucy stood in the living-room with her back to the window, her figure dark against the light. "Frances," she said. Her voice was thick. "I'm sorry."

Frances began to tremble. "Tell me."

"We've had a telegram. From Hugh. You know – Gabriel's friend. He wanted to break it gently, he said, before the War Office . . ."

"Dead?"

Lucy shook her head. "An ambush, Hugh said. They managed to get him to hospital but . . . there's not much hope. That's what he said."

Such news should never come on a day like this, with the sun sparkling on the dew-soaked lawn and the daffodils making a golden frill above the verandah edge, with spring nearly here and new life appearing . . .

She sat at the table and buried her head in her hands. Help me. Let me think. Help me think.

"Where's Sarah?" Lucy said.

"She went over to the Rectory," Julia said. "She wanted to tell your father – she's won an exhibition."

There was silence.

[208]

"Father won't tell her," Lucy said at last. "As long as Hilda or Bertha doesn't give it away ... Father won't say anything. He won't want to spoil her day."

In her mind Frances saw Gabriel lying as he had lain in his bed that first afternoon back at the Rectory three years ago; but alone now, far from home, far from family, far from her ... dying.

"I'm going to Ireland," she said. "Today. This morning. Now." The possibility of action cleared her mind wonderfully. "Sir James'll drive me to the train, won't he? ... And food, could you help Annie put some food together. Let me have the name of the hospital, Lucy; the address too, if you've got it. I'm going to pack."

The sun was slanting across the floor of her bedroom, brightening all it touched. The sky beyond the window was a clear, brilliant blue. On the wall the painted fruit of the Matisse still life glowed with vibrant colour. Impossible to believe that across the Irish Sea ... Perhaps there had been some mistake, a different name, a muddle between officers, between patients. They would laugh, afterwards, Gabriel and she ...

I'll go to Ireland, he had said. The words beat a refrain in her head. I'll go to Ireland and get myself killed ... get myself killed. He hadn't meant it; he couldn't have meant it. Could he? *And then you'll be sorry.*

There was a movement at the door. Sarah stood there, her face dirty-white, her eyes black. "It's not true," she said. "They're lying. They must be lying. He said it wasn't dangerous — he *promised* it wasn't dangerous." She pleaded with Frances, "Tell me it isn't true, Frances. It isn't, is it? It can't be true."

All Frances had ever wanted for Sarah was Sarah's happiness. If she could have lied now, she would have done so.

When she came downstairs Annie was waiting, red-eyed, in the hall.

"Oh, Annie," Frances said.

Annie's arms held her close. "There, love. There, there."

The others were outside in the lane. Sir James had turned the Daimler round and was standing beside it, ready to help her in and lay the rug over her lap.

"I'll write," Frances said. "As soon as I can. I'll let you know." She looked out of the window at Lucy. "Tell them . . ." What could she say to the Mackenzies that would comfort? Words didn't exist. "Give them my love."

She looked back as the Daimler turned the corner by the Manor. They were still there at the top of the hill, her sisters and Lucy, joined now by Annie, silhouetted against the skyline, arms raised in farewell.

"It's a sorry day," Sir James said heavily. He gave her knee an awkward pat. "A sorry day."

She knew that he thought she was crying for Gabriel but she was not. Tears for Gabriel would come later. She was crying for Sarah, whom she had tried so hard to protect and failed.

Chapter Twenty Seven

The sea was mud-coloured, flecked with white. Wind blew spray back over the deck of the mail steamer and its passengers. Frances gazed out into the rain and remembered all the times she had walked as a child with her mother beside the seashore, straining her eyes to watch her father's ship fade into the horizon. The pain she had felt then, of empty, nagging distress, was the same that gripped her now.

While she waited on the deck to disembark at Kingstown, the sun came out, shining on wet roofs and lighting up the hills behind the town. She took it as a good omen, and sat in the train to Dublin clutching her bag and telling herself that all would be well, that having got safely through the war nothing dreadful could possibly happen to Gabriel. Everything would be all right . . .

They knew nothing of him at the hospital. No-one at the main desk had heard his name. There was no record of his admittance. They told Frances she must be mistaken. When she produced Lucy's piece of paper they repeated their conviction of a mistake. She stood at the desk under the high dome of the echoing entrance hall and wondered whether it was the journey or fatigue, lack of food or fear, that was making her feel so ill.

It was a passing clerk who eventually suggested trying the military wing upstairs.

"But they're long-term patients up there," objected the girl behind the desk. "The ones left over from the war. He wouldn't be there." She turned to Frances. "You could try, I suppose. Better still, come back tomorrow. They're terribly strict, Army sisters. You know, visiting hours, all the regulations. They won't let you see him tonight if he is there."

"I'll go all the same," Frances said.

She kept her eyes firmly fixed away from the wards that led off on either side as she walked along the hospital corridors, following the directions the girl had given. Her footseps began to drag. What was she going to be told at the end of her journey?

A soldier barred her way at the top of the stairs. Light glinted on the bayonet of the rifle he held. Beyond him the corridor stretched away into the distance, deserted except for a single soldier guarding a door halfway down.

Her voice wavered. "I've come to see Major Mackenzie."

He nodded to the other soldier. "Down there. You'll have to see Sister first. She's in her office. First door you come to."

The door was open, revealing a room little bigger than a cubby-hole. Two nurses glanced up from the equipment they were sorting on the desk.

"Yes?" said the scarlet-caped one.

"I've come to see Major Mackenzie," Frances said and added – in the desperate hope, she thought afterwards, that the information might give easier entrance – "I'm his fiancée."

Sister and nurse looked at each other, looked at Frances, looked at each other again.

"Shall I get... ?" the nurse said.

Sister shook her head. "Major Mackenzie is not allowed visitors," she said to Frances.

"I do know about visiting hours. I'm sorry it's so late. I'll only stay for a moment, I promise. I won't talk to him or tire him. I just want him to know ..."

"I think you should leave these premises." There was steel in Sister's voice. "Now. At once. Before there's trouble."

"Please ..."

"At once."

Frances backed out. She waited outside the closed door. Fatigue made thinking difficult. She was sure of two things – that Gabriel was here and she would not leave without seeing him.

The soldier outside Gabriel's door gave her a hesitant smile. He was young, not more than eighteen at the most. A thick band of freckles lay across the bridge of his nose.

Frances pulled herself together. She marched up to him. "I've come to see Major Mackenzie."

The smile faded. He shuffled his feet. "They did say I wasn't to let nobody ... Did Sister say... ?"

"She said I could see him."

He wavered. "I shouldn't ... "

Frances pushed past. At that moment – she could hear them clearly – Sister and the nurse emerged from the office. The nurse exclaimed. Sister shouted. "Get her out of there!"

Impossible to tell what happened after that. Hands grabbed her wrists, held them in a grip of iron, hauled her back. She lashed out with her foot, catching bone. A man's voice: "Stop it, you devil!" Doors slammed. Women shouted. Someone screamed, on and on. A hand caught Frances hard across the face. "Don't you know there's a man *dying* in there?"

She opened her eyes. A scarlet-tabbed officer glared down at her. In the sudden silence she realised that it was she who had been screaming.

"What the devil's going on?" the officer demanded. "A

racket like that – Sister, perhaps you'd be good enough to tell me."

"I'm sorry, Major Elliot. This … woman wanted to see Major Mackenzie. She said she was his fiancée, so of course I thought … and then, when she tried to push her way in …"

He looked at Frances. "Well?"

"I only want to see him for a minute, just to let him know I'm here." Why doesn't he call out? she thought. Surely he must have heard, must have recognised her voice? Was he so near … dying? "I know it's past visiting hours … I've come all the way from Somerset."

"Ah," Sister said, as if struck by a sudden thought, and then fiercely to Frances. "What's your name?"

"Purcell. Frances Purcell."

"Ah," Sister said again. "Wait here." She went back into her office, returning after a moment with a telegram in her hand.

"This came last night," she said to the major, "from Major Mackenzie's family. They said someone would be coming. A Miss Purcell, they said. They wanted Major Mackenzie told. Why didn't you say who you were, you stupid girl? Spinning a cock-and-bull story like that."

Frances tried to pull herself together. It must have been Lucy who had sent it, it could only have been Lucy … Dear, dear Lucy. "I don't know why." She said humbly, "May I see him now? Does he know I'm coming? Did you tell him?"

Major Elliot shook his head. "He's unconscious," he said. "You'd better follow me."

If she had not known it was Gabriel she would have walked past his bed. He lay on his stomach, head turned towards the door as if waiting for her coming. His flesh was grey, stretched tightly over the bones of his face. The wound on the side of his head was an ugly lattice-work of black stitches across bruised and crusted skin. She looked down on him in silence, unable to control the trembling of her limbs. Never once during all the hours of travelling had she wondered whether he would be able to recognise her on her arrival.

"Do you want to stay?" Major Elliot said.

She nodded.

"Very well."

The door closed. Major Elliot's voice talked to Sister outside. The sound of their footsteps faded into the distance. Frances held Gabriel's hand in hers. There was nothing, no sign, no movement, to show that he knew she was there.

She stayed with Gabriel all night. She stayed because no-one suggested that she should leave and she knew nowhere to go. She watched Gabriel's face for signs of life and contemplated the possibility of his death. She knew nothing about dying; it was Mrs. Mackenzie and Lucy who helped relatives at village deathbeds. Apprehension increased her fear and despair.

Morning brought the return of yesterday's sister. She made no reference to Frances's arrival the previous evening but enquired whether Frances had been given food and drink and said that Major Elliot would talk to her after finishing his ward round.

He saw her in Sister's office. A framed photograph of the King inspecting a line of nursing sisters hung on the wall. The hyacinths on the desk were almost over, the stems leaning drunkenly over the edge of the bowl, but their scent was still strong, overpoweringly sweet, sickly. Major Elliot was distant, apologising for the previous evening's trouble but obviously holding Frances to blame.

"Why didn't you tell Sister who you were instead of trying to force your way in? How was she to know you weren't some Shinner sent to finish the job?"

Frances gazed blankly at him. The words made no sense.

"I understand you're a relation of Major Mackenzie," he said.

"His father was my guardian," Frances said. "I'm here because ... Major Mackenzie's parents weren't fit enough to make the journey." Would he send her away, she wondered? Parents had been allowed to visit the badly wounded in France during the war, she knew from Julia, but what about others?

And how badly was Gabriel hurt? "Last night," she said nervously, "you said Major Mackenzie was dying ..."

He avoided her eyes. "Haven't you talked to Sister?"

She shook her head.

He hesitated. "We can't tell ... It could go either way. He's badly injured and suffering from concussion but the problem at the moment is not so much his injuries as the infection. There is major infection."

"You can treat that, can't you?"

"We can try. There's no infallible cure. I wish there were."

"And the ... injuries?"

He rolled a pencil between fingers and thumb. He looked at her at last. "There is considerable nerve damage at the base of the spine," he said. "I'm sorry."

There was silence. Frances ran her tongue round her lips. "I don't know about these things. What effect does that have – nerve damage?"

The light was behind him; it was difficult to see his expression. "At the worst, he may never walk again. At the best" – he gave a little shrug – "he'll have difficulty in getting about."

The puffs of cloud outside the window looked unreal, like blobs of cotton wool pasted onto blue paper. If Gabriel were home on a morning like this he would persuade her to pack some lunch and her sketch book and go up with him on to the Quantocks ... It must be the sickly scent of the hyacinths that was making her feel so ill.

"It's early days, Miss Purcell. I wouldn't presume to prophesy the final outcome. Much will depend on his own determination. Meanwhile, if you wish to visit ... Are you staying with friends?"

She shook her head. "I'll find some digs."

"It might be a good idea to talk to Colonel ..."

"It's all right," Frances said quickly. "I can manage on my own." Coping with strange colonels was more than she could contemplate.

"Well, if you're sure ..." He sounded doubtful. "You'd

better have a word with Sister – she knows the best places to stay in this area. You want to be careful." He stood up, dismissing her. "I'd get some sleep if I were you, Miss Purcell. You'll be surprised how much better you'll feel." He held out his hand as he said, "I'm sorry about Major Mackenzie." He was polite, even pleasant, but he cared nothing about Gabriel. He had seen too many men die over the years to be touched by the death of a stranger now.

It seemed sinful to be undressing so early in the day, wicked to be returning to bed in the morning for any reason other than illness. Her weariness was so great that she scarcely had energy left to climb into bed. Downstairs, the landlady's dachshund kept up a ceaseless yapping. "*Quiet*, Fritz," Mrs. Gray had said when trying to converse with Frances. In England dachshunds were rarely seen these days and certainly never christened Fritz. Ireland was an alien country.

Frances lay in bed listening to the unfamiliar sounds beyond the window. Strange how street sounds echoed in daytime: hard, Irish voices, the creak of wheels and clop of horses' hooves, the rattle and clang of distant trams. She longed for oblivion. It did not come.

The unlined curtains contained too little material to meet across the window: the light in the room was scarcely diminished. Above her bed the ceiling was criss-crossed with tiny cracks, like a labyrinth of pencil lines. She tried to banish thought by transforming the cracks into abstract patterns in her mind and filling them in with colour.

When sleep finally came she dreamt of strange scenes, of empty rectories and deserted stables. She escaped at last to the familiar places and dreamt that she was coming down off the Quantocks, descending through the autumn-coloured bracken of Lady's Edge to the oaks and beeches that sheltered the stream running through Hodder's Coombe. She knew that Gabriel walked close behind her; knew too that she must not talk or look back until they reached the end of the journey. As the ground levelled out beside the widening stream and the roofs of Holford came into view she turned to laugh and exclaim . . . and saw that she was alone. She knew then that it was only her imagination and the strength of her memory that had conjured up Gabriel's presence and that that was all that was left to her.

Chapter Twenty Eight

The small square of garden below Gabriel's room was always deserted. Its grass was shaggy, the flowerbeds unkempt. Decayed foliage from last year's climbers still hung from the walls. How Gwen would like to get to work on it. Frances looked down on it from Gabriel's window while church bells rang out across the city in celebration of Easter and tried to think of Gwen, and Hillcrest, and Easter in Huish Priory – anything to take her mind away from her present surroundings.

She wondered how long a man could remain unconscious and still live. She wondered whether she should be hoping for Gabriel's death rather than praying that he might survive. "Life wouldn't be worth living . . ." he had said. Had he meant it?

Sister came to her that afternoon. "Do me a favour, Miss Purcell. One of the men in the ward wants to dictate a letter to his mother – it's her birthday – but we're short-staffed and I can't spare a nurse at the moment. I thought as you're not doing anything . . ."

Her tone allowed no refusal, much as Frances would like to have given one. She followed Sister reluctantly into the ward. She had always averted her eyes when she passed the open door, frightened of what she might see, but imagination proved worse than the reality. There was nothing to upset even the most squeamish. Unpleasant sights were discreetly hidden under blankets and bandages, or covered with plaster. Heads turned to watch her as she entered, though not all.

Sister stopped at a bed under a window. "Fusilier Hudson," she said briskly. "Tell Miss Purcell what you want to say and she'll write it down for you. If you ask her nicely I don't doubt she'll post it for you too. Writing things on the table, Miss Purcell." The starch in her apron crackled as she went out.

Lack of skill was not the reason for Hudson's illiteracy. He was in plaster from his chest down. One arm was missing from the elbow, the other in a splint.

Frances sat down and picked up pencil and paper. "Don't go too fast," she warned, "or I won't be able to keep up."

Her worries were unnecessary. She remembered, as Hudson struggled to find something to say, how Gabriel had hated having to censor his men's letters during the war. At that time the inarticulateness which had shocked him had amused Frances. Now it made her want to cry. And yet what could a man write about from a hospital bed? In this ward even a glimpse of the outside world was impossible: the windows were too high for the bedridden to see out.

When at last Hudson reached the end Frances sensed that there was something still lacking. It was the man in the next door bed who told her.

"He wants to send his mam a present. It's her birthday, see? She should have a present for her birthday."

"She can't expect anything when she knows he's in hospital," Frances said, but that thought did not console Hudson. His face was unaffected by his injuries. The profile, with short dark curls that fell over his forehead in a Grecian fringe, reminded Frances of the plaster casts that had occupied so much of her time in the Antique Room at the Slade. She said slowly, "Would your mother like a drawing? I could do one if you like. Only you mustn't move. I refuse to draw people who fidget."

Hudson, as she blushed to realise the moment she had spoken, was in no condition to fidget. She borrowed pillows from neighbouring beds and propped him up. She lost all track of time. The pencil she was using was scarcely adequate – she realised that never before had she left home without packing even a decent pencil and pad to bring with her – but the familiar act of drawing, of transferring what she saw into permanent form on paper absorbed her utterly. She was astonished when Nurse Carr announced loudly, "Tea-time! Gracious, Miss Purcell, what are you doing here?" and came over with cup and saucer and a plate of bread and butter. "I *say*! Have you done that?" She picked up Hudson's portrait and took it round the ward. "Look what Miss Purcell's done."

Sister was summoned as she passed the door.

"Have a look at Hudson's picture, Sister. Go on, Nurse, show it to Sister."

Sister looked down at the piece of paper. "Where did this come from?"

"Miss Purcell did it this afternoon."

Sister raised her eyebrows. "Very good." There was mild surprise in her voice.

"I'm next," Hudson's neighbour said. "Eh, Miss Purcell?"

"Are you indeed?" Sister said.

"Is it all right?" Frances asked nervously next time Sister came into Gabriel's room with Nurse Dickens and the dressings trolley. "I don't want ... I mean, if you'd rather I didn't go into the ward ..."

"Miss Purcell," Sister said, "those men are going to be in that ward, or one similar, for the rest of their lives. They come from Lancashire, fusiliers most of them. Lancashire's considered close enough by the powers-that-be for families to visit – which it is, of course, as the crow flies. There just happens to be a lot of water in between, so it's expensive and difficult to cross. They don't get many visitors, I'm afraid. As far as I'm concerned anything that helps pass the time and cheers them up can only be useful. Don't get in the way of my nurses, that's all I ask." She rolled up her sleeves and tied a macintosh apron round her waist. "Now, if you'll leave us ..." As Frances reached the door she said, "I trust you know what you're letting yourself in for, Miss Purcell. There are thirty men on that ward, I'll have you know."

"I don't mind," Frances said.

She felt ... not comforted, but soothed. That night she had the first dreamless sleep since arriving in Dublin. The fears were still present, as deep as they had ever been, despite Sister's assurances that Gabriel was improving – "much nearer the surface than he was," was what Sister said – but now she could be calm.

She went into the ward every afternoon and drew one or other of the men, staying afterwards to help the nurses with tea. She never found conversation easy, though the drawing helped, but her time in the ward provided a kind of antidote to the hours she sat beside Gabriel, desperately searching for some sign of life, of recognition, but finding none.

She was sitting by Gabriel one evening, watching the sunset slowly drain the colour from the sky when she heard her name.

She looked down. His eyes were open.

"Gabriel?" Her voice was no more than a whisper.

"I knew you'd come," he said, gave a sigh as of relief and closed his eyes.

She sat by the bed and held his hand. A dead hand no longer. For a brief moment his fingers had pressed against hers.

The room darkened. He did not stir. She repeated his name but his eyes remained shut. After a while she left him and went slowly along the corridor. Sister was in her office, buttoning up her coat, laughing with Major Elliot. It was he who saw Frances standing in the corridor and came out.

"Miss Purcell! Is anything wrong?"

She shook her head, tried to speak and burst into tears.

"My dear girl!" He took her arm, led her into the office and pulled out a chair. "Come and sit down. Now then. What's the matter?"

She could not speak. The tears would not stop. All the

anguish of the past months, the despair of the past days, once released spilled out in an uncontrollable flood. She cried on and on until Sister called for Nurse Carr and together they undressed her and put her to bed in one of the single rooms along the corridor, the room next to Gabriel's.

It took several minutes next morning before memory came back. Relief at Gabriel's return to consciousness was tempered by embarrassment at having to face Sister after last night's breakdown.

Sister behaved as if nothing unusual had happened. "You're looking better this morning, I must say. No, Major Mackenzie's not conscious though I understand he came round again briefly last night. The night sister told him you were sleeping. I sent a message over to your lodgings, by the way, saying you'd be back tonight, so there's no need to worry about them. Oh, and Major Elliot will be back at twelve and would like a word with you then."

Major Elliot was abrupt. "Get your coat, Miss Purcell. We're going out."

"But ..."

"Hurry up."

He took her down some back stairs and out into the garden that lay beneath Gabriel's window. His car was parked in a side street. He drove in silence while she sat beside him and wondered whether she was being banished from the hospital. They had crossed the Liffey before she realised that if he intended to put her on the boat train as she feared, he would have ensured that she had her luggage with her as well as her coat.

He stopped in a pleasant square of Georgian houses south of the river and helped her out of the car.

"What are we doing here?" she asked.

"Colonel and Mrs. Meredith have invited you to lunch. Don't look like that, Miss Purcell. You need friends. You'll make yourself ill if you go on as you are. You won't be much help to Major Mackenzie then. Don't think things will be easier now he's coming round. They'll be worse. I'll take you up; the Merediths have a flat on the first floor. I don't know why you should look so panic-stricken. Mrs. Meredith knew all about you when Sister telephoned her this morning."

Frances stared. "How could she?"

Mrs. Meredith greeted her as an old friend. "Gabriel's told us so much about you. If only we'd known you were in Dublin we'd have asked you round days ago. I can't think why Mr. Mackenzie didn't tell us you were here – Hugh *said* if there was anything we could do to help ..."

"Hugh?"

"When he sent the first telegram. Do come in. What about you, Major Elliot – won't you come in and have a drink?"

The first thing Frances saw in the living-room was her painting over the mantelpiece – the view of Exmoor from North Hill that Gabriel had bought last year.

"It's good to see you," Hugh Meredith was saying, "though I'm sorry about the reason for it. Sit down and make yourself comfortable."

"I'm sorry," Frances said. "I'm ... confused. I didn't realise when Major Elliot said about Colonel ... I'd forgotten your surname, I'm afraid, and if I had remembered I thought you were a major, like Gabriel."

"Well, yes, you would. I've been bumped up to lieutenant-colonel for this operation. Don't worry, I'll be back to major after it, if not lower. There are wartime brigadiers walking about as captains now, I understand. That's the trouble with peace-time soldiering. Though I suppose you're all right, aren't you, Elliot? Not much movement in the medical corps. Now, how about a drink? Julia, what will you have? A sherry?"

"I'm not Julia," Frances said, taken aback. "I'm Frances."

Hugh Meredith turned and stared. Mary gaped. "*Frances?*" she said. "You can't be Frances, surely? Isn't Julia the nurse? I mean, we took it for granted, when Sister said Miss Purcell ..."

"Yes, well." She was uncomfortably aware of Major Elliot's curiosity. "I am Frances, I'm afraid. Julia's at home."

"Does Gabriel realise you're here?" Mary said.

She nodded. "Yes."

"I'm glad," Mary said simply.

"You've seen your painting?" Hugh said, quick to change the subject. "It's given us great pleasure. We both agree it's our favourite wedding present."

"Gabriel was determined to have a West Country scene," Frances said, "because of the homesickness. I thought it might make it worse but he was sure it wouldn't."

"He was right. She takes it down from the wall occasionally and sits and looks at it until she feels better. A cow or two might have helped even more, but you weren't to know that."

"I don't think," Frances said, beginning to smile, "that there are many cows on top of North Hill."

"You did that, did you?" Major Elliot said. He sounded surprised. "Miss Purcell has begun drawing the men in the ward," he told the Merediths. "A Herculean task. I don't think she realises what she's taken on."

"It's what I'm used to," Frances said. "It keeps my hand in. Helps pass the time too."

An hour in the Merediths' company restored her equilibrium. It was not that they encouraged unrealistic hopes – they had been given details by Major Elliot and were as concerned as Frances about Gabriel's future – but they were more confident than Frances in Gabriel's ability to cope with his situation. They were kind, they were sympathetic, and they were amusing too about a life in Dublin that under the surface Frances sensed was very far from amusing. She was sorry when Hugh said that he should be returning to the Castle and would drive her back to the hospital before he did so.

"I'm glad you've come," he said in the car, "and not only for Gabriel's sake. It'll do Mary good. She's ... we're expecting a child in the autumn, you know, and things have been difficult. She has to rest a lot. Having you here will take her mind off her own problems. Do feel you can come and see us whenever you want – Mary gave you our telephone number, didn't she – and if there's anything we can do, please don't hesitate … We'll visit Gabriel as soon as Major Elliot allows it. I shall have to talk to him as soon as possible, anyway, to see what he remembers. I think that it was sheer chance that he was the one caught in the ambush – we thought at first that it might be rather more sinister – but we must be absolutely certain before we remove the guards."

Frances looked out on the Dublin streets as if on another world. Buildings were pockmarked with bullet holes, some still collapsed in rubble. People hurried to and fro, preoccupied with their own affairs, unaware of Gabriel's suffering and her own unhappiness. Someone, somewhere, was presumably the cause of it. She felt remote and detached, separated by the glass of the car window from the world she had once known. The hospital when she reached it felt like home.

Chapter Twenty Nine

Frances was grateful for the Merediths' comforting presence in Dublin. Major Elliot's words, that things would get worse rather than better, had passed her by at the time but the memory of them returned later. She had assumed that once consciousness returned Gabriel would be on the mend and life would improve. Her assumption was wrong. Infection still remained, though receding, and he was in terrible pain. To have to sit beside him and watch him suffer was an ordeal for which Frances was utterly unprepared.

She talked. She tried to distract his thoughts with memories of past happiness. She read to him – poetry, stories, everything Mr. Mackenzie sent – and wondered as she did so whether concentration on saying the words eased her mind more than listening did his. She sat while he crushed her hand in his and remembered as she watched him how he had distanced himself from her on his way back to the front. Sometimes she wondered if he even knew she was there.

Sister insisted that Frances continue to draw in the ward. "It does wonders for morale, having you there. Someone different to look at – out of uniform too – you'd be surprised at the difference it makes." It was the men she was considering, not Frances. "Have a word with Fusilier Preston, Miss Purcell. Third bed on the right. He's going through a bad patch at the moment; having his portrait done might cheer him up. And Gregson at the far end is a mite put out because you've sketched Peterson next door and neglected him. I'm afraid silly little things like that matter a lot when you're lying in bed all day."

Frances did not object. She was ashamed to admit it, even to herself, but there were times when she was thankful to escape from Gabriel's room. Her inability to do anything to help his pain left her emotionally exhausted. To hold a pencil between her fingers again was surprisingly comforting; concentrating on the planes of a stranger's face restored her to a sense of normality.

She was surprised by the strength of her relief at being reunited with Gabriel. He rarely complained – it might have been easier if he had – and there were occasionally glimpses of the old Gabriel, self-deprecating and mocking. She saved up the news of Sarah's success for days until she judged he was well enough to appreciate it, taking pleasure in anticipating the familiar, crooked smile.

"I knew she'd do it," he said. "All the same . . . little mouse at Oxford. Now I feel really old."

While Gabriel was immobile in bed it was not difficult to avoid talk of the future. On the few occasions he had tried to broach the subject she managed to turn the conversation away and was thankful that he did not persist. Once he was allowed out of bed, however, she knew that she would be unable to delay discussion any longer.

She waylaid Major Elliot as he was leaving one morning after his ward round. "Could I have a word with you?"

"Yes, of course." He took her into Sister's room, shut the door and pulled out a chair. "Now. What's worrying you?"

She took a deep breath. "I was wondering about Major Mackenzie. About his being able to walk. Or not walk, rather. I wondered what you planned to do about telling him."

Major Elliot looked surprised. "He knows. I told him – oh, soon after he came round. Hasn't he discussed it with you?"

She shook her head.

"Strange," Elliot said. "I would have thought ... I know he's talked to Sister."

Perhaps it wasn't strange at all, Frances thought. Perhaps when Gabriel had let her change the subject so easily it was out of consideration for her, remembering her inability to face anything unpleasant. Perhaps it would have helped him, to be able to talk.

Elliot glanced at his watch. "It seems to me," he said, "that we need to talk at greater length than I can manage at the moment. Would Major Mackenzie object if I took you out to lunch? Half past twelve?"

"Oh," Frances said, taken aback, "well, all right. Thank you."

"Lunching with Major Elliot?" Gabriel said. "What for? Has he got designs on you?"

"You're not jealous, are you?" She stared. "You are! Of Major Elliot – good heavens, Gabriel!"

"Of course I'm not jealous. Don't let him get you into some dimly lit underground cavern, that's all ... "

But it was to a hotel overlooking St. Stephen's Green that Elliot took her. She looked with pleasure at the elegant surroundings. "This is nice," she said. "After a time you begin to think there's nothing but your digs and the hospital."

"I owe you something for that first evening," Elliot said abruptly. "An apology, at least. I don't usually go round hitting women. I'm sorry."

She felt her colour rise. "You don't have to ... It was my fault. I don't know what happened that night ... I do lose my temper sometimes but I've never behaved like that before. I suppose I was desperate – I seemed to have been travelling for days." She paused. "How is he, really? I mean . . . you said at the beginning that he might never walk again."

"He'll walk. There's movement – you know that – and a reasonable amount of feeling in the legs. I doubt whether he'll ever manage without sticks." He waited for her to comment but she said nothing. "How will he cope with that?"

"I don't know. He said last time he was wounded that life wouldn't be worth living if he couldn't walk."

"He strikes me as a pretty resilient character. And intelligent. I don't think you should let something he said years ago worry you." He paused. "How will *you* cope, Miss Purcell?"

She stared blankly at him. After a moment she said, "I'll manage."

"Has he any idea what he might do when he's discharged? He's spent his life in the Army presumably?"

"Gracious, no. He was a don before the war."

"A don? I thought he was a Regular."

She shook her head. "He only stayed on in the Army because . . . well, because Hugh Meredith asked him to. It was" – she reddened again – "a sudden decision, staying on."

He was curious. "Which university?"

"Cambridge."

"Really. We must talk some time. I was there too."

He was less formal away from the hospital and more approachable. She could discuss Gabriel, his likely progress and probable future, with an ease that would have been impossible in Sister's office. She could not remember having seen him smile before and was momentarily reminded of Geoffrey, whose face too had been transformed by his smile.

"Tell me," he said. "What was the explanation of that curious incident at the Merediths?"

"Incident?"

"When they assumed you were Julia."

"Oh," she said, "that."

"I take it Julia's your sister?"

"One of them."

[227]

"And the Merediths expected her rather than you?"

"Apparently."

"Yet you were the fiancée. Or so you said." He sounded amused. "You don't have to tell me if you don't want. I'm just curious. Tell me about Julia."

He seemed genuinely interested in the families back in Somerset, wanted to know about Julia, about Frances's painting, about Gabriel's war service. Frances was astonished to discover, when they came to leave, that they were the last in the dining-room and the waiters were already setting tables for tea.

She declined to return with him to the hospital. "I'd like to walk over the road for a bit. It's a long time since I was among proper trees."

The trees were only an excuse. She wanted fresh air, time alone, time to think. She needed to walk, to absorb the revelation that had struck her with the force of a physical blow during the meal with Elliot, and had left her breathless and shaking. "How will you cope?" he had said. She had looked at him as at a stranger and instantly known.

We shall marry.

Perambulators were out in the Green. Nursemaids were enjoying the sunshine while their small charges fed the ducks. Spring would soon give way to summer. Frances stood on the bridge across the lake and looked down on a weaving mess of eels shining under the surface of the water. She had known subconsciously for weeks. Only now in conversation with Major Elliot had it surfaced in the form of words. Marriage was the only way out.

She walked the length and breadth of the Green. She was frightened as well as exhilarated. "I'll manage," she had told Elliot. She had no idea how, but manage she must. She could not endure another winter like the last. Life without Gabriel was not worth living, her work no adequate compensation. Without Gabriel it fell away; with him it flourished.

She walked back to the hospital, oblivious of her surroundings, oblivious even of the ruins of Sackville Street and the army convoys driving down between them. She was filled with tremulous excitement, but more than anything else she was filled with relief. The time for decision-taking was past; she had no other choice.

Gabriel was sitting up reading. "That was a long lunch," he said.

She sat on his bed. After so many years of refusal she felt ridiculously shy. There was, after all, no hurry. "I think he wanted to talk about you," she said. "About your future, that sort of thing. He asked a lot of questions. He was quite helpful really. He does seem pleased with your progress, Gabriel."

"Talking of progress," Gabriel said, "you haven't heard the latest news. Sister came in while you were out and said she was going to put me in a wheelchair and wheel me up and down the corridor." He pulled down his mouth. "Such exciting lives we lead these days."

"I'd be happy to push you all the way to the Merediths if they'd allow it," Frances said.

"I don't think that's likely, alas. Incidentally, did you know that Elliot and Sister nearly had me transferred to the military hospital once I was off the danger list? Sister let that one out this morning. The only reason I came here, I gather, is because I happened to be blown up round the corner and wasn't fit to be moved. The military hospital takes officers and is better at rehabilitation – more suitable for the likes of me, Sister said. I said I'd rehabilitate myself on my own, thank you very much. Better the devils you know than the ones you don't, I told her."

"I'm surprised she didn't summon an ambulance straight-away and have you carted off," Frances said, marvelling at the high spirits the prospect of venturing out of his room had induced. "Why weren't you transferred, then?"

"Elliot and Sister decided the military hospital couldn't cope with the two of us. Or perhaps it was because they thought you and I would be a bad influence. I wouldn't take kindly to strict visiting hours, I can tell you that."

"Nor I," Frances said. "Do you know, I quite like it here." She was surprised to discover that she would be sorry to leave. After those dreadful, unhappy early weeks she had settled down, become used to the routine, could feel affection for the men in the ward, the nurses, even for Sister. One of these days she might brave Sister's wrath and make watercolour sketches to work on when she returned home.

"You're very quiet," Gabriel said.

"I didn't realise," she said slowly, "that you knew ... about, you know ... I thought they'd break it to you gradually, bit by bit, over the weeks."

"Ah," he said. "So that's it. No, I'm afraid Elliot believes in telling you the worst as soon as you can take it. Quite brutal he was, I couldn't help thinking at the time – and out of the blue, too, before I'd begun to suspect a thing."

"I wish you'd made me talk."

"Well ... I didn't know how much you knew. I didn't want to upset you. You were having a rough time yourself and – I daresay you won't believe this – I didn't care. It was soon after I'd come round; all I could think about was getting free of that damned pain. Perhaps that's why Elliot told me. He promised me it would go eventually, more or less; I think I felt that not being able to walk was a small price to pay for that. Now ... well, I've grown accustomed to the idea. Of course it's not ... what I would have chosen, but you've only got to think of poor Bill Roberts to know how much worse it could have been."

"Yes. I know."

He reached for her hand. "We'll manage, my love. I may not be able to go up on the Quantocks any more but I'm damned sure I'll get up to the stables again, even if I have to drag myself on hands and knees."

Chapter Thirty

The idea that Frances should draw those who nursed him came from Gabriel. It was difficult to tell from letters from home what exactly was wrong but his parents seemed to have been ill ever since his accident. Gabriel hoped that by being able to put faces to names mentioned in letters the Mackenzies might feel closer and more involved with hospital life.

"And when I say everybody," Gabriel said, "I mean everybody. You wouldn't mind sitting for Frances, would you, Sister? We don't want anyone missing from the Rogues' Gallery."

"Talk like that, Major Mackenzie, and I'll make sure no nurse sits for Miss Purcell either. Yes, of course, if you really want me, but I won't have everyone gawping while she's doing it. You'll have to come to my flat on my afternoon off, Miss Purcell. How about tea next Wednesday?"

"Now look what you've done," Frances said, exasperated, after Sister had left. "Tea with Sister – can you imagine it! What do I talk to her about?"

Her fears were groundless. Out of uniform Sister was far from formidable. "You'll have to tell me what you want," she said. "How should I sit? May I carry on with my knitting? I'm trying to finish this before my sister's baby arrives."

She was busy with a matinée jacket. Mary, too, was knitting baby clothes when she posed for Frances. Babies were imminent everywhere.

Sister and Frances sat in companionable silence while Frances worked. Sister's complexion was smooth and delicately coloured; her hair, released from its cap, light brown and gently waving. She was younger than Frances had realised. She produced tea when Frances paused for a rest and home-made biscuits. There were flowers about, family photographs and books. The furniture was no different from that provided in most rented accommodation apart from an upright piano standing against one wall.

"I've never come across a piano in a flat before," Frances said. "Do you play?"

Sister shook her head. "It's Major Elliot's. He rents it from a firm in Sussex Street. It's convenient to keep it here; he can practise when I'm working. That's how he relaxes, you know – playing the piano, and fishing."

Frances was surprised. She remembered how she had come across Major Elliot laughing with Sister the night Gabriel regained consciousness. Were they friends?

"I was his theatre sister during the war," Sister said, as if sensing the question. "We met in France. I was his anaesthetist, in fact, though I shouldn't admit it. Nurses weren't allowed to give anaesthetics – one of those stupid rules that no-one took any notice of up at the front."

Frances's visit to Sister had an unexpected result: she became desperately, overwhelmingly homesick.

"But why?" Gabriel said. "I'd have thought the Merediths' flat, if anywhere ... always so comfortable and welcoming."

"I don't think it was the flat," Frances said. "I think it was the flowers. She had anenomes, in a glass bowl. I can't get them out of my mind. You know what anenomes are like – those thick, fleshy stems, a pale apple green, and then the petals above, such brilliant colours. The sun shone through the water onto the table. It looked like stained glass, the reflection on the table. It was ... I don't know ... the colour, I think."

"I do feel very badly about keeping you from your work all this time. Does Denis know you're here?"

She shook her head. "I keep meaning to write but I never do."

She had put off writing to Denis ever since Christmas. As far as she knew, he was still planning an exhibition for her within the next twelve months. She was embarrassed at having to write and tell him that lack of exhibits made such a plan impossible; even more embarrassed at having to explain why she would be staying in Ireland when Denis might reasonably expect her to be concentrating on her work at home.

Another problem was the allowance she still received. She had been happy to take it while Denis could recoup the money from his commission, but she could not continue if she gave him nothing to sell ... Her worries about money would have been eased had she known how long she was likely to be in Ireland. Pride made her refuse to touch the sum Mr. Mackenzie had transferred to a Dublin bank for her use, except for Gabriel's needs. While her present situation had nothing to do with Denis, the lack of work for him to sell did. She wrote, grateful for past generosity, and told him that an allowance was no longer required.

His reply was surprisingly sympathetic. He made no reference to a future exhibition, said that he understood the difficulties she was facing and was happy to carry on with her allowance. If she felt strongly about it, he suggested, they could discuss it when they next met.

"He's taken it very well," Frances said, thankfully. "He sends you his regards — here, you can read it yourself if you like."

"Poor fellow," Gabriel said, when he handed the letter back. "You'd better write and put him out of his misery."

"Misery?"

"It's obvious, isn't it? He's terrified we'll get married. He's always regarded me as the big, bad wolf."

"Oh, Gabriel, how absurd!"

"It's true. He couldn't hide his relief when he discovered I was on my way to Ireland last autumn, and even then I got the impression he'd have preferred India, as being further away ..."

"Last autumn .. ?"

He looked sheepish. "I asked him to frame the Merediths' wedding present."

"I see," she said. "Did you check on the price by any chance?"

He grinned at her. "He told me I'd got it cheap. As you said. He takes a fair whack of commission, doesn't he?"

"It's not unreasonable. He's given me an allowance since the day I left the Slade and never pushed me or tried to get more work out of me than I'm prepared to give. I don't suppose he made any profit out of me for years. He won't this year, either. I didn't realise, you know, before the war, but being taken on by Denis was the best thing that could have happened to me, from the work point of view. I do need someone behind me, someone I can talk to, who understands. I hate dealing with people and money and galleries, and he's so good at all that."

"Oh yes, I don't doubt that he's a good chap."

She watched him. "It may be absurd, his regarding you as the big bad wolf," she said slowly, "but he's right about the rest, isn't he?"

"What do you mean, 'the rest'?"

"Our getting married."

In the long silence that followed she could feel her heart thumping against her chest. At last Gabriel said, lightly but with visible effort, "Really, Frances, you gave me quite a turn. Now it's you who's being absurd."

"I want to marry you," she said.

"It's impossible. You must see it's impossible."

"You always said if we both wanted it enough ..."

"That was before all this ... happened. Darling, how *could* I marry you ... now ... when you always said it wouldn't work before?"

"I've changed," she said desperately. "I want to marry you. It's different now. I have changed, Gabriel, really I have. You must believe me."

"No," he said. "Don't tempt me. It wouldn't work. I couldn't do it to you. It wouldn't be fair. Please, Frances, don't ... Go away."

He was close to tears. She did as he asked and left, not because she wanted to leave but because she saw that staying would upset him more. She took refuge in the waiting-room at the end of the corridor where she sat on the hard settee and stared dry-eyed at a dark Victorian painting of Zeus turning himself into an unidentifiable tree, until she felt able to go out and talk to the men in the ward as if the world was the same as it had been that morning, or yesterday, or in the years long past.

"Parcel for Major Mackenzie," Ross, the medical orderly, said, standing in the doorway. It rattled faintly as he handed it to Frances.

"If it's from Julia," Gabriel said, "it's for you. I asked her to send it."

"You did? Whatever is it?" She guessed, before she'd torn the paper away, by smell and weight alone. "Oh Gabriel, my paints!"

"Some of them, anyway. I hope they're what you need. I thought Julia would know what to send and what not. Are they all right?"

She had emptied everything out on the bed and was going through it. She nodded, unable to speak.

"It was your being so homesick that made me think," Gabriel said. "I should have realised weeks ago – I don't know how you've managed without colour for so long. Only, Frances, do listen. You know how Sister complains about the number of books I have around, gathering dust and cluttering everything up. Books are bad enough, but paints would be ... impossible. I had to be very diplomatic. She'll get used to it in the end, but not if you go round being high-handed."

"How can you say things like that? You know I'm the soul of tact these days. No, of course I'll be sensible."

"What about an easel? It looks as if Julia balked at sending that. You'd better buy one if you need it. You didn't get a birthday present from me this year; I'll give you that."

She blew her nose hard. "Oh dear ..."

He smiled at her. "There must be a thousand images jostling about in that pretty little head of yours. Why don't you go off and make a start?"

"I could go down to the garden – would you mind? It'd be out of Sister's way, too. I really want to paint the ward but I suppose I'd better wait. You could sit by the window and we'd still see each other." She flung her arms round him. "Oh Gabriel, I do love you."

Another parcel from Julia followed soon after, delivered this time to Frances's digs. It was 'Morning Mist', Frances's painting of the hens outside the stables that she had painted for Gabriel the previous autumn.

Frances took it over to the waiting-room. Visitors were so rare that she was the only person she knew to use the room; she took Zeus down and left him in a corner, replacing him with her own painting.

"There's a present for you," she said to Gabriel. "From me, in the waiting-room."

"Why don't you bring it in here?"

Frances shook her head. "Sister'd only say it was clutter. You'll have to go and see it there."

"What are you waiting for, then? Fetch me a wheelchair."

"That's not good enough. You've got to walk."

"Frances! You know how long it takes me to get from my bed to the window and back."

"Then you'll have to practise a bit more, won't you?"

"You're a hard woman," he said, but his curiosity was aroused. "What is it, anyway, this present?"

"Something I wanted to give you last year but didn't."

"Why not?"

"It didn't seem ... tactful."

He looked at her. "'You can't have me – how about a painting instead?' Was that it?"

She gave him a rueful smile. "Something like that."

Sometimes in the afternoons, when Gabriel was supposed to be resting and Sister had gone late to lunch, Frances lay in his arms. Drowsing in the summer heat, eyes closed, bodies entwined, it was easy to forget the present and think themselves back into the past, remembering times spent in the stables, among the dense summer grasses of the orchard, up on the deserted Quantocks, but Gabriel's memories were more recent when he asked one afternoon, "You know the letter you wrote me – the one Lucy brought up to London?"

She was instantly awake. "Yes."

"Did you mean what you said?"

"Of course."

"I couldn't make up my mind whether you did or not. It was a pretty radical step to take, wasn't it – become my mistress?"

"If it would have kept you in England . . . and anyway, I . . . I didn't think you'd mind."

"Mind? No, I don't suppose . . . Oh, Frances, did you ever think how hard you made it for me? It would have been so easy up in the stables, wouldn't it? No interruptions, couch handy, you more than willing. It was all I had to fight you with. I thought that if I held out long enough you'd marry me in the end to get into my bed. Well, you were right, I suppose, and I was wrong. That's how we'll finish up, you and I."

The hospital wing was beginning to stir after its rest. Orderlies were laying out trays in the kitchen, dropping cutlery with an intermittent clatter. Nurses' voices sounded in the ward, jollying the men. Soon they would be bringing round the tea.

How could she have ever thought . . .? The tears spilled over.

"It's not enough," she said. "I want more than that. I want to marry you."

Chapter Thirty One

Days slid into weeks, weeks into months. It was difficult, looking back, to remember those early, dreadful days or even to recall Gabriel's despair and depression over his first attempts to walk. Now he could lumber efficiently if slowly up and down the corridor, though his inability to control his legs still filled him with fury.

"I'd come to terms with not being able to get you to do what I wanted but to have one's own legs rebelling . . ."

Sister said it would be two years before the full extent of his disability would be known. Until then, he could be expected to improve, though much would depend on his own determination and exertion. As for returning home – "I shan't be free of you until the wounds have healed," she told him, "and that's likely to be some time yet. Early autumn, I'd say."

Frances was relieved. She had feared Gabriel might be discharged before she had been able to do all the painting she planned. There was the uncertainty about their future, too, which overshadowed the prospect of their return to Somerset. Was Gabriel to go back to his mother at the Rectory while Frances herself returned to Hillcrest? The thought of being separated after so long together was unendurable.

Fusilier Hudson had been transferred from the ward to a single room, while Major Elliot tried out a new surgical technique on him in an attempt to improve his lot. Hudson was the first patient Frances had come to know in the ward and probably for that reason her favourite. She helped his parents when they arrived soon after the operation and when they returned to Lancashire she sat in Hudson's room and talked to him, painting first him and then the view of the garden from his window.

Major Elliot called in most evenings, often sitting and talking with Gabriel before he left. It never occurred to Frances to wonder why he should start visiting more than once a day, or relate it to the frequency of his visits when Gabriel had been so ill, until the morning she arrived and saw sunlight pouring through the open door of Hudson's room. She walked slowly down the corridor, knowing what she would find. Hudson's room was empty. His few possessions rested on the stripped bed, the glass jar in which he had kept the piece of shrapnel that had finally killed him glinting in the sun.

Sister came quickly out of the ward.

"My dear, I'm sorry. I'd hoped to catch you and tell you . . . Come and sit in my office."

"What happened?" Frances said.

"It was his heart. It wasn't able to take the strain. In the end it gave out. There was nothing we could do."

Frances sat in Sister's chair and looked down at her hands in her lap. "Could I paint in there?" she said.

Sister hesitated. "What do you mean?"

"If I could paint the room . . . With Hudson's things in it. It'd only take a couple of days. I wouldn't be in anyone's way."

"I really don't think, Miss Purcell . . ."

"Please."

"Would it be sensible, Miss Purcell?"

"Please," Frances said again.

Sister brought Frances a mug of tea. "My dear," she said gently, "are you sure this is wise?"

Gabriel came at lunchtime and leant on his crutches in the doorway. "Can I do anything, or do you just want me to keep them away?"

The thought lurked under the surface of her mind as she painted that this was the scene that might have greeted her on her arrival here in the hospital all those weeks ago: the cold, empty room, the few possessions left behind. By portraying it she was acknowledging her own thankfulness, as well as paying tribute to those less fortunate, the Geoffreys and Antonys, Hudsons, and others whom she had never known nor been able to help.

When she finished she left the hospital and walked for hours in the streets outside, unaware of her surroundings, until she slowly came back into the real world.

"It's like that, is it?" Gabriel said, with one glance on her return. "You'd better lie down on my bed and get some sleep. I'll deal with Sister if she complains."

When Frances woke Gabriel was sitting at the bedside reading Housman. He smiled at her. "All right?"

She nodded.

"May I see it?"

"Later." She sat up. "Roles reversed," she said.

"Yes." There was understanding and affection in his eyes. "Still tired?"

She nodded. She was emotionally exhausted. "I was excited when I was doing it. Now I don't know. I'll probably hate it when I look at it again."

It was Sister who suggested the outing, one afternoon when Mary was sharing a pot of hospital tea with Frances and Gabriel.

"Why don't you invite Major Mackenzie to lunch one of these days, Mrs. Meredith? It would do him good to get out of this place once in a while and there's nowhere else he can go unless I pack him off to the military hospital at Phoenix Park. I'm sure he'd rather have your company than that."

"It would be wonderful," Mary said, "but could we get him there?"

"Colonel Meredith has a car, hasn't he? If we put him in a wheelchair at this end and take him down to the hospital entrance, Colonel Meredith could pick him up there. Do you have stairs?"

"They wouldn't be a problem. There are plenty of army people in the house who'd be able to help heave him up."

"One of the most irritating things about my condition," Gabriel complained, after Sister had departed, having agreed a day with Mary, "is the way people arrange things over my head, as if I hadn't a mind of my own. No-one asked *me* if I wanted to go, you'll notice."

"Of course," Mary said, "if you don't want to come ..."

Transporting Gabriel proved to be easier than anyone had anticipated. By now he was reasonably competent with crutches, provided the surface was flat, and it was only the stairs that gave him trouble. When at last he staggered into the Merediths' flat he was flushed and elated.

"I never thought it would happen . . . to be back here again. Oh, and there's Frances's painting on the wall. I still prefer the hens, you know. Thank heavens you wouldn't let me have it last year. Don't forget, Frances, you promised to show me the rest before we go."

There was hilarity over the meal, as if none of them could believe its reality. When afterwards Hugh brought out the brandy and cigars and they sat reminiscing over the times they had shared together it was impossible, as Gabriel said, to remember that the hospital existed. Only Frances was quiet. Until today it had not occurred to her to consider how hard the last months must have been for Gabriel, how difficult for someone used to solitude and the countryside to be immured for so long between the same four walls.

She watched him now, arguing over the Irish situation with Hugh, and ached with sadness for his lost past. She knew how much Hugh's friendship meant to him but it was a friendship that lacked the depth and sparkle of his old intellectual and idealistic ones. The friends of university days no longer remained, having either been killed in the war or by becoming conscientious objectors distancing themselves from Gabriel as far as the dead themselves.

He looked up at her now and smiled. "How about seeing what you've done? Would you mind, Mary?"

The Merediths had given Frances their spare room as a storage place for her work. It was destined to become the nursery in time and a cot was already in place with baby things heaped between the bars, but the rest of the room was filled with Frances's paintings.

"We'd better make sure I'm discharged before the baby arrives," Gabriel said, "or things are going to be very awkward in here. I hadn't realised you'd done so much."

"I'm surprised myself," Frances admitted. "It may have been a dreadful summer from every other point of view but as far as my work's concerned it's been like, well, 1917 all over again. You'd better sit in that chair over there. There aren't many drawings because I let the men keep their own, and you've seen most of them anyway."

The watercolours were generally studies; her own form of shorthand in colour and outline to help with future work she planned to do on her return to England. The rest were oils, the great majority painted in the hospital, though there were some of the garden beneath Gabriel's window. There were studies of the ward from different angles and in different lights, the long lines of beds with their immobile occupants, and of hospital life, orderlies preparing food in the kitchen, nurses serving meals, and probationers carrying out the simple everyday tasks, rolling bandages, padding splints. There was one of the corridor stretching into the distance with blocks of light from open doors falling across the floor in dazzling patterns while in the distance, too far away to be recognisable, a solitary figure with crutches resting wearily against the wall.

There was a long silence when she came to the end. She waited for Gabriel to comment. He pulled himself to his feet at last and manoeuvred himself to the door. "You're right." He did not look at her. "You have changed," he said, and went out to join the Merediths.

She stayed crouched on the floor, still holding up the painting of Hudson's empty room, and began to shiver. She was as deflated by Gabriel's silence as she had been by Denis's lack of understanding the previous December. Not for years had Gabriel failed her. Now he had left her with scarcely a word.

She looked down at the painting by her side, at the harsh lines and abrupt angles of the hospital room, at the impersonal yellows and whites and the hard blue in the shadow and she saw it then with sudden despair as symbolic of life as it would be without Gabriel: cold and empty and without heart.

Chapter Thirty Two

Frances's first reaction to the idea was panic; Gabriel's enthusiasm.

"Really, darling," he said. "Anyone would think Elliot had suggested a weekend at the North Pole, instead of two days in a fishing pub outside Dublin. I'd like to try my hand at fishing. I'll have to find something to keep myself occupied when you get back to your landscapes. It'll be fun. You're becoming positively middle-aged, do you know that?"

He was right, of course. Now that visits to the Merediths had become regular events he needed further challenge and more walking practice in other settings. Elliot said the hotel would be ideal, and movement about it well within his capabilities. Elliot himself had been a frequent visitor since the time he had treated its owner after a traffic accident in Dublin. "And that's the best part," he told Frances and Gabriel. "Nolan finished up in a wheelchair. I'll make sure you can borrow it for the day."

The weekend had Sister's approval. "It'll do you both good to get away. Nice for Major Elliot, too. He's on his own too much. As for me, it'll be like a breath of fresh air being free of the pair of you for forty-eight hours."

"There's another advantage you won't have thought of," Gabriel said, when alone with Frances. "It'll give us a chance to get to know Elliot better. Did you know that he's been writing to Julia?"

Frances stared. "No. What about?"

"He wouldn't say. He was embarrassed, I think, that I knew. I gather Julia was afraid you were going to end it all in the waters of Liffey when you arrived, and wrote and asked him to see you didn't."

"*Drown* myself?" Frances said. "Whatever made her think that? How ridiculous."

"You must have given that impression. Elliot thought so, too."

"Well, perhaps . . . How do you know, anyway? About Julia and Elliot. Did Julia say?"

Gabriel looked sheepish. "Sarah let it out in one of her letters."

"Oho," Frances said. "I don't know about intelligence services in Dublin, but it seems to me you've been running a pretty efficient one in the Purcell household for years."

"There's no need to be so touchy." He sounded amused. "The poor child has to write about something."

"What did the poor child say about me last winter?" Frances asked.

"Nothing. There seemed to be general agreement at home not to mention your name. Very odd, it was; almost as if you'd ceased to exist. Only Father kept saying you were so unhappy didn't I think it might be a good idea if you came over and talked to me."

"And did you? Think it was a good idea."

"It was too late," he said. "Could you see yourself as an army wife?"

She thought of Mary, and shook her head. "That doesn't matter now, though, does it? You won't be in the army much longer."

"We're not getting on to that subject again," Gabriel said.

Sometimes she wondered whether they ever would. The subject was forbidden; as apparently was any mention of her paintings. He had made no reference to her work since that day in the Merediths' spare room. If he was unwilling to comment she would not force him to do so, but she was upset nevertheless.

Elliot took Gabriel fishing the first afternoon. "There's no need to look so agitated, Frances. We'll fish from the bridge.

He can't possibly fall in. Won't you join us? I've borrowed a lady's rod."

She shook her head. "I think I'd rather walk, if you don't mind."

She left them together and climbed up through the woods that ran beside the stream, looking back to see the two figures dwindling in size as she drew further away. She was pleased by their growing friendship. Elliot came in two or three evenings a week, to lie back in the armchair Sister had found him, put his feet up on the bed and drink and talk with Gabriel. They had more than their war service in common. Although their paths had not crossed in Cambridge, Elliot being older, they discovered mutual friends and acquaintances, similar interests, and the fact that they had been on the same Fabian summer courses. "Funny to think of that," Gabriel said to Frances. "Not that either of us can remember the other. Elliot couldn't stand Beatrice Webb either." He sounded pleased.

After a while she came to a clearing between the trees and sat down on the swollen podded stems of last spring's bluebells that grew round its fringes. She leant her head back against the hard, uneven bark of a tree trunk, and watched clouds move across the sky as she thought about Julia. She wondered about Elliot. She had always found him so reserved and formal, except with Gabriel, that she could not imagine how correspondence with Julia could have ever begun.

Next day Elliot announced that he intended fishing on his own. "You two can entertain yourselves. Nolan's promised to let you have his wheelchair, and his wife's packing food for the day. Why don't you go to the salmon pool? It's not far and it's private. Nice to paint, too, I would think, from the woods."

They set off, Frances pushing Gabriel in a wheelchair piled high with crutches, food and their belongings. The dusty road stretched like a white ribbon away from them to distant woods. Cows in the far-off meadow and two scrawny hens in the verge were the only things alive in the landscape other than themselves. Peace enveloped them. It was impossible to believe that half the country was actively engaged in trying to overthrow the British government, or that back in Dublin army vehicles were rushing men armed to the teeth through crowded streets.

Elliot had warned Frances in the car. "Be careful what you say while we're away. There's no need to worry as long as one keeps off politics. I've never had any trouble. They know I'm only here for the fishing. Assume that everyone you meet is a Shinner," and when Frances protested, he said, "Oh, yes, it's true. I don't doubt Nolan would be out trenching roads and shooting policemen himself if he weren't stuck in a wheelchair. I have doubts about that street accident, to tell you the truth. More like a brush with a Crossley tender than a Dublin tram, I've always thought."

Frances had never talked politics and was not going to start now, but she had noticed Gabriel's close attention to the conversations going on around them the previous evening, and was relieved to be getting him away for the day. She herself felt almost light-headed with delight at being able to wander in open country again after so many weeks immured in hospital and town.

Elliot had given them directions but his definition of 'not far' was obviously that of a car driver rather than of one pushing a wheelchair. They came to the woods at last and beyond the woods found the salmon pool lying limpid below the meadow banks. Frances left the wheelchair behind a wall and together they made their way slowly down towards the river, Frances restraining a helping hand with difficulty. Sister was insistent that Gabriel be left to manage on his own – a dictum Frances often thought unnecessarily cruel but one she obeyed nevertheless.

When the meadow made its last steep incline down to the river, Gabriel stopped. "I could go further, but heaven knows how I'd get up again. Let's stay here."

She made a return journey to the chair for the rest of their belongings and returned to find him massaging his legs.

"Let me have that rug," he said and laid it out over the grass. "He's a good chap, Elliot. Every comfort provided. Come and lie down. I've just realised this is the first time we've been alone without fear of interruption since you came to Dublin. Let's make the most of it."

After a while he stirred. "Shouldn't you be working? We'll go back to Dublin and you won't have done a thing."

"It's all right. I'm not painting this weekend. You know how I need to study the ground first." Like Professor Tonks, the ex-surgeon who could never understand how it was possible to draw from life without a knowledge of anatomy, Frances was mystified by those attempting to paint landscapes without walking the contours first. "I'd like to paint this some time though. Do you think you could persuade Major Elliot – David – to bring us again? Sister says he comes quite often."

"We'll have to see. It'd be nice, wouldn't it? I feel quite different here. Alive. Part of the human race once more."

She had brought pencil and paper with her, and after lunch began drawing him as he lay with eyes shut in the shade of the trees. She knew every detail of his head, every bump, every hollow; knew the way his hair grew and the lashes curled; remembered the pattern of his ears and the chipped tooth beneath the firm mouth. But his face had changed during the last months; there were lines now that had not been there a year ago. Saddened, she wondered how she could have expected him to behave towards her as if nothing had happened between them.

He had turned his head and was watching her. "What's Denis going to think of your paintings?" he said.

She sighed. "He'll hate them. He said last year everyone wanted to forget the war. They won't want reminding about the men left over in hospitals, will they?"

"You'll show them to him, though?"

"Oh yes. Then it's up to him. He knows that I paint what I see. If I'm stuck in hospital for months on end that's what I'm going to paint."

"I'm sorry," Gabriel said.

"Sorry?"

"If it hadn't been for me ..."

"You don't understand. It's what I want to do. I don't want to leave yet; I've got plans for others." She said, "You never told me what you thought of them."

"No. I don't think I could have said anything at the time, even if I'd wanted to. I haven't stopped thinking about them since."

"You'd seen a lot of them before."

"I know, but when you see them together ... Do you remember what you told me after your last exhibition? That it was only seeing your paintings all hanging together that made you realise what you'd been trying to do – that you hadn't known before? I didn't understand what you meant then, but I do now. Seeing these together I thought they were ... powerful. Unbearably so."

"I was surprised myself, when I showed them to you," Frances admitted. "And when I say Denis'll hate them, I don't mean he won't like them as paintings. He probably will, but he certainly won't want to exhibit them. Don't worry, Gabriel. Denis and I get on very well. We were bound to have professional differences some time or other."

"In a way, it was a relief. Looking at them, I mean. I've felt guilty all the time, letting you stay in Dublin when I knew I should have made you go home, but seeing them made me realise ... It hasn't done you any harm, has it? Your work's gained, surely? I take it that business you wrote about last Christmas soon sorted itself out?"

She looked at him in surprise. "No. Not until after I came to Ireland. Didn't you realise that? When your father told you I was unhappy, it wasn't only you. The business of painting was mixed up with it, too. Until I came here I hadn't done anything worthwhile for months – since you left really." She looked away from him, at the curve of the pool below the meadow. "I need you more than you need me, even now, Gabriel. I always have. I didn't realise it before, but it's true." He was silent. She said, "I wish you'd written last Christmas. I needed your help. You never answered my letter."

"I did. I tore it up before I could post it. I wanted to help, but I knew that if I didn't make the break ..."

"You wrote? What did you say?"

"That an artist who didn't doubt or question what he or she was doing wasn't likely to be much of an artist. You've never suffered the black moods I get. Because of that, perhaps, I felt that when you did fall into the pit it would be a deep one. I don't know that I said anything that would have helped. It was no good telling you to snap out of it and not worry; I know from my own experience what useless advice that is. All I could say was, talk to Julia and take one day at a time."

"Denis said that, too. It didn't help. I'll tell you what did — and I only realised it myself recently. Sitting in that ward, day after day, drawing those men. It was like starting at the Slade all over again. At home I was thinking about myself all the time. Here I was concentrating on the drawing and when I wasn't drawing I was watching. The men. You. Sister and the nurses. Especially the nurses. They're all so much more use in the world than I could ever hope to be. It seemed horribly self-centred to be getting hysterical just because I couldn't paint pretty pictures any more."

"You're doing yourself an injustice," Gabriel said. "Pretty pictures, indeed. There was something else I thought, too, though. People like Nash are lucky. To be in the right place, at the right time ... To have some idea why you've been put here, what's more ... that doesn't happen to many. Most of us have to struggle on unknowing."

"I suppose so." She hugged her knees. The discovery that Gabriel had cared about her distress, had wanted to help and had tried, filled her with gratitude. "I'm glad you wrote, even if you didn't send it."

The sun had drained colour from the landscape. Down in the pool a fish broke the smooth surface with a sudden plop.

"Do you think there really are salmon in the river?" she said. "It looks very tempting, doesn't it, the water?"

Gabriel smiled. "Why don't you?" he said. "We haven't seen a soul all day. If someone comes along I'll distract their attention – throw a fit or something. Go on."

"Do you remember before the war, at St. Audries?" she asked.

"Very well."

She hoped he'd say more but he was silent. She stood up and went slowly down to the pool.

The cold caught her breath. She stood motionless, toes curling over the stones on the river bottom. Her flesh was coloured peaty brown below the surface of the water. She took a deep breath and swam out of the shadows to join the dragonflies darting in the sunlight at the centre of the pool. She turned over and let herself float. The sun was warm on her face, hot on her closed eyelids.

She let the sun dry her when she came out and finished off with her petticoat. It was very hot. She felt as if the day were waiting for something indefinable, as if nostalgia were hovering round the corner . . .

"I've never swum naked before," she said when she returned to Gabriel. Her clothes caught on still damp skin. "Nothing pulling at your neck, no weight dragging you down – it was wonderful."

"I know. We used to swim in Byron's Pool in the old days."

She stared. "You hypocrite! You were shocked that time I suggested it."

"I wasn't shocked. It wasn't sensible, that was all. You'd be surprised what it's like, growing up in a rectory. Suppose some busybody had come along afterwards and said to Mother, 'Oh, Mrs. Mackenzie, you'll never believe what I saw the other day – your son dancing with that Purcell girl *naked* on the beach at St. Audries . . .'"

"You should have told me that was the reason."

"Oh, Frances! You'd have pranced off and done it out of sheer devilment."

"You do have a poor opinion of my character," she said.

He smiled. "Realistic, I've always thought. Here, give me a

comb and I'll do something about your hair. You looked like a water nymph with it floating out behind you. Very Pre-Raphaelite. If you could have seen yourself you'd have reached for your paints at once."

"I was thinking," she said, as he began to tease out the tangles. "There's no reason why you couldn't swim once everything's healed. You don't have to use your legs. Though I don't know where. It's too shallow at Minehead."

"How about Byron's Pool?" She twisted round and stared at him in astonishment. "We talked a lot yesterday, Elliot and I," he said. "While we were fishing, and later, when you'd gone to bed. About me and my future. He didn't think Cambridge would be impossible. Difficult, but not impossible. I thought I ought to set things in motion when we get back; write some letters." He said slowly, "It may seem extraordinary to you but until this weekend I've never considered life beyond the hospital. It was as if I didn't think I had a future outside. I suppose the fact of getting away and behaving like a normal human being — talking to strangers, getting dressed on one's own — lord, you don't know how long that took me — coming downstairs to breakfast and staying up late at night ..." He hesitated. "Frances, it's no sort of life to offer anyone. You, least of all ... with your work ..."

She was very still. "But if it's the life I want ..."

"How can you be so sure?"

"You were, once," she said.

The power of the sun had waned when at last they moved.

They looked back from the road, over the meadow to where the river drifted into the salmon pool and out again, to the far bank and the hills beyond.

"Strange," Gabriel said. "I always thought it would be up on the Quantocks ..."

She looked back over all the years that they had been together and saw the truth for the first time: that action that is right at one time need not be right for ever.

If they had not misunderstood each other in those letters last year, she thought now ... If she had even once during the final leave wondered whether he might be right and she wrong ... If she had only once doubted her own certainty ... who knew what then might or might not have happened?

She would have to live with that thought every day of her life.

"I don't know what you're waiting for," Gabriel said. "I'm not going in that ... pram. I'll walk back under my own steam."

She looked at him; looked away at the road as it stretched into the distance, thin, white and dusty, winding its way between the trees, now hidden, now revealed, until at last it emerged from the shadows of the wood into the sunlight beyond.

"It's so far ..." she said.

"What does that matter? We can take as long as we like. We've got all the time in the world."

AWAITING DEVELOPMENTS

Judy Allen

A Whitbread Book of the Year 1988
Winner of the Friends of the Earth
Earthworm Award
Shortlisted for the Carnegie Medal

For some time, Jo's secret haven has been the beautiful garden of The Big House nearby. Now she is dismayed to learn that the site has been sold to a property developer, who plans to cover it with new flats and houses. To have any hope of stopping him, Jo must gain the support of her neighbours — most of whom are complete strangers. Naturally a shy girl, will she have the courage to make a stand?

This award-winning novel is a story that will stir the hearts of anyone concerned about the state of our environment.

"Full of humour and genuine feeling...a highly attractive novel."
The Observer

THROUGH THE DOLLS' HOUSE DOOR

Jane Gardam

Claire and Mary love the dolls' house and its curious assortment of residents: the outsize Dutch doll, Miss Bossy; the General and his troop of Trojan soldiers; the miserable Small Cry; the mysterious Sigger... But little do the girls know of the extraordinary lives and adventures, past and present, of this resourceful band and the marvellous stories they have to tell.

"An original story...wry and funny, and full of a sharply poignant sense of the passage of time."
Jill Paton Walsh, Books For Keeps

KISS   FILE JC 110

Linda Hoy

Julian Christopher doesn't know it, but since the age
of fourteen he's been under surveillance as a suspected enemy of the state. His diaries have been
stolen, his activities carefully monitored. But when
he joins the Radical Christian Fellowship, he invites
attentions of a more personal, insidious and dis-
turbing nature – throwing even his sexuality into
doubt . . .

"An angry and sincere story about betrayal."
TES